SHOTGUN ROMANCE

By Elizabeth Spaur

First Print Publication: August 2018

© 2018 Elizabeth Spaur

ISBN – 10 is 1-7325343-3-0

ISBN – 13 is 978-1-7325343-3-9

Cover Art and Logo by Kristina Mull © 2018

Cover Photo © Hrecheniuk Oleksii | Dreamstime.com

Dedication

To my husband, who stands beside me no matter what and who always has faith in me.

AND

To my brother Bruce, who supports me and buys my books, even though he doesn't read romance.

Acknowledgements

Writing a story is a solitary exercise. Getting a book out to the world is a team effort. I couldn't have done this without the Thervs: Margo, Mia, Diane, Kristina and Karen. Thank you all for your critiques and beta reads.

Thank you to Beverly, Heidi and Charlene. I couldn't ask for more supportive friends.

Thank you to Lillie Applegarth of Lillie's Literary Services. You went above and beyond.

Thank you to Kristina Mull, cover designer extraordinaire.

If you're interested in learning more about what's next for the Gridiron Knights and the folks who live in King's Folly, be sure to sign up for my newsletter.

SHOTGUN ROMANCE

He had no faith in love. She had no faith in men. They've got nine months to find faith in each other.

Since the night his life had taken a dramatic left turn, Nick Jacobs had been searching for a chance to prove he was the man he'd always wanted to be. When his old friend calls him and offers him a chance to help rebuild the Cormac University football program, he thinks this is his shot. He didn't count on falling for Olivia or getting her pregnant. Can he juggle all his responsibilities and prove to himself, once and for all, that he's worthy of love?

After the traumatic loss of her mother, Olivia Valenti shut herself off from the world. Running the Cormac University English department is a dream come true. She didn't think she would ever want or need anything else. One night with Nick in Las Vegas and motherhood is on the horizon. Can she open her heart to Nick and build the home she never knew she dreamed of?

An instant attraction and a night of celebration leads to an unexpected pregnancy, which Nick and Olivia are determined to face together. Unfortunately, their pasts and present are about to collide, and old secrets will challenge the foundation they're trying to build their family on. Can they learn to let go of the past in time to share a future?

Will they realize that love always wins?

Welcome to Shotgun Romance, the second book in the Gridiron Knights series set in King's Folly South Carolina, where football is king, and the locals have something to say about everything. When you come for a visit, you'll never want to leave.

This is a stand-alone romance. It can be read and enjoyed on its own. If it's your first taste of the Gridiron Knights, check out Second Chance Option and find out how Tess and Cade found their happily-ever-after.

Chapter 1

It is a truth universally acknowledged that English professors should not drink tequila. It was the devil.

The bright Las Vegas sunlight filled the room and shot through Olivia Valenti's brain causing an ache to roll through her entire body. She inched her hand to the side, hoping to find a pillow. Once she had it in her grasp she would decide whether to cover her eyes or suffocate herself with it.

Instead of sliding on to one of the downy soft pillows that only seemed to exist in high end hotels, her hand met flesh. Rock. Hard. Flesh. Her hand splayed on a set of taut abs that clenched underneath her wandering fingers. Warmth seemed to jump from the unfamiliar skin to her palm and up her arm.

She heard a rumble come from the warm body next to her and held her breath as she ran through the events of the night before in her mind. It might hurt to think, but she needed to get her act together.

Her friends Tess and Cade had gotten married last night. Their friends and family had joined them for the ceremony and reception at the Mandalay Bay. The hotel was across Las Vegas Boulevard from the American Ninja Warrior course, where Tess became the first woman to finish stage three.

They'd celebrated Tess's accomplishment and her wedding to Cade the night before with amazing food and lots of booze. Olivia hadn't gotten drunk. Her blessing was that alcohol didn't affect her judgment or behavior. Her curse was that it did give her a hangover like she'd had enough to drink to fell an entire football team.

Olivia huffed out a breath.

Oh, right.

Tequila shots, arguing Star Trek and Star Wars with Tess's brothers, and him. Nick Jacobs. The man who'd starred in every one of her fantasies since she'd met him three months ago.

He'd led her out on the dance floor last night and held her there for the rest of the night. A willing prisoner.

After the bride and groom had taken off, the party had split into gamblers, partiers and Nick and Olivia, who'd ended up kissing on the elevator and all the way up to his room.

In all her wildest fantasies, she'd never imagined she would actually end up here with him or that some of the things they'd done last night were biologically possible.

Oh my God, I had sex with Nick Jacobs.

She was torn between the squeals of delight coming

from excited Olivia and the shrieks of fear from terrified Olivia.

Was he awake? Olivia opened her eyes and let them adjust to the bright lights before they focused on the man next to her in bed. His face was turned toward her and relaxed in sleep. She missed his beautiful blue eyes.

Olivia took the edge of the sheet and lifted it carefully with her thumb and forefinger and glanced down. The bright light shone through the sheer cotton. Even with the memories of last night roaring through her mind she couldn't process what she was seeing.

She was naked. He was naked. They were naked. She was naked in bed with Nick Jacobs. Naked from Old English *nacod*; akin to Old High German *nackot* naked, Latin *nudus*, Greek *gymnos*. At the sound of his snort, she dropped the sheet and turned her gaze to his face. He was still asleep.

Thank God.

The question now was, what would Beatrice do? As a Shakespearean professor, she often tried to think about what some of her favorite heroines would do in delicate situations.

Olivia had never been in a more delicate situation than waking up in a room with a naked man after a night of amazing sex. Wasn't there a protocol for one-night stands? This couldn't be anything else could it? After all, he was Nick and she was...well...Olivia.

She lay in bed for a moment glancing around the room and wondered what to do. Did he want her to be here when he woke up? What if he did and she left? What if he didn't and she stayed?

What if I stop asking myself and make a choice? What if he wakes up while I'm trying to think of what I should do?

Panic filled her at the thought of him waking up and finding her here if he wanted her to be gone. If he wanted to see her, he could come find her when he woke up.

I'll leave a note.

Olivia slid out of the bed, thankful for the high-end hotel sheets that allowed her to do so with only a whisper of sound. Once she stood next to the bed, she took a moment to steady herself. She really needed to not drink. Ever. Or at least she should reserve her drinking for nights before mornings when she could actually face Nick. He'd made a hangover cure after her last girls' night out with Tess, Delilah and Charlie that had miraculously made her feel better.

For a moment, because of the tiny little people sticking needles in her brain, she thought about waking him up. But they were in a hotel, so the odds of him being able to get what he needed to make the cure were small. And she was naked.

She padded quietly around the room and collected her clothes. Thank God he hadn't torn anything in his haste to get her naked.

Heat rushed through her at the memory of how their passion had exploded once they'd made it to his room. The fact that her panties hung from the curtain rod was all the evidence anyone else would need.

It wasn't like she was a virgin. She'd had two vaguely satisfying affairs in the past. But what she'd experienced with Nick was bigger and more overpowering than any-thing she'd ever felt before.

After writing him a quick note to tell him she would be in the café if he wanted to join her for breakfast, she picked up her shoes and let herself out of his room.

Excitement rolled through her at the thought of meeting him over a meal in the bright light of day. Maybe this was the beginning of something amazing.

She was so deep in thought as she approached her room, she didn't notice the tall blonde leaning against the wall next to the door to Olivia's room.

"Walk of shame?" Delilah drawled.

Heat rushed up Olivia's neck and into her cheeks. "No."

She refused to be ashamed of her night with Nick.

Delilah studied her. "Hmmm."

"Why are you here?"

"I came to see if you wanted to get some breakfast. Color me shocked that you weren't in your room." Delilah didn't sound shocked at all.

Olivia fished her key card out of her purse and inserted it in the door. The little green light went on and she hoped she could get into her room without too much effort. Delilah followed her inside before she could close the door.

"So, how was it?"

"I have no idea what you're talking about."

"You and Nick were glued to each other on the dance floor when Charlie and I left to hit the blackjack table. I'm guessing you're coming from his room." There was a hint of censure in Delilah's voice.

"Where I was last night is no one's business but mine."

"I'm trying to look out for you. You don't have a lot of experience."

"How do you know that?"

Delilah had all but glued herself to Olivia's side when she decided to be Olivia's best friend. It was lovely, in an odd, unsettling way, having someone so interested in her life. But Olivia hadn't been able to open up about anything

6

meaningful. She'd been on her own for so long that she wasn't used to anyone showing anything more than a superficial interest in her life.

"Olivia." The one word was all Delilah seemed to believe needed to be said.

"Fine. I don't have a lot of experience. That doesn't mean I can't, as a grown, professional woman with two doctorate degrees make a decision about where to spend my evening."

"Don't get all sassy with me. I'm on your side." Delilah snapped.

"How is this a situation involving sides?"

"You spent the night with Nick Jacobs."

"And?" There didn't seem to be a point in denying it.

"And, he's a little..." It looked like Delilah wanted to choose her words carefully.

Goosebumps popped up along Olivia's arms. Delilah never thought before she spoke.

"Rough around the edges."

Olivia blew out a breath. "He's nice."

"He's a giant box of secrets."

What was that supposed to mean?

"We all have secrets, Delilah." Olivia knew her new friend had her own demons that she refused to share.

Delilah crossed her arms and stared at Olivia. "You're not going to listen to me, are you?"

"Not about this." For some reason, Olivia needed to pursue this thing with Nick, whatever it was.

"Fine. That doesn't mean I won't look out for you." With that cryptic statement, Delilah turned and let herself out of Olivia's room.

Instead of letting herself obsess about the meaning behind her friend's words, Olivia quickly stripped down and got in the shower. She had about forty-five minutes to get ready for her first official date with Nick.

Was it a date?

Maybe not, but Olivia had never felt this way about anyone before and she was going to take a chance, for once in her life, on something she really wanted. It was time to take a risk. In the months she'd known him, she'd seen Nick's devotion to his friends and his loyalty. A date for breakfast didn't seem like that much of a leap.

He wouldn't hurt me.

Nick snapped awake at the click of the door. He bolted up and glanced around. Olivia was gone. Panic slid through him at the thought that she'd left without a word to him.

Before he could jump out of the bed and follow her, he noticed the note on the bedside table. He picked it up and glanced at it.

Good morning, I hope you slept well.

He couldn't help chuckling at the formality of the note.

I'll be at the café for breakfast in an hour. If you're hungry, and want to, you can meet me there. –Olivia

Breakfast with his dream girl.

Hot damn.

He jumped out of bed and went to take a shower. A few minutes later, he let the steamy water pound on his shoulders. He tried to focus on anything but the memories of last night. He'd been fantasizing about the hot English professor since the first time he'd seen her. Last night proved his imagination when it came to her was completely inadequate.

Who knew the buttoned-up woman could be so inventive?

Once he was out of the shower and dry, he got dressed and packed up his clothes. It had been awhile since he'd been to Vegas. Watching his best friend's fiancé kick ass in American Ninja Warrior followed by the wedding was a pretty awesome trip. Everything that happened with Olivia made it the best night of his life.

If someone like Olivia could give him the time of day, maybe he could finally put that night behind him and really have a second chance, not just go through the motions of one. It was a long shot, but last night proved it was worth a try.

He whistled as he left his room to meet Olivia for breakfast, their first date. Hell, his first date in more years than he wanted to count.

"What's got you so happy this morning?"

He jumped and spun to his left. Delilah was propped up against the wall next to his doorway looking like she hadn't matched everyone drink for drink last night. It was the first time someone had gotten the drop on him in a long time.

"Shit. Where did you come from?"

The blonde arched an eyebrow. "Don't mess with her, Jacobs."

"What are you talking about?"

She stood from the wall and poked her finger in his chest. "I'll let Olivia get away with a lot because she's one of my best friends. You are a friend of my other best friend's husband."

"Meaning?"

"I haven't been hit with a stupid stick. I know you spent the night with Olivia. I also know you've had your eye on her since you two met."

"And?" The old feeling was back in the pit of his stomach. The look in her eyes was familiar and unwelcome. It was the same look he'd gotten from most of the people that lived in the tiny Alabama town he'd grown up in. The one that said he wasn't good enough to wipe the dirt off their shoes.

"I'm glad you're not trying to play me."

"Would I be able to?" He rubbed the back of his neck, suddenly exhausted.

"Nope. Been there, done that, and I'm divorcing the son of a bitch."

Despite the lead pellets that had made themselves at home in his stomach, he laughed. He would never admit it, because she didn't need an ego boost, but he liked Delilah. You always knew where you stood with her. Too bad it turned out where he stood was a shitty spot.

"I'm not joking with you." She wagged a finger in his face.

His visions of a fun breakfast with Olivia disappeared like smoke in the wind. "I didn't think you were."

"You need to be careful with Olivia."

"She's a grown woman." Hell, even he could tell he was getting defensive.

"It might look like she is, but she's socially stunted. It's the genius disease."

"You're not giving her enough credit." Olivia was one of the most amazing women he'd ever met.

"You might be giving yourself too much."

"What the hell does that mean?" Familiar feelings of anger laced with shamed rolled through his gut.

"We both know why you lost your ride to college. The whole world knows your criminal history and why you never got your shot at the pros. It's a miracle the Gills didn't use it to tank Ed and Cade's plan for the football program."

He was used to people throwing the past in his face. Funny, he hadn't expected Delilah to do it.

"Your point." This conversation had gone sideways fast and his good mood was gone. He needed to be somewhere else. Anywhere else. Now.

"After her failed attempt to dazzle the board she's under a microscope at the university. She's the youngest department head in Cormac history and it might do a lot of damage to her career if she gets mixed up with you. She's going to have to deal with some narrow-minded pricks for the foreseeable future. So, if you're just in it for a good time get out now, before you destroy another life."

With that pronouncement Delilah turned and sauntered down the hall. Funny how a woman could shred a man and then casually walk off as if nothing had happened.

Story of his life.

Nick turned around and went back into his room. He glanced at his watch. He was supposed to meet Olivia in a few minutes, but Delilah's words rang in ears. It didn't matter that the only life he'd destroyed when he was a teenager had been his own. It didn't matter that the mistake he'd made had been covering for someone else. It didn't even matter that everything he'd done at the time he'd done because of love.

Love was an emotion he didn't believe in anymore, which was why he had no business meeting Olivia for breakfast. He needed to end this before it began and, in a way that he couldn't take back. If he'd learned anything about Olivia in the last few months, it was that she was his Achilles heel. She could make him forget all his good intentions and the lessons he'd learned the hard way.

Nick booted up his laptop. It was time to remind himself of all the things he'd thought he could leave behind when he took the job at Cormac. Apparently, the universe agreed because there was a flight out from Las Vegas to Birmingham in an hour. He could rent a car and drive the rest of the way to the little town he'd put in his rear view mirror a long time ago.

For a minute, he thought about sticking around and going to find Olivia. Maybe he could lay the whole story out for her and see if she'd give them a shot. Except, his days as the golden boy, football hero were long gone. Fourteen years ago, he'd believed everything would work out if he did the right thing. He was wrong. The last few months in King's Folly had made him forget the basic facts of his life.

Hell, might as well take swim in the reality pool.

Three planes, one car ride and thirteen hours later he stood in front of the rundown trailer that had passed for his childhood home in Nowhere, Alabama.

"You need money?" His mother's voice, hoarse with too much yelling and too many cigarettes, came from behind him.

So much for "hello."

"I ever ask you for any?" They both knew he hadn't since he'd gotten his first job when he was nine.

"You in trouble?"

He'd forgotten how negative she was. "I can't just come visit my mother?"

"Why are you here?" The suspicion in her voice told him she didn't believe he would. She was right.

14

"Was in the neighborhood." That was a laugh. He'd made it his life's mission to be as far away from this neighborhood as he could since he was eighteen.

"Right. Pull the other one."

He shrugged. "Maybe I needed a reminder."

"Of what?" She stood in front of him, rigid.

Was it weird that he suddenly wished his mother would just hug him and tell him it's going to be okay? "Where I came from."

She snorted. He'd barely seen his mother since he'd gotten out of the service. She'd made it clear when he was eighteen that he was on his own, even after what he'd done for her.

"Wouldn't think you'd need to lay eyes on this place to remember that." There was something in her expression.

It looked like regret, but he couldn't be sure. Maybe the years he'd been away from her were helping him really see her. He blew out a breath. All the positive changes in his life lately had made him think he could finally leave this place behind for good. Delilah had reminded him that the past never stayed buried. This little detour on the way back to South Carolina drove it home.

A deep sigh drew his thoughts back to the moment.

"It's a mystery how me and your daddy made you boys.

Two ex-cons without a pot to piss in having two damn heroes for sons." It almost sounded like she was proud.

"I'm no hero." He never had been.

She crossed her arms. "I'll never understand why you did what you did, but we both know you didn't kill that girl."

"Didn't stop it from happening." It was a mystery to him why people tried to make excuses for him. Not doing the right thing was sometimes more catastrophic than doing the wrong thing.

"Proving you were young and stupid like most eighteen-year-old boys. Could have been just like your daddy. Taken the stint inside and rolled all the way downhill. Instead you took the out. Joined the Navy. Got yourself a chest full of medals." There was definitely pride in her voice.

How did she know that? He didn't think his mother cared about what happened to him after he'd left the courtroom that day. It would take a lot to convince him she'd even cared before.

"That judge used to stop by until Simon took off. He'd tell your brother how you were doing. I might have listened in from time to time."

Her begrudging tone forced him to look at her, really

16

look at her. She's been beautiful once. Before his father and life had leached the color out of her once brown hair, weathered her face and dulled the blue eyes she'd passed on to both her sons.

She rummaged through her beat-up purse for a few seconds and pulled out a cigarette. Trudging over to what passed for a lawn chair in front of the trailer, she lit up then sat down. As she took a long drag on her cigarette, she nodded to the pile of nylon and aluminum on the other side of the steps. He picked his way through the overgrown crab grass then sat, careful not to put his entire weight on the rickety chair.

His mother blew out a long puff of smoke. "It's not like I dreamed of being an ex-con and working as a truck stop waitress when I was a little girl. I had dreams." She paused and stared off into the distance.

Moisture pooled in her eyes as if she was thinking of the girl she'd once been. After a moment, she blinked the moisture away, like it was never there. "The first time I saw your daddy I thought he could make all my dreams come true. My mama told me he'd burn them to the ground."

She coughed. It was a hacking cough that sounded like she might lose a lung any second.

"He rode into town on his Harley and I thought when I

17

jumped on the back of it that I was done with small towns forever." His mother laughed. But there was no humor in her voice.

Nick wasn't sure what to say. They'd never talked about stuff like this before. Hell. He'd never talked about anything with his mother. His memories of her were mainly watching her leave for work, if she was around at all.

"Turns out my mama was right, which still burns my ass. After your daddy got finished torching my future, it was all I could do to keep a roof over our heads and food on the table when you two were boys. I didn't have time to do more. Maybe I should have." She sighed.

What was he supposed to say to her? Her excuses were as familiar to him as his own. He had plenty of friends with single mothers who'd busted their asses to provide for their kids and loved them at the same time.

As if she sensed his thoughts, she answered his unasked question. "I know there are women out there who do it all. Probably even women who went through worse than me. Truth is your daddy broke my heart and prison broke the rest of me. I didn't have it in me to keep fighting. Not even for my boys."

"Why didn't you let the state keep us?" Their brief stint in foster care hadn't been great, but they might have landed in a better home if their mother had let them go.

She cackled. "The one thing life never beat out of me was my stubborn streak."

That wasn't an answer. "Is there a reason you're talking about this?"

"I was never a good mom. Your daddy wasn't a good example of what kind of man you should be." She took another drag and blew out a puff of smoke, careful to blow away from him.

"He wasn't an example of what a human should be."

She cleared her throat. "Somehow. We managed to make two sons any mother would be proud of."

Shock rolled through him like he'd been zapped with a cattle prod. Of all the things he'd expected his mother to say, that wasn't one of them.

"Surprised you. I know it seemed like I didn't care. Truth is I did. I didn't have it in me to rise above my garbage to be there for you. That's on me."

"Not sure what you're looking for from me." He wasn't sure he knew how to comfort her, or if she would even let him.

"You don't owe me anything. Fact is, I'm lucky you're talking to me at all."

"You're my mother." That simple truth was at the heart

of his choices fourteen years ago.

"For a while anyway." She sounded resigned.

He shifted in the seat. The creak from the chair made him think he should stand up before it collapsed. "What's that mean?"

"I've got cancer. Stage four and no insurance. Doc gives me a year without treatment."

A year?

He looked past her bravado to focus on her. She was stick thin and there were circles under her eyes. Fatigue was etched in every line of her face. Calling her a crappy mother would be generous. But he'd sacrificed his future for her freedom once and she'd brought him into this world. Could he really let her leave it without a fight?

He ran a hand through his hair. "Shit. Simon and I can help with treatment." The bike shop they owned in King's Folly had started strong, thanks to Simon. There wasn't a lot of extra cash, but they could find a way.

She held up a hand. "Nothing to do. Only option is buy more time, but I'm not sure I want any."

"Mom." He hadn't called her that in more years than he could count.

"Been giving up my whole life. I guess there's no reason to stop now." She dropped her cigarette on the dirt patch next to her chair and tamped it out with her foot.

"Fuck that."

Her eyes widened.

He was surprised by his own vehemence. The thought of her crawling off to die made him want to find his old man and beat the hell out of him on principal.

"I don't deserve more." Defeat swirled around her, as visible as the smoke from her cigarette was a moment ago.

"World would be a sorry place if we all got what we deserved." God knows he'd always gotten more than his due.

"Can't argue with that." The hint of a smile played at the corners of her lips.

"You got anything keeping you here?" He couldn't imagine the answer to the question would be "yes."

She stared at him, her eyes blank, still not following where he was going.

"You're going to pack whatever you can't live without. Then you're coming to South Carolina to live with me and Simon. We'll get you into treatment. Maybe all we can do is buy you more time, but we're going to use it to put what's left of our family back together while we still can."

She didn't answer. Instead, she fished another cigarette out of the pack. Her hands shook as she tapped the end lightly on the pack then lit up. The shaking spread through her body as she took a drag on her cigarette and blew the smoke in his face.

He'd spent twelve years in the Navy. Before that he was one of most highly recruited offensive guards Alabama high school football had ever seen. He recognized a defense when he saw it.

"This ends today." He snatched the cigarette out of her hand at the same time he grabbed her purse. The half-empty pack of cancer sticks was on top and he snatched it out of her bag as he stomped out the lit butt.

"Who the hell do you think you are?" She stared at him with an expression he couldn't identify.

"I'm your son." Emotions he couldn't, or wouldn't, name rolled through him like a storm coming off the ocean.

"Hasn't meant much up 'til now."

"To either one of us," he agreed. "That changes too."

"What's got into you?" Her voice shook.

"Buddy of mine convinced me everyone deserves a second chance. Gave me mine." He still wasn't sure he deserved it, but he'd promised himself he would earn it.

"What's that got to do with me?"

"I figure everyone includes you."

Her eyes were wide and filled with something dangerously close to hope. "I never did a damn thing for you or your brother growing up."

"You gave us a roof, fed us, clothed us. From what you just said, seems to me you did your best. Maybe it's time you let someone do their best by you." He couldn't identify most of the feelings rolling around in his gut, but he did his best to ignore the feelings of betrayal that had been stewing since that night fourteen years ago.

She didn't seem to be able to respond. He wasn't sure if that was a tear building in the corner of her eye or a reflection. If he hadn't seen the moisture in her eyes a few minutes ago, he would have bet his savings on it being a reflection. She cleared her throat and looked at her feet.

He took her silence as agreement. "Let's go in and get what you need."

After a moment, she stood and went inside the trailer. He followed her. Nothing had changed, and everything had. It was neater than he remembered. That might be the fact that she didn't have two boys underfoot, or it might be that she'd changed in the years since he'd left.

His gaze was drawn to the wall next to the door as his mother disappeared into the back of the trailer. There were several framed photos. All of them were him and his brother. There was a framed copy of an article covering his return from his first deployment. It wasn't a well warn scrapbook wet with her tears of regret, but for his mother it was almost as meaningful.

"Take those."

Her voice from behind him made him turn. She stood there with a suitcase in one hand and a half-filled canvas bag in the other. He glanced at his watch. Twenty minutes had passed while he'd been caught up in the evidence his mother had given a damn about her sons.

"That all you want?"

"It's all I have that's worth taking, except for those." She nodded towards the pictures.

He carefully took them off the wall and handed them to her. She wrapped them in scarves and placed them in the bag like they were precious to her, making him feel about six inches tall. Had he ever noticed that beneath the screw you exterior his mother gave the world she actually gave a damn about her sons?

"You got your ID?"

She nodded.

"Okay. We're driving to Birmingham then I'll get us on a flight to Charleston. My truck is at the airport there." He'd been on three planes already today and wasn't looking forward to two more. But the flight time was half the drive time.

"We're going to fly?"

"Easiest way to get there."

"I've never been on a plane before." Her voice suddenly sounded so small.

And it was possible to feel lower. He and his brother had seen the world. Sure, they'd done a lot of that touring in Humvees seeing parts of the world where getting a tan came with dodging gunfire. Still, they'd left her behind. Never once bothering to consider that maybe, as much as she hadn't been there for them, it wasn't because she didn't want to be.

"It'll be fine." He picked up her suitcase in one hand and took her hand in the other. "I'll be with you from now on. Every step of the way."

It was just as well he'd walked away from Olivia. Between his mother, his jobs and his brother, he wasn't going to have anything left for her.

If he had anything worth giving in the first place.

Chapter 2

She glanced at the instructions she'd committed to memory the first time she'd read them. Of course, she'd re-read them ten more times just to make sure there wouldn't be any misunderstanding. The row of twenty plastic holders that housed the immunoassay strips all had two pink lines.

Pregnant.

Apparently, tequila induced passion didn't include safe sex. In the weeks since she'd left Las Vegas she'd stopped asking what would Beatrice, or any other Shakespeare heroine for that matter, would do. They wouldn't have a freaking clue. Especially now.

She was going to have a baby. Everything she'd done to avoid her mother's fate had been for nothing. Unmarried and pregnant. Her life had somehow landed on the same trajectory as her mother's, which wasn't good, all things considered.

Olivia pressed her hand over her belly, picturing a chubby little boy with blue eyes and his father's smile. Motherhood was her reality now, she wouldn't consider any other options. The question was, what was Nick going to think about being a father?

Would he want to be? She'd spent a pathetic hour at

breakfast that morning in Las Vegas. It only took her about fifteen minutes to realize he wasn't going to meet her there. Not the first time a man had disappointed her. For some reason, she hadn't expected it of Nick. Resolved to forget him, she'd enjoyed a leisurely meal reconstructing her emotional defenses, pretending a little piece of her heart hadn't broken that morning.

The flight back to South Carolina was interminable. Delilah had monopolized the conversation and, for some reason, had spent a majority of the flight complaining about how unreliable men were. She had to give her friend credit. Whatever Delilah did, she did with enthusiasm, whether it was called for or not.

Ever since Delilah had declared she was Olivia's new best friend she'd made a point of being around. It was endearing and annoying at the same time. No one had ever pursued any kind of relationship with Olivia with such fervor.

She wished she trusted the new friendship enough to confide in Delilah, or Tess or Charlie. But life had taught her that trust was too dangerous to give away. It gave others power over you. Power they always used to hurt you.

She placed her hand over her belly. First things first. She

needed to protect this baby and make sure she did everything right. Once she saw the doctor, and confirmed the
pregnancy with the appropriate laboratory tests, she would
talk to Nick and tell him he was going to be a father. Whatever his reaction, she would handle it. It wasn't just about
her anymore.

Three days later she stepped out of the doctor's office
and into a brick wall. A brick wall that felt very familiar.
Nick's arms steadied her as she looked up into his concerned blue eyes.

"Sorry. Are you all right?"

She nodded. The doctor had just confirmed that she and
Nick were going to be parents in thirty-seven weeks. As if
she'd summoned him, he was here.

"Olivia?"

She nodded again. For an English professor, she had an
appalling inability to use her words around him.

"You're kind of freaking me out here. Can you say
something? Anything?"

"I'm pregnant," she blurted.

Well that was one way of telling him. The color drained
from his face and he swayed a little. For a split second, she
was worried he was going to pass out. She wanted to
steady him, but if he went down she would go with him.

"Nick?"

"Are you sure?"

She pointed to the office behind her. "The doctor just confirmed it."

"How long have you suspected?"

"A couple of days. I wanted to be sure before I told you."

She braced herself for the cliched response. The insulting question about paternity that told a woman the man she'd been with thought she was a slut or stupid.

"How are you feeling?"

Once again, he defied expectations. "Physically I'm fine."

He nodded. The silence stretched between them like a high wire at the circus. She realized that they were in a building that housed medical offices only.

"What are you doing here? Are you all right?"

"My mom had an appointment with a specialist. She left her bag. I was going to grab it."

"Your mother?"

"Stage four lymphoma. We were going over treatment options."

"I'm so sorry." She put a hand on his upper arm wanting to comfort him, but not knowing how.

"Thanks. I guess I can add more to my plate now." He nodded towards her stomach.

His choice of words made her want to smack him. "You don't have to."

"What does that mean?" He narrowed his eyes.

"It means I'm a healthy woman, with a good job that's not physically demanding and I'm financially secure." She was actually quite well-off but didn't need to broadcast it. "You don't have to add anything else to your plate." Maybe she could kick him.

"I don't know what you want me to say."

If she knew, she might tell him. "I hadn't planned on telling you this way."

"But you did plan on telling me."

"Of course, I did. But I wasn't going to blurt it out in a public hallway."

"Okay." The way he drew out the one word made her feel like a wild animal he was trying not to corner.

"You clearly have a lot to handle already."

He narrowed his eyes. "Doesn't mean I don't take care of my responsibilities."

"That's not what I meant." The last thing she wanted was to be just a responsibility to anyone. Ever again.

"Say what you mean, then."

She hoped he didn't mean to sound as sharp as he did. "You're worried about your mother and she's probably waiting for you. So why don't you take a little time to get used to everything. When you know how involved you want to be we can sit down and talk about how we're going to move forward."

When he didn't respond immediately she turned and walked down the hall, shoulders tight, head held high.

That could have gone better.

Later that night, Olivia studied the calendar she'd just finished. She'd worked back from the baby's due date and included all the critical milestones and dates. The minute she'd gotten home she'd done what she'd been too shell shocked to do at the doctor's office and scheduled all her follow up appointments.

The next thirty-seven weeks were laid out. A few weeks were set aside for redoing the room next to her office to make it a nursery. She needed to research early development and color, so she could choose the best decorating scheme for the baby. Another item on her growing to do list.

Her thoughts were interrupted by a knock on the door. Wondering who would be here this late she went to her front hall and peeked out the window overlooking the front

31

porch.

Her body heated, the way it always did whenever she saw Nick. She opened the door.

"Hi." Words continued to fail her.

"Hi." He shoved his hands in his back pockets. "Can I come in?"

She stepped aside and shut the door after he'd made his way into the front hall. "Sure."

He looked around. "Nice place."

"Thank you." She loved living on the beach. "Do you want something to drink?"

"Water if it's not too much trouble."

"Sure."

He followed her toward the kitchen but stopped at the breakfast room table where her lists and calendar were laid out. She watched him out of the corner of her eye as he studied her afternoon's efforts while she poured him a glass of water.

She tapped him on the shoulder making him jump. His gaze had been focused on the date circled in bright red ink on the calendar. Her due date. He turned back to her and took the water from her, which he guzzled in a couple of seconds.

"Thirsty?" She couldn't keep the humor out of her

voice.

"Freaked out."

"I can relate." Her pregnancy felt surreal.

He ran a hand through his hair. "I don't know how good I'll be at this."

"It's new to me too." She'd spent so much of her life detached from others. The prospect of an instant bond with her baby terrified her.

"Yeah, but you're a better person than I am. I'll probably be a shitty father."

"What makes you say that?"

"Never had a good role model. My dad's an ex-con. I haven't seen him in more than twenty years. Hell, he could be back in prison for all I know."

"Maybe he's sharing a cell with my father."

The minute the words were out of her mouth she cringed. She never talked about her father. Ever.

"Your dad's in prison?"

She nodded. It was her least favorite topic. The look in his eyes told her she wouldn't be able to get away without answering some questions. There was no way she would answer them all.

His blue eyes were warm with sympathy. "Why?"

"Murder," she whispered.

33

"Who'd he kill?"

Could she say the words? "My mother."

"Are you serious?" The shock in his voice was clear.

"Do you think that's something I would joke about?" Anyone who knew her at all would know that sarcasm wasn't something she indulged in.

"Sorry. It's just…not what I expected at all."

She shrugged. People saw what they wanted to see when they looked at her. Usually, their perceptions were completely off the mark.

"How long has…" He stopped talking, as if it was his turn to be at a loss for words.

It was odd, how much she wanted to talk to him about things she hadn't spoken of in years.

"He murdered her when I was sixteen, almost fourteen years ago. He got life without parole."

"Where did you go?"

"I was already in graduate school. I was basically eman-cipated."

"Didn't you have any family?"

"My grandmother. We weren't particularly close, but she did her best." The standard answer came out of her mouth. For the first time in a long time, she really wanted to tell someone the truth. But the truth meant trust and she hadn't trusted anyone since the night her mother died.

Who was she kidding? Nick had some kind of pull on her. It was all she could do to keep herself from blurting out all her secrets. How could she trust him with them when she couldn't trust him to show up for breakfast?

"At least I had my brother when things went south."

She latched onto a different subject. "He looks like you."

"You've met?"

She shook her head. "Delilah pointed him out to me when we were at lunch."

"Oh. So…"

"Why did you come over tonight?"

"I wanted to tell you that I'd be here for you and the baby."

"Oh. How?" Her stomach turned to lead. Could she do this? Let him be part of their lives?

He blinked. "However, you need me to be."

"I want you to want to be involved." She sounded like an idiot, even to herself.

"I'm here for you, and the baby."

"But?" There was always a but. Nothing good had ever happened to her that hadn't been followed by something that minimized it. It was her least favorite word in the English language.

"I don't know how to say this without sounding like an asshole."

"I find just telling the truth is the best policy." She'd spent her entire childhood swimming lies. The same thing was not going to happen to her own child.

"There's a reason I decided meeting you for breakfast was a bad idea."

If he'd slapped her it wouldn't have hurt more. "I don't intend to use this child as a way to pretend we're more than we are."

His eyes widened. "What do you mean?"

"I mean, I'm not stupid. Quite the opposite. I didn't mistake you standing me up as a declaration of your undying love. It was clear what it was."

"What was it?"

"A rather graceless kiss off." It took all her strength to keep from crying at the memory.

He winced. "I'm sorry. I just —"

She held up a hand. "We don't need to rehash it. Neither of us expected to be here. It's not about us. It's about our child. If you want to play a role in our baby's life, I want that too, but you need to promise me you plan on being there. I don't want you to say one thing and do another.

36

I'd rather do this alone than be abandoned when you re-think your options."

"I guess I deserved that." He pinched the bridge of his nose. "I'll be honest. I've never seen myself as the long-haul kind of guy."

"I hate to tell you this, but babies are a long-haul situation."

"I know." He ran a hand through his hair. "I'm messing everything up."

Olivia had been teaching long enough to know this could go around in circles for a while. She took his hand and led him away from the calendar and lists to the sun porch off the kitchen.

"Sit."

Her dog, well puppy really, who'd been ridiculously quiet since the knock on the door stood up from her bed next to the couch, one of many throughout the house, and started barking.

"Hush, Kate."

"I didn't know you had a…is that a dog?"

"Don't make fun of her." Olivia sat on the end of the couch closest to the mutt she'd adopted.

Her friend Tess, also a veterinarian, had guessed Kate had some German Shepard and some Pekinese and a bunch

37

of other breeds that would require DNA testing to confirm. It didn't matter what kind of dog she was. The minute Olivia had seen the pup she'd fallen in love. Mongrels had to stick together.

The mongrel in question had stopped barking. Instead, she'd taken up a defensive position in front of Olivia and was growling at Nick.

He laughed. "Sorry. She's just…it's a she right?"

"Yes. Her name is Kate."

"*Taming of the Shrew*?" He hunkered down and held a hand out to Kate.

He knew Shakespeare. The look he gave her told her she hadn't hidden her surprise very well.

"Not all jocks are dumb." He snatched his hand back as the puppy snapped at him.

"I didn't think you were dumb. Kate's a common name, not many people would associate it with Shakespeare."

"I liked that one." He stood when it became clear Kate wasn't warming to him. "*Much Ado About Nothing* is my favorite though."

"Mine too. I always thought Beatrice and Benedict were the best couple."

"Yeah. I liked that he stood up for his girl and her cousin against his friends. He knew what was important."

She was struck momentarily speechless. She'd been mocked by some scholars for her defense of the play.

"I...think that's a brilliant point."

He blushed. It was endearing to see a man of his size turn red at a compliment from her.

"Thanks," he mumbled.

"I meant it when I said I didn't want you to feel pressured into doing anything you don't want. It's best for the baby if we both want to be involved. Children are extraordinarily intuitive. They can tell when someone doesn't really want to be with them."

"I want to be a part of this kid's life. I do. I also want to help you."

"But?" There was that word again.

"I don't know how good I'll be at it. I didn't show up in Vegas because I knew I was no good for you. I figured standing you up was like ripping the band-aid off. It would hurt less in the long run."

He was the most confusing man she'd ever met. It was her luck that she would be forever tied to a man she was wildly attracted to but didn't understand. The same thing had killed her mother.

Was she always destined to follow in the woman's footsteps? Because that would not end well.

◀▦▶ ◀▦▶ ◀▦▶

This wasn't going well. He wasn't sure how he thought it could go. When he'd realized he needed to let Olivia know he would stand by her and help her with the pregnancy and the baby, he'd gotten in his truck to drive to her place. She only lived down the beach, but it might as well have been another planet. Their differences had grown bigger in his mind and any attempt to come up with a plan for their conversation went out the window.

He still couldn't believe he was going to be a father. When had his life spun so far out of control?

"Nick?"

"Sorry. Just thinking. Look, I know I'm no prize. I came here to tell you I want to help." He ran a hand through his hair. "Don't know what kind of father I'll be, but I'll do my best by this baby, and you."

Speeches weren't his thing. He figured this was the best he could do. Hopefully, it was enough.

"I appreciate that."

Her response could be more lukewarm, but he wasn't sure how. Of course, given what he'd learned about her parents, he was guessing she didn't have a lot of experience with dependable men. He may not be relationship material, but he was reliable. Once he committed to something, he was all in. Not that she had any evidence of that.

"So, it looks like you've got a schedule going already." He jerked his head toward the kitchen. His stomach had done back flips when he'd seen the due date circled. March eighteenth. He was going to be dad on March eighteenth.

Fuck.

"I like to come up with a plan when I can. It doesn't always work out, but it's a good place to start."

She was pretty cute when she retreated behind her professor wall.

"Yeah. I should probably do one of those calendars. Keep everything straight."

"I know you have a lot to do with the football program and your business with your brother. With your mother sick, too, I don't expect – "

"It's obvious you don't expect much from me." That burned in his gut.

She shrugged. "I've been on my own for a long time."

"Just because I didn't plan on being in this place with you, doesn't mean I'm going to let you down. My schedule might be tight, but I'm going to be here for you and the baby. But I get it. I have to walk the walk, not just talk the talk."

She nodded. "I know everyone thinks I have my head in the clouds because of my chosen profession, but I've had two feet planted on the ground for most of my life."

He understood what she was saying. "I'd say we both got stuck with facing reality when we were young. I say we work together to make sure our baby gets be a kid for as long as possible. We can figure it out together as we go."

"That sounds reasonable." Her shoulders relaxed slightly.

That was progress.

"You mind if I copy down the dates you've got organized?" He nodded toward the calendar on the table. "I'll get you a copy of my schedule, so we can match them up. Maybe we can have lunch together in the next couple of days start figuring things out."

"That would be fine."

Nick moved to the table and stared down at the calendar that documented the next eight months of Olivia's life. He tried to hide his smile. The color coding was cute as hell, but he didn't think she'd appreciate him pointing that out right now.

Once he'd gotten all the dates copied down he left her with a handshake. A freaking handshake. The best night of his life had resulted in a baby and all he was doing with his kid's mother was shaking hands.

Story of his life.

Later that night, Nick sat on his back porch listening to the waves of the ocean break against the shore. Beach front property wasn't cheap, but he and his brother had gotten a great deal on this house. It was rundown and in foreclosure. The owners wanted to get out before the bank took it. So, he and Simon had gotten the property for a steal. After seeing Olivia's upscale home, he felt like he was back on the other side of the tracks.

His brother had always wanted to live on the beach and Nick didn't really care one way or another. He had to admit, the sounds of the beach at night were relaxing. Too bad he was too keyed up to appreciate it.

He turned at the sound of the sliding glass door. His mother came out on the porch.

"If you're out here to sneak a smoke, think again." He wasn't sure why he was so gung ho to fight for her life, when she seemed so ambivalent herself.

"Nope. Looked like you had something on your mind. God knows you've got no reason to come to me with your problems, but since we're trying to do this mother son thing, I thought I'd come out see if you wanted to talk."

Simon followed their mother. "You don't want to talk to

her, you can talk to me."

He shrugged. "You both might as well know. I'm going to be a father in March."

"You sure it's yours?" His mother's question pissed him off.

"Yes." The anger in his voice was obvious.

"Don't get pissed at her. I would have asked if she hadn't." His brother sat in the chair next to him.

"Olivia and I hooked up at Cade's wedding."

His brother whistled. "Olivia? *The* Olivia is pregnant with your kid?"

"Who's this Olivia?" His mother's rasp hadn't started to improve since she quit smoking.

"She's a professor at the university. Nick's had the hots for her since he met her."

"I wouldn't say that." Nick felt heat slide along his neck.

It looked like his mother wanted to reach out to him for a minute but clenched her fist instead. "What's wrong with her?"

"Nothing's wrong with her." He wasn't thrilled that this conversation had turned into defending Olivia to his mother and brother.

"Then why aren't you with her?" His mother sounded curious.

"Because I'm not good enough for her. She deserves better than an ex-con with a past like mine."

His brother stared at him. "That bullshit was expunged and it's ancient history. So why don't you tell us what's really going on."

For a minute, Nick thought about arguing. His past would never be history. But, he was too tired to have this argument with his brother again. "I'm not going to talk about it. I'm telling you both, so you can help me keep my shit together over the next eight months."

"I can go back to Alabama. Get out of your hair." His mother pinched her lips together.

Simon snorted. "Yeah right, Mom. Nick and I are going to send you back to Alabama to die. Not happening."

Their mother shrugged. She'd been walking on eggshells since Nick had brought her home. Once Simon had found out what was going on, he'd gotten on board with the plan. But the three of them hadn't shared a home in fourteen years, they were all dancing around each other without dealing with anything other than immediate concerns.

"Olivia's a good woman. Got a good job and a career of her own. I need to be there for her, but it's not like she's going to need me to do everything for her. We can figure it

45

out, it might mean you need to carry a little more around here." Nick looked at Simon.

A throat clearing drew their attention to the side of the porch. Bob Moore, Nick's mentor stood there.

"Didn't mean to eavesdrop."

"But you did anyway." Nick couldn't help smiling. Bob was a legendary coach and learning to take over the strength training for the university from him was an opportunity Nick never thought he'd have in a million years.

Bob shrugged, but didn't say any more, at least not about the eavesdropping. "Sounds like you got a pretty full plate."

Nick shrugged, trying not to show how much this man's opinion mattered to him. The only person other than Bob he was dreading sharing this news with was Cade. His boss and best friend was one of the men he respected most in the world. Not to mention Cade's new wife was one of Olivia's closest friends. Cade and Tess both might have a thing or two to say about the situation.

"I can handle my responsibilities." He looked at his mother. "All of them."

"Don't doubt you can. But I know a thing or two about some of those responsibilities. I can help you with some of it."

46

Bob had lost his wife after a hard-fought battle against cancer. Nick knew he would need the man's strength and wisdom to get through this.

"I'm not going to turn down help. But I'm not asking anyone to pull my weight."

"Didn't think you were." The older man crossed his arms.

"I know you didn't come by just to listen in on our conversation." Bob wasn't the kind to just show up anywhere.

"Nope. Got off the phone with Ed a little while ago. Seems the Gills have regrouped and are planning some new kind of ass hattery."

Damn. The Gills had tried to prevent Ed and Cade from taking over as co-head coaches of the Cormac football team a few months ago at a meeting of the Board of Trustees. It had been epic. The Gills had had their asses handed to them by Tess and the Board. Seems they didn't learn their lesson.

"Do we know what they're up to?"

"Not yet. We're having a meeting in the morning. Want to make sure we got our plans laid out and tight. No room for them to worm their way in and mess things up."

"What time?" Nick tried to remember what Olivia's calendar looked like tomorrow. Their conversation earlier had

47

left a lot up in the air. He hated that. It was better when things were laid out and he know what was expected of him.

"Eight. Ron's office."

Nick nodded. He fished the small pad of paper out of his pocket that held all of Olivia's dates to make sure he wasn't going to have to let her down right away. There was nothing baby related on her calendar tomorrow. Good. "I can be there."

Bob nodded. "Once we finish the meeting, you and I are going to meet. We'll go through the schedule. We've got some time to get everything in order."

Nick nodded. With the sanctions the football team was facing they would have a smaller than usual roster this fall and no games to train for since this season was cancelled. But he'd be working with Bob to run the strength programs for the other sports.

The good thing about the set-up Ed and Cade had come up with was that the younger coaches had a chance to learn the job from the ground up working with some of the best coaches college football had ever seen before they had to fly solo.

"I'll see you in the morning." Cade shoved his calendar

in his pocket. His note pad full of notes paled in comparison to Olivia's neatly organized planner.

Bob nodded and with a last glance between Nick, his mother and brother wandered back the way he'd come with a wave of his hand.

The next morning, Nick sat at the conference table in the athletic department with Bob, Cade, Ed and Ron Jackson, Cormac's athletic director.

"We've got commitments from all my guys," Ed said. "They'll be back and ready to go by the middle of August."

Cade nodded. "My team will take a little longer to assemble. Most of them still owe the military a little time on their current enlistments. Ben, Frankie and Boomer have a few things to wrap up and will be here sooner than the rest."

"I'd be worried about your entire crew not being here sooner if we had to get a team ready to play this season." Ed rubbed the back of his neck.

"I know." Cade nodded. "Since the upcoming season is cancelled for the Knights, we don't have to worry about a game schedule or training for one. I've arranged for some practice games with some of the local varsity teams. That should give the players we do have some experience playing under our coaching system."

"Couldn't we at least arrange some games with community colleges?" Nick couldn't imagine many college athletes being thrilled about going back to playing high school players.

Cade shook his head. "The local junior colleges have league play and full schedules. I am working on building relationships with some of the junior colleges because we can get some great talent from them once we can start recruiting again."

"Which will be when?" Nick looked around the room. It was hard to put a team back together without players.

"Recruitment ban is officially lifted after the national championship. No going after eligible players until then."

"Most of the top high school players will have signed commitments by then." Nick had been committed to his top choice the second the rules allowed him to sign.

Ed chewed on the butt of his perpetually unlit cigar. "The very best high school players have been committed to schools for years. Hell, a school out west got a commitment from a nine-year-old player."

"Nick. You and Cade both know there's plenty of talent that doesn't get picked up for one reason or another." Ron gave them both pointed looks. "We're going to have to get creative finding players the first couple of years. Not look in the obvious places. We're going to be looking for athletes with talent, hunger and drive. The kind of players who will stick with a program while it rebuilds. Who'll take pride in being part of the rebuilding we're doing here."

He didn't disagree. The former coaching staff had gotten rich while sucking the football program dry and breaking every league rule they could. Nick was a little surprised Cormac didn't fold the team outright after the sanctions that were imposed. They needed a miracle to rebuild the team and this plan Cade and Ed had might be it.

They spent the next few hours talking about logistics and trying to figure out ways the Gills could potentially mess with them. Gill Senior was still an influential alum, even though he'd been forced to resign from the Board of Trustees after the recent meeting. He and his son were sneaky bastards and Nick wouldn't put anything past them. Everyone agreed they needed to keep their eyes and ears open.

"If there's nothing else — " Ron started stacking the papers in front of him.

"I have something to say. An announcement really."

All eyes turned to him.

"Olivia Valenti is pregnant and I'm the father. She's due in March. So, I'll have a lot on my plate. Bob and I are going to work things out so my job doesn't suffer, but I wanted you all to hear it from me." The words poured out of Nick's mouth. "No jokes about shotgun weddings, either. We're figuring out what's next. I don't want anyone putting pressure on her."

Cade cleared his throat. "Does Tess know?"

Was Cade pale?

"Better yet, does Olivia know you're telling people?" Ed asked, a look on his face Nick couldn't figure out. Was he trying not to laugh or puke?

"I imagine Olivia will tell Tess. She's only a few weeks along so I'm guessing she's not going to go wide with it for a while, but I've made a commitment to you all and the program and I want to make sure all my cards are on the table."

Looking at the expressions on the faces of the other men, all of whom were or had been married, Nick felt his stomach seize up. "What?"

"Son." Ed grimaced. "You've just violated the first major rule of relationships. You don't share your woman's business without her permission."

"I'm sure she'll understand. She's a logical woman."

Bob chuckled. "She's also loaded up on hormones and in the first trimester of her pregnancy." He held out his right arm and pointed to a small scar on his forearm. "Got that when my Barbara was pregnant with our first. I told Ed she was pregnant before she told anyone else. When she found out she stabbed me with a fork."

Nick winced. He couldn't imagine Olivia reacting like that, but then again, Bob's wife, from all accounts, was one of the sweetest women that ever lived.

Shit. Olivia's going to kill me.

Chapter 3

I'm going to kill him.

Olivia hung up the phone after her conversation with one of her best friends, who had called to tell her that she would be there for Olivia, whatever she needed. Tess had also made it clear that she'd found out about the pregnancy from Cade who'd found out at a coaches' meeting. Apparently, Nick had announced it to everyone there.

Olivia paced her office. The contrast of the sea foam green and cream fabrics against the antique walnut woods usually soothed her. She'd painstakingly chosen every item. It was an exact reproduction of her mother's home office. The only thing that was missing was the mini version of the desk and chair, which her mother had made for Olivia.

Should I order a desk and chair now for my baby?

She put her hand over her stomach. Would her child need a sanctuary like the one her mother had given her?

Bad idea to go there. She shook off the thought and resumed pacing. Her anger built with each step. Was it too much to be able to decide when she told people about her pregnancy? She was only a few weeks along. What if something happened? Then she'd have to deal with all the pitying looks. There had been enough of those in her life after her mother's death. Pity was useless. It was the emotion people expressed to make themselves feel better about someone else's pain without actually doing anything to try and alleviate it.

If this was a cartoon she was sure steam would be coming out of her ears. She wanted to hit something. Or throw up. It was impossible to tell if that was the anger or the baby. Although it was probably too early to be the baby. Anger it was. Anger at Nick. Anger that built with every step across the carpet. As she was contemplating the next course of action there was a knock on her door.

"Come in," she said without thinking. She wasn't prepared for visitors.

The door opened, and the object of her fury stood there, in all his glory.

"You have some nerve." She couldn't find anymore words for what he'd done.

He held up his hands. "I know. I screwed up."

"Screwed up? This is more than screwing up. This is a total violation."

Nick stepped into the office then shut the door behind him. "That's seems a little exaggerated."

"Exaggerated? Exaggerated? We haven't even had a serious conversation about how we're going to co-parent this baby. I'm not even through my first trimester. We definitely didn't come to a decision together about how we were going to tell people."

"I know, but — "

She held up a hand. "Now, thanks to your big mouth it will be all over town by sunset."

"None of the people I told will spread it around." He sounded defensive.

"This is a small town. Once news like this is out, it's out." She started pacing again. Her mind zoomed along dozens of tangents. "I'm going to have to tell the dean. He's going to have things to say about me being single and pregnant. They're going to try and force me out of my job." She knew she was being irrational. None of those things were likely to happen.

He stepped in front of her and put his hands on her shoulders. "Stop. Breath."

It was like she was no longer in control of her body. Instead of calming down she punched him in the nose. A sharp pain shot up her arm.

"Ow. Ow. Ow." She shook her hand then stared at her knuckles, which were already turning red.

Horror shot through her as she looked up at him. Nick was rubbing his nose, staring at her with an expression that was equal parts frustration and amusement. "We're going to have to work on your hook, Slugger."

He glanced down at her hand and scowled. "We need to get some ice for this." Nick cradled her hand in his.

"I'm so sorry. I don't know what came over me." She'd never hit anyone in her entire life. Even when they deserved it.

He massaged her hand, careful of the reddening knuckles. Tingles zipped across her skin, resurrecting memories of their night together.

Nick chuckled. "I guess I bring out the best in you." He blew on her knuckles.

It was all she could do to ignore the fluttering in her belly. "You bring out something in me." With her other hand, she swept a curl that had slipped from her bun out of her face.

He laughed. His laugh was the best thing she'd ever heard. It was soothing, like drinking hot cocoa on a cold night by the fire.

"I am sorry. We've got a lot going on with the team and this is a big deal for me. I'm used to giving my men all the important intel. I should have talked to you before telling anyone."

It was a sweet apology accompanied by a reason for his announcement which didn't feel like a justification. Still, it was a violation, one that couldn't be ignored even for an apology accompanied by twinkling blue eyes.

"I wanted more time before I had to make any announcements." It wasn't unheard of for a woman to be unmarried and pregnant, this was the twenty-first century. But it was a small southern town. Someone was bound to open their mouth and try to make trouble for her.

"I know it's a small town, but no one I know is going to spread gossip about us." He sounded like he actually believed it.

"You hope."

"I know. Cade told Tess. I'll bet fifty bucks that Tess hasn't even told Charlie or Delilah."

That seemed unlikely to Olivia. "They're her friends."

"So are you."

It was odd, thinking of herself as having real friends. She'd spent so long holding the world at a distance, it gave her a jolt every time she realized someone had gotten through some of her defenses and none of her recent efforts at rebuilding had succeeded in pushing anyone out.

"Why does that surprise you?" He sounded surprised.

"Honestly?"

"Between us, from now on, only the truth, the whole truth and nothing but the whole truth."

She wished she could believe that. "That's a tall order."

He shrugged. "We're having a kid. We need to be able to trust each other."

Olivia sighed. "You're right." It was going to be easier said than done.

"Don't sound so happy about it."

"I'm happy about the baby. I'm freaked out about it, too." She'd leave the issue of trust out of the discussion for now. It wasn't a conversation she was prepared to have with him.

"You and me both." He scrubbed his hand down his face.

"I've been on my own for a long time. I'm not used to people actually caring about me or being involved in my life." She'd been on her own since her mother died. With few exceptions, she hadn't made any lasting connections since that night.

"You're going to have to get used to it. Once Delilah knows she's going to be impossible to shake."

"Why do you say that?"

He shrugged but didn't answer her question.

The look on his face told her there was something he didn't want to tell her. So much for trust. "What do you know?"

"I know a lot." He evaded her question.

"About Delilah?"

Nick studied her but didn't say anything.

"The truth, the whole truth and nothing but the truth," she reminded him. If he really meant it, he needed to start now.

"Fine. She cornered me when I was heading downstairs to meet you for breakfast in Vegas."

"What did she say?" Anger rolled through her again. Delilah had something to say about everything. The thought that he would let her get in the way of meeting for breakfast gave her pause. Was that all it would take to make him run again? One snarky comment from a nosy friend?

"She's protective of you."

She would deal with Delilah later. "What did she say?"

He looked up at the ceiling. "She wants you to be happy."

"What did she say?" She enunciated each word. If he didn't answer her soon she might punch him in the nose again.

"She warned me not to hurt you." He still wouldn't look her in the eyes.

"Why?"

"She thinks I'm not a long-haul kind of guy and that you deserve that."

She yanked her hand out of his and started pacing the room for the third time. If this kept up she wouldn't need to get any other exercise today. "She's got more nerve than a set of lips."

"Than a what?"

His bark of laughter stopped her mid-pace. "What?"

"You said more nerve than a set of lips." His smile soothed and irritated her at the same time.

"I know." She tilted her head.

"What's that mean?"

"The lips have the highest concentration of nerve endings in the human body." She didn't understand why he was confused. It was common knowledge.

Wasn't it?

"Really?"

So much for common knowledge. "Yes."

"That's funny." He chuckled.

"Thank you."

"You're welcome."

She pinched the bridge of her nose. "What were we talking about?"

"I almost don't want to say."

"Why?" Was he always going to hold things back from her? How could they have any kind of relationship if he did that?

"Because we'd gone from you pissed off and pacing to us having a conversation." Nick smiled.

"Oh."

He ran a hand through his hair. "Delilah just reminded me of something I forgot for a little while."

"What's that?"

"I don't believe in love."

She started pacing again. It seemed impossible to contain all her nervous energy. "What do you mean you don't believe in love?"

"What do you mean what do I mean?"

Olivia stopped and faced him. "It's a simple question."

"No. It's not."

"It should be," she mumbled.

"What's that mean?"

"Love is more than an emotion. It's an action. It's as real as the sensation of pain I felt when I punched you." It was a lesson she learned at her mother's knee. Anyone could say the words. The people who meant them backed them up with deeds.

"That's your opinion." He sounded frustrated.

62

She wanted to hit him again. "It's a fact."

"How can you say that?"

She threw up her hands. "I teach literature. It's filled with the range of human emotions, including love."

"This is an insane conversation." He ran a hand through his hair again.

"You started it." She moved to the small sofa and sat, suddenly exhausted.

How could he not believe in love?

"How about we get back on track."

"Which track? I think we've been down a few since you showed up." She normally hated being unable to follow a conversation. Somehow, with Nick it was frustrating, but not annoying.

"First. I hope you'll accept my apology for talking about the baby before you were ready."

His pronouncement about not believing in love had actually made her forget the reason she'd gotten mad at him in the first place. His apology had sounded sincere. She could even understand his logic. But he'd broken her trust for a second time. How could she rely on him?

"I understand why you did it."

He let out a breath. "But do you accept my apology?"

"I believe you're sincere. But you're going to have to

give me some time. It was a major violation, taking the choice of when to announce my pregnancy away from me."

"I know. I am sorry. Tell me what I can do to make it up to you?" He sounded a little desperate.

"I'm going to need you to be patient. We haven't really spent a lot of that together if you think about it. It's going to take more than a few minutes for me to process this and get over it. To trust you not to do it again."

Nick ran his hand through his hair for a third time.

He seemed to do that when he was frustrated.

"I know myself well enough to know I'm going to screw up again. I need to know how long I'm going to be in the doghouse."

"I can't answer that right now. The best I can do is tell you I won't harp on it. You messed up, but you've apologized. Now you have to give me time to move on from it." She'd become an expert at moving on from betrayal over the years.

He studied her for a moment before he nodded. "Okay. Next, we need to figure out what we're going to do. How we're going to handle the pregnancy."

"You really want to be involved?" She chewed on her bottom lip.

His gaze focused on her lips for a second before his blue

64

eyes looked into hers. "I've said so, haven't I?"

"You've also said you don't believe in love. That makes me wonder why you want to be a part of this child's life."

"I'm sure I'll love our child."

That made no sense to her. "How, if you don't believe in the emotion?"

"You're twisting my words."

"I'm not. I'm trying to understand how you can't believe in love, but want to parent a child, an experience I believe should be all about love." Raising a child without love was cruel. She should know.

"Fine. I don't believe in romantic love."

She rubbed her forehead. "You are so confusing."

"Do you think I'll be a bad father?"

The hint of vulnerability in his voice tore at her heart. "Quite the opposite. I think you'll be an amazing father."

"Why?"

"You're an honorable man, who fights for what he believes in and stands by the people he cares about, dare I say loves." He also took responsibility for his mistakes, but they'd talked enough about his bad judgment for one day.

He mumbled something as a deep red blush spread up the back of his neck.

"What?"

"Thank you."

"You're welcome." Had they made progress? She couldn't tell.

"So, what's next?"

"I have a list I've been working on." She always had lists.

He smiled. "Of course, you do."

She didn't appreciate his tone. "It helps to be organized."

"I'm not making fun of you. I like having everything in order, too." He pulled out a dogeared pad of paper with post-its sticking out in every direction.

"What is that?" The thought that he considered it orderly made her cringe.

"It's my calendar." He looked at her like it was the most obvious thing in the world.

"That's not a calendar." It was barely a notebook.

"What is it then?"

She took the pad from him and flipped through it. "What language is this?"

"English." He laughed.

"This bears no resemblance to any version of the English language I have ever learned or taught."

"Ha ha." He took the pad out of her hand. "It works for

me."

"Does it?"

"It always has."

"Have you tried to balance a full-time job as strength and conditioning coach, opened a garage and dealt with two sets of medical appointments, one for cancer treatment and the other for pregnancy?"

He stared down at the pad. "Can't say I have."

"With everything going on, maybe you should upgrade your system." Anything would be better than what he was using.

"I can't stand those freaking electronic calendars. I don't need my phone beeping or buzzing every sixty seconds."

"I think we can come up with something in between the two extremes."

"Like what?"

Olivia stood up then moved to the cabinet behind her desk. She opened the door to the cabinet and fished around until she found what she was looking for. It was a compact calendar, black and streamlined. Perfect for Nick.

He walked up to stand behind her before she could turn around and give it to him.

"What's all this?" He reached past her and started thumbing through the stacks of books and loose-leaf pages.

She felt heat roll through her body. "I like planners."

"Clearly. Aren't a lot of these out of date?"

"Most of them are blank or can be adapted." There was no way she was going to tell him about the boxes of calendars she had saved and in storage.

"So, you collect them?"

It had started as a way to keep her mother close, holding on to her planners and diaries. Somehow, she had amassed a collection over the years. "Yes."

He took the small black planner out of her hand and flipped through it. "This should work. You sure you can part with it?"

She nodded. "I give them out to students and colleagues when they need help organizing their schedules."

"I definitely need something. Do you think you could help me get my notes organized into this?"

She glanced at her watch. "I have a class to teach in about twenty minutes."

"How about I grab dinner and come by your place tonight. We can get your appointments in my calendar and start figuring out how we're going to do this."

"Okay. Can we have pizza?" She'd been craving it all morning.

"Sure. What do you like on your pizza?"

"Extra cheese, sausage, pepperoni and bacon."

He smiled. "I'll be there at six."

With that he strolled out the door leaving her to wonder how he'd done it. Minutes ago, she'd been so mad she punched him. Now he was bringing pizza over to her house, so they could organize his calendar.

I'm in big trouble.

He couldn't get a bead on Olivia. She was so much more than he thought she was, and nothing like he expected. Every time he thought he had her figured out, she showed a new side of her personality. Funny, he'd never liked complicated before her. Complicated in the form of her curvy body, brown hair and blue eyes was a whole other story.

He glanced down at the leather-bound book in his hand. An organizer. She'd given him an organizer. Nick couldn't remember the last time anyone had just given him anything just to help him out.

"What are you doing here?"

The sound of Brian Gill, Jr.'s voice threw his day straight to hell.

"I could ask you the same question, Backup." He knew Gill hated the nickname he'd gotten in college when he'd spent four years as backup quarterback instead of getting to start for the football team here at Cormac.

"I have business here."

"In the English department at Cormac? Last I heard, the board told you and daddy dearest to limit your appearances on campus to alumni events."

Gill's eyes narrowed. Score. Now Gill knew Nick was aware of his history.

"Wylie talks too much."

Anger rolled through Nick like a tidal wave at Brian's use of a nickname for Tess that she hated. "Watch it. Tess is my friend, and my best friend's wife." Backup shouldn't be talking about her at all or lurking around Olivia's office.

"What are you going to do about it?" Gill sneered.

"Why are you here, Brian?" Olivia's voice kept Nick from punching the other man.

"I need to talk to you, baby."

The endearment that slid off Gill's tongue made Nick want to do more than punch him.

"First, endearments are not appropriate between us. Second, we have nothing to say to each other." Olivia came to stand next to Nick and crossed her arms.

"Don't tell me you're dating this loser." Brian tilted his chin in Nick's direction.

"I'm not telling you anything, you craven fen-sucked lout. Why are you here?"

Nick barked out a laugh. He wanted to grab Olivia carry her into her office and lock the world out. There was something about a woman hurling Shakespearean insults that made him want her more than he'd wanted any other woman.

Brian just stood, hands fisted at his side. "We need to talk." He gritted his teeth.

"We don't need to do anything. I'm going to be late for class if I don't leave now." She turned to Nick. "Would you mind walking with me?"

He wanted to stay and beat the shit out of Gill but knew it wouldn't help his situation with Olivia. Reluctantly, he followed her out of the building.

"What do you think he wants?"

"I have no idea." Olivia kept a quick pace. "I haven't spoken to him since the board meeting in April."

"We talked about him at our meeting this morning. He and his father are going to be a problem." Nick caught up with her and took her hand. It was a good sign when she didn't yank it away.

"Why? They don't have any influence on the board anymore."

71

"Ron got wind they're up to something. We don't know what it is yet." He glanced down at her. "I don't want you alone with him."

"Believe me, I have no desire to be anywhere near him."

"I don't know what his deal is these days. After that stunt he pulled at the board meeting the only thing that's clear is that he's a wildcard. I wouldn't put it past him to try to corner you." The thought of Gill being alone with Olivia made Nick want to hit something.

"I'm an adult. I can take care of myself." The small catch in her voice contradicted the proud tilt of her chin.

"It's not just you anymore." He moved to open the door for her when they reached her classroom.

"I'm aware of my situation."

A few eager students sat at attention when he ushered Olivia into the room. One in particular made warnings echo in Nick's head. There was something off about the kid and the way the little bastard's eyes roamed from Olivia's toes up to her head and back set Nick's teeth on edge.

Some primitive part of him wanted to stake a claim on Olivia, in front of this kid and the world. She was carrying a piece of him. He should be able to make it clear that she was off limits to every other man on the planet.

Nick shook himself. Olivia had already belted him once

72

today. It was cute, but he didn't want to be responsible for her injuring her hand even more.

"Thank you for walking me to the door." She smiled at him.

He'd never understood the true power of a woman's smile until this moment, when the power of hers shot through him with the force of an exploding grenade.

"Sure. I'll see you tonight." She nodded.

His response was interrupted by the sound of a throat clearing. Loudly. He turned to face the bug-eyed little bastard who'd been eying Olivia when they walked in.

"Excuse me, Professor Valenti." The little prick stood to close to her.

Nick crossed his arms. There was something about this kid that set off Nick's radar, but Olivia didn't seem to notice.

"What is it, Clay?"

After giving Nick the stink eye, Olivia's student plastered a grin on his face. "I wanted to ask about doing some extra credit."

More students started to file in to the room. Olivia tried to step aside, but Nick refused to budge, so she ended up pressing closer to his side, giving him a chance to slide his arm around her waist. The little worm's face fell, and Nick couldn't keep the smug expression off his face.

That's right, junior. I'm not going anywhere.

Olivia glanced over her shoulder. "Actually, today's handouts will have some options for extra credit. You can choose from one of those."

Clay's face fell. "Oh. I was hoping we could discuss it during office hours, or maybe we could meet for coffee and talk about it."

"I appreciate your enthusiasm, Clay, but I am limiting the extra credit projects to those suggested with the various assignments."

"Oh. I just thought there are some interesting projects that I could do about *King Lear* for example."

Olivia tried to subtly push Nick back, but he wasn't having it. Her student put all his senses on alert and he wanted this kid to know that he would have to go through Nick to get to her.

"I appreciate your enthusiasm, but this is a summer class. I prefer to have the students stick to projects related to the syllabus. School is important, but everyone needs to try and make time to relax too. If *King Lear* is something you're interested in, you should consider taking my seminar on theme and motif in Shakespeare's tragedies. We spend a great deal of time on that play. I'm offering it this fall."

Clay's face lit up. "Oh. Yeah? Cool. Well, I should take my seat, so we can get started." He gave Nick a pointed look before stomping back to his seat.

"Interesting students you got, Slugger."

She blushed at the reminder of her outburst, making him grin. Deciding not to push his luck, he left the room. He could tease her more later.

His good mood took a nose dive when he spotted Gill lurking at the end of the hall. When he spotted Nick, the sneaky weasel took off. Nick debated chasing him down, but he wasn't sure he wouldn't beat the shit out of him on principal if he caught up with him.

He pulled out his phone and dialed Cade.

"What's up?" Cade answered after only a couple if rings.

"Backup is lurking around Olivia."

"What?"

Nick had to pull the phone away from his ear because of Cade's lack of volume control.

"What's that son of a bitch want?"

"No idea. Said he needed to talk to Olivia, but she didn't want to talk to him. I walked her to the summer class she's teaching, and he followed us here. Took off when he saw me."

"Shit." Cade's frustration was audible through the phone.

"Yep."

"We're going to have to figure out what he's up to."

That was an understatement. Nick meant what he said to Olivia about Brian. The guy was a wildcard. In one breath he'd backed his father's play and the next he'd defied him. Word was he was back in the old man's good graces, but that didn't mean anything. "Yeah."

"Olivia pissed at you?"

"Yeah. She's calmed down, but it's going to take a while for me to get out of the dog house. How long did it take you to rat me out to Tess?"

"Dude, she's my wife." Cade seemed to think that was all he needed to say.

He could understand his friend's priorities. "Sure."

"How'd you get Olivia to calm down?"

"Apologized."

"That's it?"

Nick could understand the disbelief in his friend's voice. "I let her hit me too."

"Hit you? Olivia hit you? Olivia Valenti, head of the English department, hit you?" The shock in Cade's voice rang in Nick's ears.

"Popped me right in the nose."

"She draw blood?" Cade laughed.

Nick snorted. "She hurt her hand."

"You guys a couple?"

He rubbed the bridge of his nose. "Not going to sit around and talk about my feelings with you."

"Who's asking you to? I'm trying to figure out what's up, that's all."

"What's up is we're figuring it out." He didn't want to say anything too personal to Cade, or in public. Whatever he and Olivia had he would leave it to Olivia to make it public. He'd messed up enough for one day.

"I'll let Ed and Ron know about Gill. We'll do a little more digging, see if we can figure out what's going on."

"Yeah. I'm meeting with Bob again to go over the weight room schedule for the fall. I'll bring him up to speed."

"Thanks. Talk to you later."

"Later." Nick disconnected the call and glanced at the time. He needed to meet with Bob. He decided to take the long way to the athletic building, which, coincidently, would take him along the hallway Gill had disappeared down.

Surprise, surprise, the man was still lurking.

"Gill."

"What?" The other man was sweating.

"You have a reason to be on campus, other than harassing Olivia?"

"Screw you, Jacobs. I can go wherever I want."

"Private university, which has given you specific times you can be on campus."

"So?"

"So, they can trespass you off the property if you're harassing a professor and don't have a legitimate reason for being here."

"They let an ex-con hang out." Brian waved his hand at Nick.

Reminding himself of all the reasons why he couldn't rip the man's arm off and beat him with it, Nick counted to ten, then did it again.

"No smart comments. Right, you'd have to be more than a dumb ex-con to say something smart."

"Wouldn't throw stones if I were you. And I'm not an ex-con. Do your homework, dumbass. I don't have a criminal record."

"You should."

Nick shrugged. "Don't though. And I didn't even have a

rich daddy to buy my way out of trouble. I earned it."

Gill turned red and narrowed his eyes. Nick prayed he took a swing. Self-defense was a good excuse as any for beating the hell out of this guy.

"This isn't about my old man or what he's got going on and it's not about you. I need to talk to Olivia." Brian ran a hand through his sandy blond hair. There was a look in his eyes that bordered on desperation.

"Hold your breath waiting for that to happen. Please."

Gill studied Nick for a moment. Beneath the desperation Nick wasn't positive he saw, there was something else. Regret? Couldn't be. Whatever it was, it was gone in a second as the other man put an arrogant expression on his face.

"You all may think you're big fucking deals now, but you're still the same never weres you've always been. And the old men you're working with are nothing more than a bunch of has beens." Brian said the words, but it sounded like he was reciting a script, not saying something he believed. After a brief staring contest with Nick he turned and stormed away.

They'd need to keep their eyes on the Gills. Those sneaky pricks were up to something. Nick would be damned if he'd let them mess up the first good thing he had going in his life in a long time. Too long.

Chapter 4

Maybe this was too much. Olivia studied the calendars, pens, post-its and pads of paper she'd set out before Nick was due with dinner. Order was important and, with everything so out of control since her night with him, she needed it now more than she had in a long time.

Half of her kitchen table was covered with paraphernalia. She'd left the other half empty so that they could eat there. Olivia glanced around the kitchen wondering what he thought of the open space that she'd fallen in love with at first sight. The gleaming hardwood floors and soft white and green paint gave the room the feel of an old farmhouse. Somehow it worked with the modern stainless-steel appliances.

She jumped when she heard the doorbell and almost wished she hadn't laid everything out like this. He'd think she was crazy. Better for him to see what he was getting into before the baby was born. They were a package deal.

Before she could think twice, or three times, as the case may be, she answered the door.

Nick stood there with a large pizza in one hand and a bag in the other. "Hey."

"Hi." He was on time, which she appreciated, but he was also here, which freaked her out a little.

"Can I come in?"

"Oh. Yes. Sorry." She stepped aside, and he walked right by her into the kitchen.

Nick set the pizza and the bag down on the kitchen counter. "I got some salad to go with the pizza. Figured it would be good for you and the baby."

A warm feeling started in her heart and spread through her body. He got salad because it would be good for her and the baby. Tears pricked the corners of her eyes. She couldn't remember the last time anyone had done anything for her just because.

"Slugger." He reached out and cupped her cheek. "It's just salad."

She cleared her throat. "It's sweet. Thank you."

He shrugged and pulled the containers out of the bag. "Plates?"

"Oh, right." She gave herself a mental shake as she got plates, forks and napkins out. She set them on the counter. "Something to drink?"

"Whatever you have is good."

Olivia opened the refrigerator. "I have sweet tea, water and orange juice."

"Sweet tea is good."

She smiled. "Delilah likes to say it's the house wine of

the south." She took the pitcher out and closed the refrigerator door. "I must be a southerner at heart, because I prefer it this way."

"My buddy's mama used to say, 'if sweet tea can't fix it, it's a serious problem,'" he drawled, thickening his accent and making her belly flutter. It was too early in the pregnancy to blame it on the baby.

He took the pitcher from her and she turned to retrieve some glasses from the cupboard. She set them down then he poured their drinks as she scooped salad onto their plates.

"I have a couple of dressings. Could you grab the balsamic for me?" She watched him as he put the tea back in the refrigerator and surveyed the contents.

He grabbed two bottles and handed her one. He poured a liberal helping of honey mustard on his salad as she used a smaller amount of her preference. When they were done, she led him to the kitchen table.

They ate in silence for a few minutes. It was weird how comfortable she felt. She wasn't usually good with silence when she was with other people. Somehow, with Nick, she felt more comfortable than she'd felt in a long time.

Once they'd finished the salads he stood. He waved for her to stay in her seat. "I'll take care of this. You sit."

He took the dishes to the sink and came back with two plates of pizza. He handed her a plate and took his seat.

"Thank you. This is perfect." She picked up a piece of pizza, loving the string of melted cheese that connected the slice in her hand to the one on her plate. If she was alone, she would have played with the cheese. *What the heck?*

She hooked her finger through the string of cheese and wound until it separated from the slice on the plate. Then she stuck her finger in her mouth. She realized he was staring at her and felt the heat rush up her neck into her cheeks.

"What?"

"You're cute as hell, Slugger."

"I wish you wouldn't call me that." She wasn't thrilled about the reminder of her impetuous behavior.

"Why not? I think that punch you tried to throw earlier was cute."

"Why on earth would you think that was cute?"

"You were pissed and let me know it. It's not like you did any damage."

"Do you want me to take a swing at you every time you make me angry?" She wouldn't be able to do that. Violence was never the answer and she was still reeling from the fact that she hit him earlier. It made her wonder if there was more of her father in her than she'd let herself believe.

He laughed, his blue eyes sparkled with warmth and humor. "No. I have a feeling I'll piss you off more than a few times, and I don't want to you feel guilty about taking a whack at me again."

"Why do you think you'll keep making me angry?"

He shrugged. "I'm me and you're you."

"You believe we're incompatible." It felt like there were a ton of rocks in her stomach.

"Nope. Just different. We need to figure each other out, make adjustments. Like any good team."

"Team?"

Red rose up the back of his neck and spread to his cheeks. "I figure that's what we are now."

"I...I've never been part of a team." Even when her mother was alive, it never felt like they were a team. Olivia felt like she was more of a burden than an asset.

He studied her for a moment while he took a bite of his pizza. After he finished he took a sip of his tea. If she had to guess she would say he was choosing his words with care. Nick didn't talk much, so when he did it meant something.

"Most teams aren't in sync when they form. They have to practice together, get to know each other's rhythms and habits. Learn to trust each other. After they settle in, they can play as a unit. I figure it'll take us some time to get

84

there."

"You sound so sure we will." She wished she could feel his certainty. Since her mother's death, the only sure thing in her life was that she was alone.

He shrugged. "Neither of us are quitters."

She wanted to argue with him, but that would involve telling him things she'd never told anyone else. Any response she had on the tip of her tongue was interrupted by her dog Kate, who came barreling in from the sun porch barking like she'd heard a can of Alpo being opened.

"Hey, girl." Nick leaned over and tried to hold out his hand for her to smell. The pupped nipped at his fingers.

"Kate," Olivia admonished as she scooped her friend off the floor. The little bundle of fur shook in her arms, focused totally on Nick and growling.

"I guess she doesn't like me."

"It's odd. She never behaves like this."

"You have people over to your house a lot?"

Olivia shook her head. She usually went out to meet people, when she did go out.

He smiled. "She doesn't want to share you. Understandable. Let her run around, get used to me."

The tilt of his lips made her want to taste them.

"Olivia?" Nick tilted his head.

His warm voice drew her out of her fantasies, or was it the stuff of them?

"Olivia." He snapped his fingers close enough to her that Kate tried to take a nip out of them.

She jumped, and Kate growled. "Sorry."

"Where'd you go?"

Heat rushed up the back of her neck. There was no way she was going to tell him that. "Just thinking."

"About?"

"Um. How we should deal with Kate." Hopefully he believed that was all that was on her mind.

"Sure." He clearly didn't buy a word of her excuse. "Let her run around and get used to me. She's still little. Won't hurt me if she gets a few nips in here and there."

Olivia looked down at the ball of fur in her arms. The growls seemed to be abating, so she shrugged and set the pup down on the floor. Kate immediately dove for Nick's boot.

Wow. Kate really wants to take a piece out of him.

"I'll put her in my room." She didn't think Nick could actually get hurt, but he couldn't want to put up with the little dog's aggressive behavior.

Nick chuckled. "Leave her. Let's finish our pizza then you can show me how to organize my life." He nodded at

86

all the planning paraphernalia she'd laid out earlier.

"Okay." A warmth slide through Olivia with his understanding and patience with Kate.

It was the most entertaining dinner she'd ever had. The pizza was delicious, and Nick was entertaining when he relaxed. The funniest part was Kate. She went from yanking on the hem of Nick's jeans to dashing a few feet away and preparing to pounce. Then she would pounce and try to wrestle with his leg. Finally, she curled up at Olivia's feet, panting. Every once in a while, she would open one eye and growl at Nick to let him know she wasn't done with him before going back to sleep.

An hour after dinner Nick rolled his eyes at Olivia. "Really? Color coding?"

"You need it more than I do," she tried to explain.

"How do you figure?"

"Look at your schedule. You have two jobs and, between your mother's treatment and my pregnancy, two sets of regular medical appointments. If you color code them you can tell at a glance what each thing on your schedule is."

"And I need to do that at a glance because?" He scrubbed his hand down his face.

"Imagine you wake up and take a quick look at your

calendar. If you see the colors and you know you have a meeting with Coach Moore and the next thing on your calendar is an appointment with your mother, then you'll know when your meeting with Coach Moore needs to end."

"Huh?"

"It's almost thirty minutes from the university to the hospital where your mother's getting her treatments. If the appointments are color coded, you know you need to leave the meeting with Coach Moore at least an hour before your mother's appointment."

"I guess that makes sense. I just don't see myself carrying a bunch of colored pencils with me."

The image made her smile. "That's what the post-its are for."

He looked like he was ready to run.

She nibbled on her thumb for a second. "It's too much isn't it?" She'd been accused of being too much before.

"It's something."

That was clear as a muddy pool. "I like this system."

"That's good. You should have a system that works for you."

She didn't know why she wanted to cry. It couldn't be because he thought her organizing was stupid. That was a ridiculous reason to cry. She tried to tell herself to suck it up, but felt the tears start to slide down her cheeks.

"Hey. Hey. Don't cry. I'll carry a dozen colored pencils with me."

That's so sweet.

"It's not that." She didn't know if she could explain why she was crying.

"Then what is it?" He pulled her off her chair and onto his lap, wrapping his arms around her.

"You think I'm weird." It was a feeling she was used to. You can't graduate college at eleven and not experience it. She didn't think he would make her relive those feelings.

"I don't."

"You do. You think I'm a crazy, color-coding, planner collecting freak," she wailed.

He rubbed his hand along her back. "That's not true. I think you're cute as hell."

She sniffled. "Really?"

He reached out and grabbed a napkin then tilted her chin so he could gently dab away the tears on her cheeks. "Really."

"Okay." She hiccupped.

"You want to tell me what that was really about?" He set the napkin on the table then cupped her cheek in his hand.

If she knew herself, she could decide whether to tell him. His warmth calmed her senses, but didn't give her any clarity.

She shrugged. "I just don't understand how we got here."

"What does that mean?"

Wasn't it obvious? "I mean look at you and look at me."

"Seriously. What are you talking about?"

"I'm the geek. The girl who started college when she was seven. You're the star football player who went on to serve his country. Why would you ever be with me?"

He looked irritated. "I barely made it through high school. You've got a couple of doctorates. Hell, I got this job by the skin of my teeth. The question is, what the hell would you want with me?"

"I don't understand." He was wonderful. She knew there was something that happened to keep him from playing football in college, but it obviously hadn't stopped him from doing amazing things with his life.

He was silent for a moment, like he was trying to figure out how to not say something. "My point is, life is all about timing. Maybe if we'd met at a different time, we wouldn't have connected."

"I've never known anyone like you." Until she'd moved

to King's Folly, she'd never known anyone outside of the academic community.

"Right back at ya." He smiled.

"So, what do we do?" It made her uncomfortable. Not having a clear picture of what to expect of the future.

"Keep doing what we're doing. Spend time together. Make plans for the baby. You're absolutely right I need to be more organized." He eyed the supplies laid out on her table. "I just may not be as organized as you are."

She sighed. "I just wish it wasn't so complicated."

"You and me both." He rested his forehead on hers. "We'll figure it out though. Together."

When he touched her, she felt like anything was possible. "Together."

Finally in agreement, they spent the rest of the evening organizing his calendar in a way that worked for him. They seemed to have an unspoken agreement that weightier topics could wait. By the time he left, Olivia felt like they had laid the first bricks in a solid foundation for their relationship. She still wasn't clear what that relationship would be. But she felt hopeful for the first time about the two of them.

The next morning Olivia was going over her schedule for the day when her doorbell rang. She approached the front door with caution since she wasn't expecting anyone.

There was a reason she loved the windows that ran along each side of the door. All she had to do was peek through one to see who was there. The sight of Tess, Charlie and Delilah on her front porch made her want to hide.

"Don't even think about running." Delilah banged on the door. "We saw you peek out the window."

Olivia took a deep breath and opened the door. "What brings you by?" She tried to sound nonchalant.

Delilah pushed into the house followed by Charlie and Tess. Tess mouthed "I'm sorry" and squeezed Olivia's hand.

"What's going on with you?" Delilah demanded.

"Why does something have to be going on?"

Delilah threw up her hands. "Something is up, and Tess knows what it is, but she won't tell us, which is totally against the code."

"Delilah, you need to calm down. Olivia's not going to tell us anything with you on a one of your bitch-pages." Charlie huffed.

"What's a bitch-page?" Olivia wasn't sure who to look at.

"It's like a rampage, but instead of running around all uncontrolled and violent she runs around and acts like a bitch."

"Who asked you to come anyway?" Delilah pushed Charlie. "We decided. I'm Olivia's Charlie. You already got to be Tess's Charlie."

Olivia didn't want to point out that Charlie was Tess's best friend because she'd stuck by her from the beginning.

"You're nuts." Charlie crossed her arms. "No wonder Olivia avoids you."

"Take that back." Delilah pushed Charlie again.

"You push me one more time, blondie, and it is going to get ugly."

Before Tess or Olivia could say or do anything, Delilah pushed Charlie who pushed back. In seconds, the two women were rolling on the floor locked in combat.

Tess grabbed Olivia and pulled her away from the action as Kate came bounding into the room at the sounds. In no time, she was hopping over the two women like she was jumping through a doggy obstacle course. Her yips combined with Delilah's and Charlie's yells echoed through the room.

Olivia stared at the spectacle.

When did my life descend in to total chaos?

Before she or Tess could come up with a plan, Cade and Nick appeared out of nowhere. Cade let out a sharp whistle, which did nothing to stop the combatants who were clearly angry about more than their verbal back and forth a few moments before they ended up on the floor.

Giving each other a resigned expression, the two men moved forward to separate Delilah and Charlie. They bent down and each of them came up with an armful of writhing, shrieking, pissed-off female.

"Enough." Nick's bellow was followed by a growl from Kate who latched on to his jeans like they were made of ham.

The sound of his deep voice, raised in anger, quieted the two women instantly.

"She started it," Delilah mumbled.

"Did not," Charlie shot back.

"I don't care who started it." Nick's voice was filled with exasperation. "You don't come in to Olivia's home and start a brawl."

"Who died and made you king of Olivia's home?" Delilah eyed him speculatively.

He looked at Olivia and shrugged before he reached down to grab the puppy who dashed away into the kitchen before he could get a hold of her. The pup growled at him from around the corner.

"Nick is the father of my child." Olivia announced

Delilah whipped around and stared at Olivia, a look of

shock mixed with hurt filling her eyes.

Olivia was really starting to miss the days when she was a lonely social misfit. It was so much easier then.

Hearing Olivia announce he was the father of her child sent a warm, loopy feeling rolling through Nick's bloodstream. When Delilah turned her gaze from Olivia to him, his blood froze.

Shit.

He didn't want to be on Delilah's bad side. No one wanted to be on her bad side.

"You're pregnant?" Charlie broke the silence.

"I am."

"And you told Tess before you told me?" Delilah pouted.

"Technically, I didn't tell Tess." Olivia crossed her arms and glared at Nick. That one glance let him know she blamed this whole clusterfuck on him and he was not completely forgiven for sharing the news before she wanted to share it.

Which, yeah, he probably owned this one. These four women were tight. Odds were, Olivia would have told her crew at the same time. Instead, he'd screwed up and set up a situation where one of her girls found out before the others did.

Shit.

Trust was a fragile gift and he'd done nothing to make himself seem worthy of it to Olivia.

He let Charlie go as Cade released Delilah. When neither woman made a move for the other, Nick stepped over to stand next to Olivia and Kate dashed out to nip his heel before retreating back to the kitchen.

What the hell was up with that dog?

"What does that mean?" Delilah moved into the kitchen and flopped down on the nearest chair.

"It means Nick told Cade who told Tess, and when I found out Nick told anyone without discussing it with me, I punched him." Her cheeks turned a cute shade of pink that made him wish they were alone.

"You punched him?" Charlie smiled then took a seat as far from Delilah as she could.

Nick still couldn't figure out the dynamics of these women. They were so different and, other than Tess and Olivia, who both had giant brains, didn't seem to have anything in common. As a group, they bickered all the time, especially Charlie and Delilah, but if you came for one of them, the other three were right up in your face telling you

96

to back off. He respected that friendship, even if he didn't understand it.

"We got together in Vegas. We weren't sure about pursuing a relationship, but I found out I'm pregnant, so we're trying to figure everything out now." It seemed like she chose her words carefully.

Nick wasn't happy with the ambivalent tone in Olivia's voice. All things considered, though, he knew he was lucky she was speaking to him at all.

"Are you happy? About the baby?" Charlie watched her intently.

Nick's stomach clutched. He got more excited as he adjusted to the news, but he'd been afraid to ask Olivia how she really felt.

She smiled at her friends. "I am."

The truth that rang in those two simple words made Nick feel like he'd just picked up a fumble on the other team's goal line and run it for a touchdown.

"Obviously, Nick and I have a lot to figure out, but we're both happy about the baby." She put her hand in his and squeezed.

That small gesture made him feel stronger than he'd ever felt in his life. He wasn't sure what he could say to add to Olivia's statement. Before he could think of something

Delilah burst in to tears.

"Of for the love of — " Charlie stood and stomped over to where Delilah was sitting. She sat on the arm rest and threw an arm around Delilah's shoulders. "What's gotten into you now?"

"We're going to be aunts," Delilah wailed. The sound made Kate start to howl.

He turned to Olivia who had a sweet smile on her face for a second before she started to laugh. Her laugh made his insides turn into the center of a chocolate lava cake. He put his arm around her and pulled her close. She looked up at him and kept laughing. All he wanted to do was kiss her, but he didn't want to mess up the moment.

"Who wants coffee?" Olivia slipped away from him and ambled to the other side of the kitchen and over to the coffee maker on the counter.

Nick took that moment to step away from the chaos and followed her. "I'll help."

He grabbed some mugs from the cupboard as she brewed the coffee. The wails from the other side of the room subsided. He glanced over his shoulder and noted their friends were now lounging around the table, which was still covered with Olivia's lists and calendars.

"Should you be drinking coffee?" He looked back at

Olivia.

"I'm going to have juice. There haven't been any conclusive studies on the impact of caffeine on human pregnancy, but I don't want to take any chances."

"Okay." He wasn't sure what to say, so he turned back around to face their friends. He didn't want to be one of those guys who followed his woman around monitoring everything she ate or drank during her pregnancy, but he didn't want her taking any chances either, with herself or the baby.

"So, you're due in March." Charlie studied the calendar.

"I am." Olivia moved over to the table to set out the cream and sugar.

"I guess what happened in Vegas didn't stay there," Delilah joked.

Charlie punched her lightly on the shoulder. "Seriously, Delilah? That joke is staler than a month-old cookie."

"So, what can we do to help?" Thankfully, Tess took control of the conversation before Charlie and Delilah could start up again.

"For now, nothing. Nick and I still have some things to figure out between the two of us before we need to call in the troops."

"Well, whatever you need. We're here for you." Tess

looked from Olivia to him. "That goes for both of you."

"What's going on with Nick?" Delilah strode up to the counter to pour herself a cup of coffee.

Tess gave him a questioning look, and he nodded. The less he and Delilah talked right now the better it would be.

"In addition to the baby, his job at the university and opening the garage with his brother, his mother is undergoing treatment for cancer."

"Classic rains it pours situation, huh?" Delilah looked at him, something other than anger and annoyance in her expression. "Been there, done that, gave the t-shirt to the Junior League rummage sale."

He shrugged. It was still strange, having anyone outside of his brother know his business.

"Okay. So, I'll be your mom's chemo buddy. Did Olivia trick you out with your own calendar?" Delilah left the room for a few minutes and came back with a bright red planner. It might have come from Olivia originally, but it was all Delilah now.

"Umm." He didn't know what to do about it when Delilah was on a roll.

"Relax, Conan. I've been down this road. The cancer gene runs in my family."

"Cancer gene?" Did his family have a gene he needed to

100

worry about? Could he have it or pass it on to his kid? His heartbeat raced.

"Yeah. Fortunately, it skipped me, but I'm a veteran of the cancer wars. So, I'll help." She flipped through her planner.

"You don't even know my mom." Why would she help his mom? Delilah barely tolerated him.

"Doesn't matter. I know what she's going through. I also know you won't be able to handle the really tough stuff."

"You don't know me" He'd served in combat and helped the medics with some of his wounded friends. Why wouldn't he be able to sit with his mother in a state of the art hospital where there were no explosions or gun fire?

"I know you're a man. I know you're her son. Stuff is going to happen during treatment that she's not going to want you to see. I can help with that. Plus, as a cancer fighting sidekick, I kick ass. Team Derringer four, cancer zero."

Nick wanted to argue, but he noticed that Olivia gave him a little shake of her head. He hoped she'd explain later why he was agreeing to let Delilah help him with his mother.

Pretty soon, the six of them were gathered around

Olivia's master schedule. Everyone was making notes on their own calendars and Delilah was making plans to show up at his house and introduce herself to his mother.

Warmth bloomed in his chest and spread through his body. He caught Olivia's eyes and the small smile that played at the corners of her mouth. Being part of a team was a familiar and welcome feeling. Since he'd gotten out of the Navy he'd been floundering, looking for his next team.

He had his brother, but they'd both been deep in their own stuff since they'd each gotten out of the military. They were close, but watching his friends rally around him had made Nick realize he and Simon weren't as close as they could be. It was time to do something about that.

Later that day he was going through schedules and training calendars with Bob for the various university teams. They were working on the strength training and weight room schedules.

"You're going to be a busy man," Bob noted.

"You're telling me." Busy was good, though. It was better than having time to stew in your own stuff. He studied his mentor. It had been a long time since Bob had been in the game. "You up for this?"

Bob gave him an assessing look. "Don't think this old

man can handle it?"

"You've been retired for a while."

"Yep. Retired so I could try and get my Barbara through her cancer fight. We bought her some good years, but it ended up in her brain and that was the end of it." Bob's voice sounded thick.

"I'm sorry."

Bob nodded. "Truth is, since I lost her I've been looking for something to do. The kids and grandkids are great, but they have their own lives. When Ed came to me with this idea I jumped at the chance to get back to what I do best."

"I'm a little worried I'm in over my head," Nick voiced the thoughts he hadn't shared with anyone else.

"Why do you say that?"

"I know about football and I know about strength training, but I gotta admit I don't know shit about some of the other sports."

"Neither did I when I started. I'd been an assistant coach in a community college for a couple of years when Ed tapped me for this job. He said I knew what I needed to know to get started and I was smart enough to learn the rest."

Nick shrugged. He wasn't sure what to say.

"I'm going to tell you something, kid. Most people are

never ready for the good things that come their way. We tell ourselves we'll be fine staying in our lane and anything else is out of reach. I've spent most of my life focused on the road in front of me. I didn't go looking for detours or opportunities."

"Sounds like a smart way to go." The detours in Nick's life had usually started with catastrophes.

"I got lucky. I had people who saw things in me that I didn't see myself."

Nick shifted in his seat. The conversation was going in a direction he wasn't sure he was comfortable with.

"Ed showed up and offered me a job I didn't think I could do. A few months later, I met my Barbara. We crashed in to each other in a doorway on this campus. She was the most beautiful woman I'd ever seen, and I was just a dumb country boy trying to do a job I still wasn't sure I could do."

A blind man could see the point Bob was trying to make. "I get it."

"Do you? I know you've got a lot on your plate, but I figure if I could pull off the ride I've taken in my life, you can too."

"How do you figure?"

"You're already a better man than I could ever hope to

104

be."

Nick wouldn't be surprised if his jaw hit the floor. "Are you kidding?"

"When your country called, you stepped up. When it called me, I got every deferment I could get. Not proud of it, but there it is."

Did Bob think Nick would think less of him after that confession?

"You shouldn't confuse me with Cade. I didn't walk away from a career in the pros to serve. My choice was prison or the military. If things were different I would have been playing defense for Alabama, not serving my country." Nick looked down at the papers in front of him.

"Cade's a good man. So are you."

Nick shrugged as he felt the heat creep up the back of his neck.

"In some ways, you're a better man than Cade is."

Nick looked up from the paper he'd been pretending to study. A jolt shot through him at the ridiculous statement. "Don't push it."

"I mean it."

"Did you forget the part where he chose service over a multi-million-dollar contract and I chose it over ten years behind bars?"

"No. I also didn't miss the fact that Cade was raised by a father who set an example every day for what kind of man he should be. He had a road map. Hell, he had a couple generations of men who showed him the way. Your father was a bastard. No man worthy of being called a man would want to follow in his footsteps. You made it here on your own steam."

Nick started to speak, and Bob held up a hand to stop him.

"You screwed up. No question. We all do. The mark of a good man isn't that he always does the right thing or that he never fails. It's that he learns from his mistakes and picks himself up when he's down."

Nick sat back. He wasn't sure he bought what Bob was trying to sell, but the man's admiration for him touched him somewhere he thought had died a long time ago.

He cleared his throat. "Thank you."

The silence spread between them for a moment, thick and filled with things that still hadn't been said. Finally, Bob slapped a hand on the table and broke the moment.

"I figure that's enough of that for now. We've got a lot to get done in the next couple of weeks. Fall sports training starts soon and we need to be ready."

Nick nodded. The knots in his stomach loosened as they

moved on to talk about work. With so much going on in his life, he needed to be able to spend time in his comfort zone, collect himself. He appreciated Bob's opinion, but right now he was only worried about Olivia's opinion.

What would she think if she knew the truth about him?

Chapter 5

Truth was a funny thing. It usually wasn't as bad as people believed it was when they hid it, and miles worse than they thought it was when they shared it. A knock on the door drew Olivia from her weighty thoughts.

"Come in."

"Apologies for the interruption." Professor Rushford Avery's smooth English accent was one of the many reasons his courses were so popular with the female students. Olivia wouldn't be surprised if he single-handedly doubled the enrollment of women in the STEM programs at Cormac.

"You aren't interrupting anything but my wayward thoughts."

He smiled. It was a gorgeous smile. In one of the ironies of life the smile of the eminently suitable Professor Avery didn't melt her bones the way a single grunt from Nick did.

"Your thoughts appear to be diverting again." His voice drew her attention.

"It's my turn to apologize. I'm easily distracted these days." For more reasons than one.

"No need to apologize. I'm the one that interrupted your day."

Olivia stood and moved to the sofa by the window. It was a more comfortable place to talk. She waved toward the other side of the sofa. "Please, have a seat, Professor Avery."

"Call me Rush." He sat in a motion that struck her as elegant and masculine at the same time.

"What can I do for you, Rush?" Why didn't he make her insides go crazy the way Nick did?

"I've been approached by two parties with a similar proposition who are seeking vastly different outcomes."

"I'm afraid you're going to have to translate that for me." She'd only spoken to Rush a handful of times and wasn't sure why he would seek her out for advice of any kind.

"Two different people have approached me about taking on the role of academic coordinator for the athletic department."

She was still confused as to why he was bringing this dilemma to her. "I see. I didn't realize you were a fan of American sports."

"I'm not, really. I know enough about cricket and rugby to carry on conversations with my brothers when we're together, but athletics has never been one of my primary interests."

"Are you considering the offer?" She knew he was dedicated to academics.

"It's an intriguing proposition. I've read some horror stories about young athletes, men in particular, finishing with a degree but an inability to manage their own money, or even read."

She nodded. "There are definitely some tragic stories out there."

"Which is why I'm interested in exploring the opportunity. I know you're friends with some of the new coaches for the football program. It's the competing objectives of the two offers that concern me."

"Who approached you?" She had a feeling she knew at least one party.

"Ron Jackson and Brian Gill."

Her stomach tightened at the thought of what the Gills could be planning now. "Senior or Junior?"

"Senior." There was enough disdain in Rush's voice to make Olivia relax a little.

"What did he want you to do?"

"He wanted me to make sure the football team wouldn't make the minimum grade point average for the conference."

Olivia sat back. Just when she thought the Gills couldn't sink any lower. The memory of falling for Junior's false charms filled her with shame. If her new friends hadn't rallied around her, she might have left Cormac after being humiliated by him. She stood and moved to her desk to get her cell phone, so she could make a call. Nick answered after one ring.

"You okay?"

The concern in his voice warmed her from head to toe. "I'm fine. I have a question for you."

"What?"

"What would happen to the football program if your team couldn't achieve the minimum grade point average set by the conference?"

He was silent for a moment. "Why do you want to know?"

"Humor me and answer my question before I answer yours."

"There were some stipulations included with the sanctions, minimum requirements the team has to meet every year. If we fail to adhere to the sanctions or don't meet those requirements for one year, the sanctions are extended by a year. If it happens for two years it basically kills the program. Now why do you want to know?"

"Because Gill Senior just asked the potential new academic coordinator to guarantee that the football team

111

doesn't make grades."

"What?" He barked, forcing Olivia to pull the phone away from her ear.

She moved to sit in the chair opposite Rush as she listened to Nick talking to someone in the background. The conversation wasn't clear, but she was sure she heard "the bastard" a couple of times. There was a muffled sound, like someone grabbed Nick's phone.

"Olivia, it's Cade. How did you hear this?"

"Rush came to me for advice. He said Ron approached him about the job and then Brian approached him with his proposition."

"Rush?"

She smiled apologetically at the man in question. It was rude to talk about someone in front of them. "Professor Avery."

"He's there now?" Cade asked.

"Yes."

She heard Nick yell, "Who's with her now?"

There was another few seconds of muffled conversation.

"Don't move. Cade and I are on the way." Nick disconnected the call.

"Well that sounded interesting," Rush observed dryly.

"Nick and Cade are on their way."

He leaned back on the sofa, resting an arm along back. "And they are?"

"Cade is training to take over as head coach for Ed King and Nick Jacobs is working with Bob Moore to be the strength trainer."

"How well do you know them?" Rush raised an eyebrow.

She put a hand on her belly. "Nick and I are going to have a baby in March."

Rush leaned forward. "Congratulations. It seems I've missed the boat."

"What does that mean?" She tilted her head.

"It means I've been trying to get up the nerve to ask you out for a few months now."

"Oh. I'm sorry." She didn't have another response for him.

"No need for that. It's not as if I've been pining with unrequited love. I merely think you're an attractive woman and we have a great deal in common. I thought we would be compatible."

"That's nice. I think." It was something that might have intrigued her a few months ago, but sounded too clinical now.

"It's ridiculous." He laughed. "I shouldn't have said anything."

It would be rude to tell him that between Brian's perfidy and Nick's magnetism, Rush hadn't stood a chance despite their compatibility. "I hope we can be friends."

"Of course, we can. I'm still finding my way here. I have a few American cousins I'm getting to know, but I wouldn't say not to making new friends here." He leaned forward and took her hand in both of his. "I do wish you well."

His hands felt warm on hers, but there was no spark. She smiled but didn't get a chance to respond.

"You want to keep those hands, you'll take them off her." Nick's voice came from the doorway and was filled with menace.

Rush leaned back and held both hands in the air. "You must be Nick."

"Stop scowling at the man." Olivia huffed. "He's here as a friend."

Nick crossed his arms. "We'll see."

Cade elbowed Nick out of the way and approached Rush. "Cade Maguire."

"Rush Avery."

"Ron speaks highly of you." Cade held out his hand.

Rush shook it. "I appreciate his vote of confidence, but

I'm not sure I've earned it."

"Because you're thinking of taking Gill's offer?" Nick moved behind the chair Olivia was sitting in and rested his hands on the back of it.

"Because I'm not sure why he thinks I'd be the ideal candidate for the position. I don't know much about athletics, especially American sports."

Cade took a seat on the couch. "That's why he wants you."

"I don't understand." Confusion filled Rush's voice.

"We're not just rebuilding the football team. There were a lot of things that people let slide around here during the Delano years. Academic supervision for all the athletes was one of them. Ron wants someone in charge of the program who's going to be all about their education and not their team stats."

"I see." It was clear Rush didn't understand at all.

"It's a brilliant approach." Olivia leaned back in the chair.

"You think so?" Rush looked at her, which made Nick growl.

She reached back and smacked his hand. "Stop."

Cade laughed. "She's right. If you take the job, you'll be all about making sure the student athletes get the education they should be here for. Ron wants to design a program that works with the students and their challenges and schedules but doesn't cater to them."

"I'm still not sure what you mean." Rush crossed his arms, bringing one hand to his chin.

"You must have heard stories. There was a big one in the news not too long ago. A university basically set up football courses." He used air quotes to emphasize the last two words. "They were easy A's for the athletes. No work, no effort, no education."

"I read about that. It was one of the reasons I approached Olivia. If I take on this position I want to make sure I have the autonomy I need to build a program that puts academics first. Whatever the world thinks of these young men and women, they are students first and athletes second. I believe that's why the phrase is student athletes." Rush did his own air quotes.

"That's why Ron wants you for the job. His plan is to have a liaison between you and each team, a member, or members, of the coaching staff who can work with you to make sure the athletes on their team get the attention they need," Cade explained.

"Interesting. I'm assuming I would have a budget to hire tutors and assistants." It was obvious Rush found the

116

offer more than interesting.

Cade nodded. "Absolutely."

"What do you want me to do about Mr. Gill's offer?"

"Can you string him along?" Nick jumped into the conversation.

Rush turned to him. "Why would I do that?"

"We need to figure out if this is a last-ditch effort, or a part of a bigger plan," Nick responded.

"The man's an alumnus of this school. Why would he be so interested in destroying the program?"

"He's a sore loser with an ax to grind," Nick said.

Rush took a moment and studied the other two men. "I'm not a fan of poor sports. I'll take the job."

The four of them spent the next few minutes talking strategy. Well, the three men did. Olivia didn't want anything to do with either Brian Gill, ever again.

After the plan was agreed to, Cade and Rush made their excuses and left.

"You okay?" Nick kneeled next to her and took her hand.

"I just thought I was done with the Gills, especially Junior. Do you think this is why he was lurking around me the other day? He wanted to get me to approach Rush about being an academic advisor?"

"Who know? Who cares? You don't have to see him again and this Avery guy seems like a straight shooter."

"He does. I don't know him that well. He just started last fall and he teaches in another department."

"He's got a thing for you." Nick growled.

"He does not." She wasn't going to enlighten Nick about the conversation she was having with Rush before he and Cade arrived.

"What would you call it?"

"The potential to have a thing for me, that no longer exists because he knows we're having a baby together." This possessive side of Nick was a little irritating.

"You told him?" The surprise in his voice made her feel a little guilty.

"I'm not ashamed." Which was the truth. She might not be pleased with the entire situation, but she wasn't embarrassed that she was pregnant.

"I didn't say you were. I'm just surprised you told him. Does this mean you're not pissed at me for telling the coaches about the baby anymore?"

"No. You were still wrong, and it's going to take more than a day for me to get over it. You're the father of my baby, but that doesn't entitle you to make any decisions for me."

"Could there be an anything else between us?" The expression in his blue eyes was warm.

It was a simple question, but she didn't have a simple answer. "You tell me."

He huffed out a breath. "What does that mean?"

"I'm the one who got stood up in Vegas. I'm the one whose wishes were completely discounted when you announced my pregnancy without consulting me." The memories of that interminable breakfast and finding out about his announcement from Tess left a pit in her stomach. The fragile tendril of trust she'd offered to Nick that morning had been broken in Las Vegas and smashed to pieces with his presumption. He needed to give her a reason to rebuild it.

Nick was silent for a moment. "I deserve that."

"Has anything changed besides the baby?" She needed to know if he wanted something more than a co-parenting relationship.

"No."

That one word pierced her heart like a spike through a marshmallow. "At least you're honest."

"You don't understand." He leaned forward and pulled her hand closer to his chest.

"You don't have to explain." She tried to yank her hand

away, but he held it in a firm gentle grip. "We can just be friends and be good parents."

"That's not what I mean." Nick sounded exasperated.

"Fine. What do you mean?" She stopped trying to pull her hand away.

"I chickened out." He rushed through the words.

She couldn't help it. Olivia snorted. "You're not afraid of anything."

"That's not true. I'm afraid of a lot of things. That morning I was freaked out at the thought of starting something with you and coming up short."

She wanted to tell him that was ridiculous, but the look in his eyes stopped her. He reminded her of a little boy who hoped for a treat but expected a punishment instead. It was important to choose her words carefully.

"I'm afraid of letting people in, too. Before I moved here I never spent much time with anyone outside of work. They complicated my life and I decided it was easier to be on my own." She paused. Every word revealed pieces of her she'd kept close for most of her life. "Trust is an issue with me." It felt like she ripped the admission from her chest.

His hand squeezed hers. "What changed?"

"Delilah. I believe I told you in Vegas, she's like the Borg." The other woman drove her crazy, but definitely made life more interesting.

"Resistance is futile, huh?" He smiled.

"Exactly. Before I knew it, I had girlfriends and girls' nights out and I was in Vegas for American Ninja Warrior and a wedding." It was still unbelievable that this this was her new life.

"Now you're pregnant."

It was her turn to squeeze his hand. "A shocking development, but not a bad one."

"Are you sure?" He sounded insecure.

"I'm happy about the baby. It took a little getting used to, and I still have moments where I can't quite believe it. But, I can't wait to meet our baby." That was the absolute truth. She'd never planned to follow in her mother's footsteps, and she vowed the similarities between her and her mother would end right here.

"God, I hope she takes after you." He looked sincere.

"It could be a boy who's just like his daddy." She wasn't opposed to a sturdy little boy with big blue eyes.

"Don't wish that on us. I was a hellion growing up."

"However our baby turns out, we need to promise each other we're in this together. We have to move forward together as parents. Whatever happens between us." It was vital to her that her child know only security and acceptance from both parents.

Her heart slowed, and the world seemed to stop. She knew her entire future hinged on his response.

"Agreed."

The world rushed back to full speed. They'd just crossed a major bridge.

Where it would lead was still anyone's guess.

What the hell was he doing?

He'd heard some British dude in the background and lost his shit. Cade hadn't come with him to Olivia's office to meet the guy, so much has he'd wanted to make sure Nick didn't take a swing at him.

The professor seemed okay. It bugged him that the guy seemed like he was more Olivia's speed than Nick was. Too bad for Professor Perfect Accent. Nick was here to stay. He just hoped Olivia didn't regret it.

Time to focus on something other than the other guy. "So, dinner tonight?"

"What time do you want to come by?" She pulled her hand back and he felt the loss of contact somewhere in the region of his heart.

"Why don't we go out?" He hoped she'd meant it about moving them forward.

The look of confusion on her face was cute. "Like out, out?"

"Yes, like in public, with people around."

"Are you sure?"

"I'm not ashamed to be seen with you." He prayed she felt the same.

"I didn't think you were. Are you worried about what people will say?" She nibbled on her bottom lip.

"No. Are you?" Moving forward with her would require cautious steps. God knows he didn't want to step on some IED that could blow up their relationship before they had a chance to build it.

"No."

"Then I'll pick you up at six. Are you okay with Mooney's?" The Irish-Mexican pub was one of his favorite places in King's Folly.

"That sounds good."

"Okay. Pick you up here or at your place?"

She stood then moved to her desk. "I'm going home after my next class, so pick me up there."

He nodded and left before he said something that messed up the fragile foundation they'd just laid. A glance at his watch told him he needed to get home soon anyway. Delilah was due to stop by and meet his mother.

It was a short drive from campus to his house, especially since there weren't many students in town over the summer. He got home with a few minutes to spare and was glad he did when he saw Delilah's VW pull up behind him. It was an older model, from the sixties, but looked like it had just come out of the factory.

"Nice wheels," he said as she stepped out of her car.

"Thanks. You're not so bad yourself." She smiled.

He had to admire her. A modern-day version of Dolly Parton, she never let the world see her sweat, even on a hot summer day. "I meant your car."

"I know what you meant, sugar. Your mama home?" She stared at him, a hard look in her eyes.

"She's inside. Where do you get your car serviced?" It wouldn't hurt to find out the competition for the garage and it seemed like a safer topic than whatever made her look at him like he was six inches lower than dirt.

"There are certain questions you don't ask a lady. Where she gets serviced is one of them." Delilah sauntered past him and up the front steps.

Nick shook his head. He had to hand it to her. She was

ride or die for her friends. Given her warning to him in Vegas, it was obvious her attitude toward him was a result of the news of Olivia's pregnancy. Better not to go there.

"You know my brother and I are opening a garage in town." He followed her up the steps.

She glanced over her shoulder. "Simon?"

"You met him?" He'd barely seen his brother since he'd gotten to town.

"We had a chat at Mooney's the other night."

It was good that Simon was getting out more but hearing news about his brother from someone else made Nick realize he was letting Simon down. Again.

Story of my life.

Now wasn't the time to dwell on how many people he'd managed to disappoint lately. Nick reached for the door then opened it for Delilah. He gave a little bow, indicating she should go in first.

"Manners only get you so far." She stared at him. "I'm watching you." With that pronouncement, Delilah stepped into the house and followed the sounds of life coming from the kitchen.

Nick followed her, and they found his mother and brother at the kitchen table having a cup of coffee.

"Mom. This is Delilah." He introduced the two women

and gave a quick nod of greeting to his brother.

"What's in this for you?" His mother looked at Delilah with suspicion.

Delilah sat at the table, seemingly unconcerned with the other woman's sharp attitude. "I'm on a pre-payment plan for my angel wings."

"Mom." Nick tried to warn her in one word.

"What?" she barked. "I'm trying to figure out blondie's game."

"No game, Miss. Janie."

"It's Jane." His mother stared at Delilah.

Delilah shrugged, seemingly unconcerned with his mother's antagonism.

"You know he's with that professor, right?"

"Mom." Simon joined the conversation.

"What? No one shows up and helps a total stranger with cancer treatments. She wants something."

Nick started to speak, but Delilah held up her hand.

"You want it straight? I'll give it to you. Your boy here knocked up one of my best friends, which means he's important to her. So, he's important to me."

"Why would you help me?" Jane pushed.

"Because you've got two great sons who aren't going to know what to do to help you get through this."

"Doctors can tell them what to do."

Delilah laughed. "I've got news for you. Your doctors aren't going to be able to do that."

"What do you mean?" Nick straightened. If they didn't have good doctors they needed to do something about it.

"Doctors have a lot of patients. They know everything you need them to know about the treatments you need to kick cancer's ass. But they can't follow their patients home. They won't know what you need after a round of chemo. Your doctors don't have any recipes for food that stays down when the drugs make you want to puke everything up. When that first lock of your pretty hair falls out and you're faced with the reality of what your treatment is going to do to your outside, not just your inside, your sons are going to run in the other direction."

"Now wait a minute." Simon looked angry.

"Pipe down." Delilah was on a roll. "I've helped my grandmother, my great aunt, my aunt and my mother through cancer. I know how to kick its ass and take its name."

"They all still alive?" his mom asked, obviously still not willing to give Delilah a break.

"Shit, Mom." Simon ran a hand through his hair.

"It's okay." Delilah smiled. "It's a valid question."

"You didn't answer it."

Delilah shrugged. "My great aunt and my aunt passed away, but it wasn't the cancer. Derringers know how to beat some things better than others." Her voice sounded a little choked up.

"Mom. Delilah offered to help, and we can use it. Simon and I aren't abandoning you to her, but she's right. We don't know anything about how to take care of you after your treatments. She can help us almost as much as she can help you." He didn't want to sound like he was begging. But he was begging.

"Why don't you boys step outside and let me talk to your mama for a few minutes? A little straight talk between girls should take care of everything."

"Are you sure?" His mother was in a mood, and he didn't want to make Delilah deal with it alone.

"I'm always sure." She sat up and gave him a look he recognized. He'd seen her give it to her friends more times than he could count in the short time he'd known her. Cade called it the "Delilah's ready to blow" look.

"Okay." He gave a nod to Simon and stepped out the back door. Nick stood on the porch looking at the ocean for a moment, waiting for his brother. He wanted to talk to him anyway. When Simon joined him, he turned to face him.

"How's it going?" He studied his brother. They hadn't had much of a chance to talk, especially since Nick had shown up at the house with their mother and announced they were taking her in.

"Good. The garage is on track for opening in a couple of weeks. I've got some custom builds lined up that will keep us afloat until the local business starts coming in. Found out the owner of the only other garage in town wants to start winding down. He'll give us time to build our rep. If we do our job right, he'll throw business our way as he closes in on retirement." Simon faced the ocean and leaned on the porch railing.

"I'm sorry."

His brother's eyes widened as he glanced at Nick.

"Why are you sorry?"

"You got the short end of the deal here."

"How do you figure?"

"We were going to open a garage together, fix up this place, equal partners in every way. Then I got this opportunity and we knew it meant you would be taking on more responsibility with the garage. Now there's Mom and Olivia and the baby. I feel like I'm going in a million different directions and leaving you in the lurch."

"Don't be an idiot."

129

As usual his brother, cut to the chase.

"Simon —"

"Let me finish. Yeah, a lot happened that we didn't expect, but we both know this garage is more my dream than yours. You went along with it because you thought your dream was dead. Then it wasn't. As for Mom. Doesn't matter how shitty our childhood was. She's our mother. If we can help. We help. When it comes to Olivia. That's your deal. I'm here if you need me."

It felt like his brother was letting him off too easy. "I still feel like I'm not pulling my weight at the garage."

"You don't have to. It's enough for me that you're willing to invest your savings. I don't care if you're a silent partner. Truth is I kind of prefer it."

"You sure?" Nick wasn't sure why he kept pushing it.

"I am." Simon huffed out a breath and ran his hand through his hair before turning to face Nick. "Can we stop with the self-sacrificing bullshit? Finally?"

"What the hell are you talking about?" Nick felt his brother's disgusted tone like a punch in the gut.

"You and your need to take a bullet for every fucking person in your life. You've been doing it since we were kids. It's gotten a million times worse since that bullshit your senior year. Life is finally swinging in your direction.

130

If you want to do something for me, don't try to throw yourself on your fucking sword."

Simon stormed off, leaving Nick wondering what the hell had happened. He knew his little brother had just handed him his ass. The question was, why.

It was a question he was still asking himself a couple of hours later when he pulled up in front of Olivia's house. It was a great house. A beach cottage, like his on the opposite end of the King's Folly beach. It was convenient they lived so close to each other. Of course, her house wasn't a run-down fixer-upper. It was a fully restored craftsman cottage that suited her.

He got out of the truck as she opened her door and stepped out.

"I can come to the door." Nick wasn't going to think about the need to prove he was a gentleman to her.

Olivia smiled. "I can meet you out here just as easily."

She seemed to be full of energy. He'd gotten one of those what to expect books. Obviously, he knew he couldn't experience anything with her, but he wanted to know as much as possible about what she was facing. It was important to him to be able to support her through the pregnancy and all the changes she would have to face phys- ically. This pregnancy wasn't in either of their plans and he was going to do as much as he could to help her.

So far, there was nothing to indicate that she was pregnant. It might make him a caveman, but he was looking forward to seeing her belly grow with his child. He'd never thought of being a father before now. Since he'd found out about the pregnancy, most of his few free moments had been devoted to praying that he didn't fuck it up.

"Are we going to sit out here and stare at each other, or go to dinner?" Her smile sent his heart into overdrive.

"Dinner. Absolutely, dinner." He moved to open the door for her and helped her step up into the truck.

Once he was back in the driver's seat he started the engine then pulled out of her driveway. "Hungry?"

"Starving. I didn't get lunch."

He wanted to stop the car and lecture her but figured that wouldn't go over too well. "You can't skip meals."

"I know. It was purely unintentional." She sounded annoyed.

Nothing was supposed to bother her. Not for the next eight months. Well, not ever. "What happened?"

"One of my students needed help after class. By the time I got his issues sorted out I was exhausted and took a nap when I got home instead of eating."

"Next time, try and do both." He tried to keep his tone

132

light. Olivia was pretty mellow, but he knew she wasn't going to sit still and let him boss her around.

"I need to go to the grocery store for some snack food."

He made a note to do some grocery shopping for her. "Make me a list. I'll pick up whatever you need."

"You don't have to."

"I know. But I intend to take care of you, so you might want to get used to it now. Might save us some time to argue about other stuff later." He was going to his best not to mess up, but he'd screwed up big time without realizing it already. Odds were good he'd do it again.

"Are we going to argue later?"

"Slugger, we're bound to clash. We just need to save it for the fights that matter." He knew enough about people to know that conflict was inevitable. The best relationships he'd seen were between people who knew how to resolve it, not dwell in it.

She seemed to accept that, and they drove to Mooney's in comfortable silence. The pub was busy, but not packed. He found a parking space and pulled in.

"Stay put." He unbuckled his seatbelt then got out. He may not be some fancy professor, but he could be a gentleman for her.

He hustled around the front of his truck then helped her

133

out of the passenger side. She wasn't a petite woman, thank God. At about five-foot eight, she was the perfect height for him. He took her hand as they walked into the pub together.

Mooney's was a local institution. It started as a traveling inn just after the town itself was founded and had morphed over the years into a favorite local hangout. The Irish pub had changed again in the last generation when Liam Mooney married Graciela Delgado. Now the place was known for its mix of Irish and Mexican food and its fantastic microbrews created by Graciela and Liam's daughter, Annie. The food was great, but Nick really loved the family atmosphere, since a majority Mooney clan worked in some capacity at the restaurant.

Any hope of having Olivia all to himself for dinner flew out the window when they walked inside. He spotted Cade and Tess immediately and before he could suggest they say hi quickly and get their own table, Olivia stepped toward their friends with a smile on her face that reminded him of a flash bang.

He tried to recover his senses and got to the table just in time to see Olivia pull up a chair.

"Tess and Cade asked us to join them for dinner." She smiled.

"Great." He pulled up a chair. The smirk on Cade's face told Nick he knew exactly how thrilled he was by the development.

Tess set her menu aside. "I heard you had some excitement today."

"What, the thing with the professor?" He wouldn't call it exciting.

"I'm talking about the mysterious package left in Olivia's office."

He slapped a hand on the table. "What?"

Olivia's bit her bottom lip. "How did you hear about that?"

"I'm on the board of trustees. After the Gill debacle, I get copied on every freaking e-mail. I had the triplets set up a program so only topics I care about end up in my inbox. Everything else goes straight to a different folder."

"The 'I'm never going to read it folder.'" Cade took a sip of his beer.

"Can we get back to the security issue? The one in Olivia's office?" Nick tried to control his temper.

"It was nothing, which is why I didn't bother bringing it up." She patted his hand while glaring at Tess.

"Well, not nothing." Tess looked apologetic.

"Will someone tell me what the hell happened before I

135

lose my shit?" The thought of anything threatening Olivia or the baby made him want to go berserk.

"There was a package left on my desk while I was teaching. My assistant found it and called security. It was silly. It was just a teddy bear."

"A teddy bear? What'd you do with it?" Lots of things could be hidden inside a stuffed animal.

"It's in the donation box for the children's hospital toy drive. My secretary called her boyfriend with security because she's watched one too many thrillers. By the time I got back from class the entire box had been dismantled."

"Who was it from?" It sounded harmless, but the whole situation set off his radar.

"That's why my secretary overreacted. The box was left on my desk and wasn't marked. She swears she didn't leave her desk after I left to teach class until she went in to put my mail on my desk, so she's positive she would have seen someone enter my office, but she didn't."

"So, someone what? Climbed into a second-story window to leave you an anonymous package? Olivia, this doesn't sound like nothing." Nick exchanged glances with Cade. He was relieved that the other man looked as alert as he felt.

"My secretary is amazing, but she doesn't realize how

often she steps away from her desk during the day. I wouldn't be surprised if she went out for something and forgot about it. It's really nothing."

"Still. We should go over the security for the building." He thought about who he'd want to look it over.

"Too bad Boomer's not going to be here for a few more weeks. He'd get campus security into shape in no time."

"Who's Boomer?" Olivia asked.

"He's going to be the offensive line coach. Good guy. He was injured in some kind of incident recently, so he needs to finish rehab before he can get here."

"Why would he be the one to handle security?" Olivia found Nick's friends fascinating.

"He was NCIS before his medical discharge." Cade leaned back in his chair.

"Like the television show?"

Nick rolled his eyes. "Probably not exactly like the television show, but the same general principal."

"How did he get hurt?" Tess asked.

"We don't know. He hasn't talked about it." It bothered Nick that they didn't know enough about Boomer's situation to help, but he knew is friend well enough to know that if he needed help, he would ask about it.

"Oh. Well, even if he were here there would be nothing

137

for him to do, at least as far as the teddy bear in my office."
Olivia sounded completely unconcerned.

Nick wished she would take it more seriously. "If some-one's leaving stuff for you that could be a bad sign."

"Someone's not leaving stuff." She blew out a breath. "One package was left. It's an isolated incident."

Nick didn't like it, but he knew her well enough to know she wasn't going to budge. His plans for the night were already shot because his dinner with Olivia had turned into a double date. Pushing the issue would mess it up even more. He was going to have a long talk with Cade about campus security and make sure Olivia was safe. There was no need to tell her about anything, yet.

For a second, he thought about how pissed she was about his announcing her pregnancy to the coaching staff. But this was different.

I'm sure it's different.

Chapter 6

The last few weeks had been very quiet, well as quiet as things were likely to get for a very long time. Olivia checked her watch. Nick was going to pick her up any minute for her appointment with her obstetrician. They had a lengthy discussion about whether he needed to go with her. Although he would probably say it was their first fight.

There was so much going on in his life. The team, the garage, his mother. He was a good man being pulled in a million different directions. She didn't want to be a burden. Worse, she didn't want to rely on him when the demands from other parts of his life could pull him away.

Nick had insisted. Delilah had leapt into helping with his mom and had dubbed herself Captain of Janie's cancer squad. Both Nick and Simon had gone with their mother to her first treatment. Apparently, it had been so uncomfortable, Delilah had banned them from attending any others. According to the human tornado "You don't kick cancer's ass with uncomfortable silences and decades of lingering guilt."

Delilah had taken over Jane Jacobs's schedule and set up family time for the woman and her two sons. It had been amusing to watch her friend roll through the objections lodged by all three of the Jacobs. Still, Olivia knew if Jane needed her sons they would be there.

There was something underneath the almost manic way Delilah had assumed control of the situation. Olivia knew enough about people to know there was more going on than a friend doing a favor for another friend. It seemed like a situation that warranted a girls' night. She would have to talk to Tess about it, as girls' nights weren't her area of expertise.

She looked up when she heard the knock on her door. Nick was standing in the doorway and she was struck all over again about how gorgeous he was. He kept his thick dark hair trimmed short, not quite military short, but they'd known each other long enough that she knew he got irritated when his hair got too long. His beard was trimmed and neat and his blue eyes still made her insides do the Watusi.

"You ready?"

She nodded, words momentarily escaping her. Her entire life was the English language. It was ironic that she couldn't string a coherent sentence together whenever she saw him.

Olivia grabbed her purse and moved to the doorway. As the stepped past him and into the small anteroom used by her secretary the door to the outer office opened and her student, Clay, all but tripped across the doorway.

"Professor Valenti, I'm glad I caught you. I have a problem with my assignment." Beads of sweat dotted his forehead.

"I'm afraid I have an appointment, Clay." Office hours were over, not that this particular student ever paid attention to them.

His face fell. "But this is important."

"I'm sorry, Clay. I can't change my schedule today. We have several summer tutors helping with classes. I can have Lydia get you their numbers. I'm sure one of them could help until my next office hours."

"But it has to be you. You're my professor." He words came out as a whine instead of an honest plea.

"I'm sorry. I simply can't help you right now. If you need help before the assignment is due, you'll have to work with one of the tutors."

"But —"

"Kid." Nick put his arm around Olivia's waist. "We're running late, and we need to go. You should do what Professor Valenti told you to."

Clay ignored Nick. "Can I come by your house tonight?" He sounded so hopeful and lost she almost ignored the warning bell in her head. Of course, if she had, the

141

tightening of Nick's arm around her waist would have made her pay attention to it.

"That wouldn't be appropriate."

Clay took a small step forward. "We could meet for coffee —"

"Look —" Nick's impatient tone told her it was time to move this along.

"I am sorry, Clay, but I simply can't help you today. I am sure one of the tutors can help. Now, we really do have to go, or we will be late for our appointment." Her doctor had given her his last appointment of the day to accommodate her schedule.

She took the hand that held her waist and led Nick past Clay and out of the office. It wasn't a surprise that she had to tug Nick to get him to move. He seemed to want to say something to Clay, but they were really going to be late if they didn't leave now.

"I don't like that kid," Nick growled.

"I'm not blind." Or deaf.

"You need to watch out for him."

Clay's persistence was a concern, but she'd dealt with student crushes before and likely would again. "He's a young man who has a difficult time socializing, which is why he does a lot of summer courses."

"So?" He clearly didn't care.

"I can relate to him." It hadn't been that long ago that she'd been a young student, with few friends outside of her books, and a need for human contact.

"Slugger, I refuse to believe you and that weird little freak could have anything in common."

"Freak?" She stopped and turned to him. "That's incredibly rude."

"Maybe. Doesn't mean it's not accurate." He took her hand and continued moving.

She tugged her hand, trying to get him to stop, but it was like stopping a boulder rolling down a hill from the back side.

"You were the one who said we were going to be late. We can fight and walk at the same time."

She let him pull her down the hall then out of the building because she didn't want to be late to her appointment. "I don't want to fight."

"Really? Didn't sound that way to me."

"I was simply stating that it was rude for you to call him names." She'd been called most of them and still felt the sting.

Nick didn't stop moving. "I think it's rude of him to come on to you and try and get you alone."

143

"That's ridiculous. He's my student."

"Slugger, he wants to be a hell of a lot more than that."

"He does not. Even if he does, I've dealt with students with crushes before. I can do it again." She trotted behind him. "And I wish you'd stop calling me that. It's not polite to remind me of my impulsive outburst."

"I think you kind of like it." The humor in his voice was obvious.

She snorted.

Have I ever snorted before?

"See." He sounded so smug.

Olivia clenched her fist.

I can't hit him again.

"I don't understand how you can judge him like that." She was used to people only seeing the surface. It wasn't fair to place unreasonable expectations on Nick because he was the father of her baby.

"I don't understand how you can be so blind." Now he sounded exasperated.

"I'm not blind." She'd learned at an early age to not trust what people showed her. It didn't mean she couldn't hope for the best.

"That kid is a pair of binoculars away from becoming a stalker."

They reached his truck in the parking lot and he opened the passenger door for her. He helped her up into the seat, treating her as if she was fragile and precious. It always amazed her, his ability to make her feel so protected and important, while irritating her at the same time.

"How can you say he's on his way to becoming a stalker. He's a lonely, eager student. That's all." She'd seen more students like him than she could count.

"He looks at you like you belong to him, and he hated me on sight." He shut the door and rounded the truck.

She waited for him to get in the driver's seat before responding to his last comment. "That can't be true."

He was quiet for a moment and glanced at her out of the side of his eye.

"What?" she huffed.

"What what?" He tried to sound innocent. And failed.

She wasn't going to let him get away with anything. "What do you want to say?"

He blew out a breath. "I don't want you to take it the wrong way."

"Words that guarantee that I will not like what you are about to say." Why couldn't he just say what he wanted to say?

"I clocked him the first time I walked into your class."

145

"What does that mean?" It wasn't good that she wanted to punch him again.

"It means I don't trust him. He's into you and not in a 'harmless fantasies about his hot professor' kind of way.'"

"Hot professor?" This was a ridiculous conversation, but warmth flowed through her like warm maple syrup thanks to his complement.

He rolled his eyes. "Yes. You're hot."

"You're the only one who thinks so."

"Got news for you, Slugger. Every man with a pulse thinks you're hot."

"That's never been the case before," she scoffed.

He laughed. "It's probably been the case for a long time, you've just never noticed."

She wasn't entirely comfortable with the direction the conversation was going in. "I still don't understand why you don't like Clay."

"I don't trust him. If I thought you would listen, I'd tell you to stay a mile away from him."

"He's my student." She couldn't avoid him if she was going to teach him.

"I know. Which is why I'm trying to keep my shit together. I also know you're a smart woman who doesn't take any chances. I just don't trust him, so I'm going to ask you

146

to avoid being alone with him and if he ever actively tries to get you alone, get away from him."

"I think this entire conversation is unnecessary, but I will take your opinion under advisement." How could she explain to someone like Nick the alienation people like Clay and her experienced and the importance of finding someone you could relate to?

He snorted. "You do that."

For the rest of the drive they talked about less weighty topics. The garage he was opening with his brother, the fall semester, the university's new landscaping. Anything but his protective attitude and what it might mean for a relationship.

Forty-five minutes later they were in the doctor's office. She was still only six weeks along so there was no sonogram and it was too soon to hear the baby's heartbeat. The doctor had conducted the exam without Nick in the room and Olivia had agreed he could join them once she was fully clothed.

Nick shocked her speechless by pulling out a long list of questions he'd tucked into his planner about her first trimester.

His questions were so thorough she could feel the heat

spread up her neck and into her cheeks. What really surprised was that all the questions weren't about the baby. There were almost as many questions about the potential impact of the pregnancy on her health and what he could do to help her.

It had been years since anyone had truly cared about her well-being. She didn't want to burst in to tears. To keep from crying she started reciting "The Wife of Bath's Tale" from Chaucer's *Canterbury Tales* in her head.

After a moment, she realized the room was silent. She looked up. Nick and her doctor were staring at her.

"Sorry?" Olivia assumed she'd turned beet red.

"Did you hear anything we were just talking about?" her doctor asked.

"Not really," she admitted.

"Olivia." Nick sounded exasperated. "We're talking about your health. You need to take it seriously."

"I do? I thought I'd go out and buy a pack of cigarettes and a fifth of vodka when we're done here." The overprotective caring Nick was lovely, in small doses. Today, it felt like she was getting an extra-large helping.

Her doctor coughed. The gleam in his eye made it clear he was trying not to laugh.

"When did you turn into such a smartass?" Nick asked.

She shrugged. "Delilah has practically glued herself to my side for months. She was bound to rub off a little bit."

He took a breath. "I get it. I'm pushing."

"You're being very sweet and protective, but I'm a grown woman with a ridiculously high IQ. I know how to manage my health and the baby's. Not to mention I'm young and healthy. I've done my research. All my health factors make this a low-risk pregnancy."

"Right." Her doctor jumped in. "I think we're good for today. Everything's moving along on schedule with your pregnancy. I'll see you in a month unless you have any problems."

Nick whipped his gaze back to the doctor and stared. "Problems?"

"Cramping. Bleeding. Unusual aches. Olivia knows her body and she knows what to look for."

"She does," Olivia agreed as she looked Nick in the eyes. He was going to need to dial back this caveman side or he might not survive her pregnancy.

He was never going to survive her pregnancy. He'd spent most of the night reading that what to expect book and a bunch of articles on the internet. There were at least ten drafts of his list of questions crumpled up in the trash. The protocol on whether or not he should even ask questions was unclear, but when Olivia had gotten quiet he couldn't stop himself.

The doctor had answered all his questions, until Olivia spoke up and he knew he'd stepped in it.

"I didn't mean to piss you off." He glanced at the doctor before focusing on her.

"You haven't…yet."

That would be his cue to stop talking. Although, she looked so damn cute when she was mad at him he was tempted to irritate her for the hell of it. But he'd pushed her buttons enough for one day, between the questions for the doctor and his reaction to her student trying to push her into a meeting she didn't want.

He made a note to himself to call Boomer. He couldn't get to King's Folly until he was finished with his rehab, but maybe he could do a little digging to see if that gut, Clay, had a record. Maybe this was all an overreaction.

"Do you have any other questions for me, Mr. Jacobs?" The doctor interrupted his train of thought.

He looked at Olivia and smiled. "Do I?"

"Not today."

He laughed. "Guess I don't have any more questions

then."

The doctor moved to the door of the exam room as Nick held out a hand to help Olivia off the exam table.

She stared at his hand. "I'm still early enough in my pregnancy I can stand up by myself."

"I know. I'm still a simple Alabama boy who believes in offering a hand to his lady."

His lady? Had he just said that out loud? They hadn't had any conversations about being a couple. They'd been spending a lot of time together since she'd told him about the baby. She hadn't made any comments about their future, but she'd been open to him being a part of her life. He was starting to believe they might have a chance.

Olivia turned a cute shade of pink that made him think of the roses his commanding officer's wife used to grow in her garden. He liked making her blush. It was cute as hell.

"Thanks, doc." Nick nodded at the doctor.

"You're welcome." The other man turned to Olivia. "I know you've already scheduled your appointment for next month. So, I'll see you then."

"Thank you," Olivia said.

Nick put his hand on the small of her back and guided her out of the office. "Want to grab something to eat before we head home?" Between her classes, his meetings and the doctor's appointment, it was six-thirty. Dinner time.

Her stomach rumbled and the pink in her cheeks turned a shade closer to red. "Sure."

Perfect. They decided on a little Italian place near the medical center. He had a feeling they would be finding more than a few restaurants in the area over the next eight months.

"What did you mean by what you said in the doctor's office?" She studied her menu.

"I said a lot of things. You're going to have to be more specific." He set his menu down. The lasagna special looked good.

"You called me your lady."

He nodded. "I was wondering if you caught that."

She huffed out a breath and set down her menu. "What did you mean?"

"I could be wrong, but it seems to me we're building more of a relationship than just a co-parenting thing." At least he hoped that's what they were doing.

"We haven't talked about it." Olivia took a sip of water.

"I don't want to push you and I don't want you to think I'm making moves because of the baby. Figured we could let things move along at their own pace without having to call it anything." This was all unfamiliar territory and he didn't want to screw it up. He'd made more than enough mistakes in his life.

"Until today."

He shrugged. "It slipped out. Didn't mean to say it, but that doesn't mean I didn't mean it."

"What do we do now?"

His answer was interrupted by the waitress who took their orders. He stuck with his first instinct of lasagna and his policy to go with a staple of any new restaurant he tried. Olivia was more adventurous and ordered the chicken special with some kind of cream and cheese sauce.

"Eat some dinner. Keep getting to know each other. See what happens." One day at a time was probably the best approach.

"It's that easy?" She sounded skeptical.

"Probably not. I don't know a lot of things for sure, but one thing I've learned in life is almost nothing in life that's worth having comes easily."

She watched him long enough that he started to worry she was going to tell him to hit the road. Instead, she smiled. It was the kind of smile a woman usually gave a man when she knows she's got him by the balls.

He snorted at the thought. Olivia wouldn't play those kinds of games with a rulebook and a roadmap.

Olivia tilted her head. "What's so funny?"

"You're amazing." His stomach rolled in a not entirely unpleasant way. He wondered if it was the sensation of butterflies he'd heard people talk about.

"I am?" She sounded shocked.

He wondered if he would ever get used to her sounding so surprised when people told her how awesome she was. "Why do you do that?"

"Do what?"

"Anytime I compliment you, you come back with a question that sounds like you're surprised I'm saying something nice."

She glanced down at her lap.

"Olivia?"

"I'm not used to people saying nice things to me," she whispered.

Her quiet admission ripped a hole in his gut. She deserved so much more than she'd apparently gotten.

"Get used to it." He decided he'd make sure she heard how fantastic she was every day.

She smiled. "I'll try."

"There is no try. There is only do." He used his best Yoda voice.

She burst out laughing. The sound rushed through like

a warm ocean wave.

"I wouldn't have pegged you for a Star Wars fan." Olivia smiled.

"What's not to love? Swashbuckling in space, good against evil, the good guys eventually win."

"I've always been more partial to the Star Trek world."

He remembered she had a debate with Tess's brothers in Vegas but didn't remember the details. "Why?" He didn't really care either way, but he was curious about what made her tick.

"Star Wars always seemed too limited to me. It was one world basically. The rebels versus the Empire. Star Trek has so many iterations and now it's got the movies with the alternate time line. The stories are more varied."

Her animated defense of Star Trek versus Star Wars fascinated him. Once their food got there, they talked about the two science fiction series through dinner. When she got going on a topic the only word that could accurately describe her would be vivid. The more he got to know her, the more he realized how much life and color inhabited the woman behind the reserved genius professor that she showed the world.

Nick didn't know if he'd ever taken so much time over a meal just enjoying someone's company. Almost two hours later they'd finished eating and covered the finer points of the Star Trek universe as opposed to the Star Wars movies. He'd basically invited himself to dinner at her place tomorrow to eat take out Chinese and watch episodes of one of the Star Trek series. She'd shyly admitted she had all of them on Blu-Ray.

When they finished their meal, he paid the bill and stood to help her out of her chair. He ushered her out of the restaurant, keeping a hand on her back. She stumbled a bit as they left the restaurant and he pulled her close. It had been a long day and she must be exhausted. The sun was setting. It would be dark by the time he got her home.

As they stepped on the sidewalk, a chill shot down his spine. Something was off. Nick scanned the sidewalk looking for any signs of a disturbance. At the same time, he turned so that she was between him and the building. Pulling her closer, he ushered her toward his truck.

"What's wrong?" She kept pace with him, but there was a tremor in her voice.

"Why do you ask?" He didn't want to worry her. It had been a while since he'd been in combat and he couldn't say for sure what had set him off now. The last thing she needed was to get upset for no reason. It could be nothing. His internal alarm sometimes set off an alert when he was stressed. His life could qualify as stressful right now.

"You got tense all of a sudden and your scanning our surroundings like you're expecting an attack." There was a tremor in her voice.

She was observant. He'd give her that.

"I don't know anything is wrong. Just got a bad feeling." That much was true. It could be nothing.

He felt a little better when they made it to the truck. He scanned the area again as he helped her in. His nerves relaxed a little more when she was safely in the passenger seat, surrounded by steel.

Once she was settled he moved around the front of the truck as he continued to scan the street around him. His muscles were tight, and he couldn't figure out where the threat, if there was one, was coming from. Was someone watching them? He hopped into the driver's seat and started the truck as he slammed his door shut.

"You're making me nervous." She looked a little green around the gills.

"Sorry." His senses were jangling. They may be in the truck, but there was still something wrong. He barely said two words for most of the drive home. He knew he was acting like an asshole, but he couldn't shake the feeling that there was some kind of IED in front of them that they were about to step on.

The feeling didn't lessen as they left the city limits and hit the highway. At least it didn't get worse. The dull jangling of his senses told him something was going to happen. He wished he knew what the hell it was. The sun sank below the horizon as they drove home. The spreading darkness didn't help his nerves.

They were just outside of King's Folly when Olivia reached out and grabbed his hand.

"I need you to pull over." Her voice sounded strangled.

He glanced around. There wasn't a lot of traffic on the two-lane road, but he couldn't see anything that would cause concern. "What? Why?" Nick glanced at her.

She looked pale and a green tinge had darkened her skin since they'd left the restaurant. "Pull over."

Nick signaled and pulled over to the shoulder. He'd barely put the truck in park when she threw open her door and stumbled out. The sound of her throwing up echoed in the night. Then there was silence as he threw the door open then bolted around the front of his Chevy.

When he saw her his body froze, and his heart raced faster than a rocket engine. The shadows from the night and the forest partially concealed her. He could barely make out her form in the dark. She was on her side partially curled up in the fetal position. Fear clogged his throat as he rushed to her side then knelt next to her. The gravel from the road bit into his knees, but he ignored it.

What the hell just happened?

Nick's fingers trembled as he checked for a pulse. It fluttered against his fingers like a trapped butterfly. He ran back to the truck to grab a flashlight and rushed to her side. Once he turned the beam on he slid it across her skin trying to figure out what had happened. He saw the blood trickling from the side of her head and the puke on the side of the road.

She must have thrown up and somehow tripped and hit her head. He didn't want to move her, but he had to get her to the hospital. If she'd injured her neck when she fell, though, he could paralyze her. The possibilities rolled through his brain like a freight train.

"Olivia? Slugger? Can you hear me?"

She moaned but didn't open her eyes or answer him.

Shit.

He glanced both directions down the road. It would figure that there was no traffic. Why did he take a fucking shortcut off the highway? If he'd taken another exit they'd

be on the main strip of the beach and there would be someone to flag down and get help.

He fumbled in his pocket looking for his phone. "Fuck."
Where was his phone? He patted his pockets again. His
heart raced faster than it ever had, and he felt light headed.
"Where the fuck is my phone?"

Talking to himself wasn't going to help, but he couldn't
think of what to do. He needed to get to his phone to call
someone. Anyone.

The truck. He always put his phone in the center con-
sole of the truck. It felt like it was a million miles away.
Glancing back at the truck, he rested his fingers on Olivia's
pulse again. It still fluttered. Was it to fast? It felt too fast.
But it was still there.

Panic started to set in and pull him under like a rip tide.
"Hang on Olivia. We'll figure this out."

The smell of her vomit in the open air made his stomach
clench. He'd smelt worse things in his life, but this meant
she needed him to do something. Anything. All he could do
was kneel next to her, holding her pulse like a lifeline while
his frantic mind searched for a way to help her that didn't
involve leaving her side.

The reflection of blue and red lights drew his attention
over his shoulder. The breath he hadn't realized he'd been

holding came out in a whoosh when he recognized it was a county sheriff's cruiser. Whoever got out of that car was going to get a kiss right on the mouth.

The sound of a car door slamming broke into the silence of the night air.

"Hello?"

"Over here." Whoever it was needed to get here, now. He glanced over his shoulder and saw Deputy Sheriff Lily Mooney come around his truck.

She hunkered down on the other side of Olivia. "What's going on?"

He explained what happened to her. His fingers stayed pressed to Olivia's pulse point and he tried to ignore the way his hand was shaking. As long as he felt her heart beating, it would be okay.

Lily grabbed her shoulder radio and called for an ambulance. Nick didn't know how much time passed between the call and the sound of sirens. All he could focus on was the flutter of Olivia's pulse that told him she was still with him.

Two paramedics hopped out of the ambulance and everything moved from slow motion to fast forward. Once she was safely in the back of the ambulance he jumped in his truck to follow. He sped after the vehicle carrying his whole life with Lily's cruiser right behind him.

Trying to figure out how they went from a quiet dinner together to her lying unconscious by the side of the road was like trying to untangle a knot of Christmas lights. Pulling one thread only let to another one drawing tighter.

What the hell happened?

Chapter 7

Voices carried across the darkness, leading her toward the light. Nick was there. His agitated baritone soothed her, somehow. Maybe it was just the fact that he hadn't left her alone. She didn't know what was happening, but it didn't matter. Nick would make sure she was all right.

"Nick?" Her voice sounded weak and breathless.

What happened to me?

A warm hand engulfed hers. "Olivia? You back? Come on, Slugger, open your eyes."

She tried, she really did, but her eyelids felt like they were glued together. "Thirsty." Uttering that one word took all her strength.

"She can have some water. A few sips." Olivia didn't recognize the voice. A moment later a straw was pressed against her mouth

It took every ounce of energy to purse her lips and draw in some water. The cool liquid slid along her tongue and down her throat, easing the burning sensation that lingered there. She tried to grip the straw in her teeth as it was pulled away.

"Doc said a few, Slugger. Can you open your eyes for me?" Fear laced through his voice.

The pleading tone in Nick's voice forced her to lift her lids. Pain shot through her as the light hit her eyes. She tried to lift her hand to cover them, but her arm felt like it was being held down by a pile of sand bags. A gentle hand shielded her eyes and a large body blocked out the light.

"Olivia?" His beautiful blue eyes were filled with fear. "Baby?"

A soft caress moved across her abdomen and rested there in a protective gesture that eased the fear roaring through her body. "The baby's fine. You will be too."

"Happened?" She couldn't seem to form a complete sentence.

"The doctors believe the food poisoning made you sick. When you threw up, you were dizzy and fell over and hit your head. You knocked yourself out, but your scans are clear. So they don't think you have a concussion."

"You?"

"You were the only one that got sick." He sounded irritated.

"How?" She couldn't grab onto any of the thoughts rolling through her mind.

"Could have been chicken or the cream sauce. The sheriff's department called the restaurant. We haven't heard if there are any other cases, yet."

"Oh." His words seemed to make sense, but somehow her fractured brain wasn't processing anything. "Sure about the baby?"

He nodded. "So far so good. I got you right to the emergency room and we got you treated right away."

"Risks?" As her mind cleared, she latched on to the details.

A throat cleared. Olivia shifted her head to see a woman standing patiently by the door.

"Professor Valenti, I'm Dr. Wyatt. I'm an obstetrician and I specialize in high risk pregnancies."

"Risk?" The panic that had only just eased built again. Was she going to lose the baby?

"Doc. Maybe we can do this later." The warning tone in Nick's voice was clear.

Olivia put her hand over his, the one that rested on her stomach and squeezed. "Now."

He scrubbed his other hand down his face then nodded.

"Food poisoning can be dangerous during pregnancy, particularly if the infection spreads to the baby. At this point, you're still in your first trimester. There are no signs of miscarriage, but there are some concerns. Based on the information Mr. Jacobs gave us, you're still too early in your pregnancy for there to be a fetal heartbeat."

"What does that mean?"

"It means that for now we are operating under the assumption that you still have a viable pregnancy. From this point forward, we are going to treat this as a high-risk pregnancy and since I specialize in helping women bring pregnancies like this to term I would like to handle your care for the rest of your pregnancy." Dr. Wyatt's voice was matter of fact and she maintained eye contact with Olivia.

Tears pricked the corners of her eyes as she turned to Nick. She wanted this baby so much. The thought of losing it sent spikes of pain rocketing through her.

"What do you think?" She needed him to tell her it was going to all right.

"I think it's your choice. Dr. Wyatt updated your doctor on the situation and her recommendations. He's on board if you want to make the switch."

Everything was happening too fast. She tried to piece it all together. They were having dinner, then they were driving home. The vague sense of nausea lingered. It felt like there were layers of cotton between her and rational thought.

"Do you want me to switch?" His opinion was important to her. They baby was his too.

He glanced at the doctor, who stepped forward and patted her leg.

"I'll let you two talk about it and I will check in on you shortly." She left the room.

The whooshing of the door shutting behind Dr. Wyatt mixed with the beeps from the machines Oliva was hooked up to echoed through the room.

Despite the noises, it felt like she was drowning in silence.

"I like Dr. Wyatt." His smooth voice rolled across her skin, soothing her frayed nerves.

"Do you think we should switch?" She wanted to hear what he thought since he'd spent more time with Dr. Wyatt than she had. Well. Conscious time.

"Well, she's definitely closer. She teaches at the medical school and has an office there. Once you're cleared to go back to work, it will be more convenient for you."

"Do you trust her?" That was the most important part.

He scrubbed a hand down his face as if to hide the guilty expression that had flashed across it with her question.

"What?"

"I had a lot of time to wait in the emergency room."

"And?" What was he hiding?

167

"I called Boomer and had him run a quick background check on the doc."

"I —" That was incredibly intrusive and, oddly, one of the sweetest things she'd ever heard.

"I know. It was shitty. But I didn't know what was going on and you weren't waking up and I didn't know Dr. Wyatt from Temperance Brennan. I wanted to make sure you were in good hands."

"So you trust her." She knew if he'd learned anything that worried him, Dr. Wyatt wouldn't still be treating her.

He nodded. "She's tops in her field. It's like King's Folly is a magnet for hot geniuses."

"Did you just call her hot?"

A deep red color stole up the back of his neck. "You, Tess, the doc. You're all hot. It's an objective fact." He let out a breath. "I know you like those."

She couldn't identify the sensation rolling through her. Her skin felt tighter and she wanted to scratch Dr. Wyatt's eyes out. *Was this jealousy?*

"For the record, I prefer literary nerds to science geeks." His smile eased the tightness of her skin and made her relax a little.

"Nice save."

"I thought so." He chuckled but sobered up quickly.

"Anyway, she finished medical school at fourteen and she's been practicing medicine for fifteen years. She's board certified in obstetrics and gynecology and surgery, with a specialty in fetal surgery. The doc was recruited by a bunch medical schools and is a top-rated teacher."

"Is that all?" It was a surprising amount of information. How long had she been unconscious?

He had the grace to look a little embarrassed. "It's all Boomer could get on short notice."

This was a weird conversation, all things considered. Oddly enough it was also calming.

"You think I should switch to her." It wasn't a question.

"I think you have a good doctor, but things just got way more complicated and you deserve the best. Seems like that's Dr. Wyatt."

Tears pricked the corners of her eyes. This morning she had a routine, low-risk pregnancy. Now, she was faced with the possibility that her baby could already be gone.

Nick leaned over. "The baby is fine." His tone of voice brooked no argument.

"But—"

"No. They baby is fine," he repeated. "We're going to do everything the doc tells us to do to make sure of it."

She took a deep breath as if she could draw his strength

into her and give it to the baby. "Okay."

"Okay." He leaned down and kissed her forehead. His warm lips lingered, and a warmth spread from through her entire body from that simple contact.

Please, God. Let him be right.

Oh, fuck. Let me be right.

Nick shifted in the piece of furniture the nurses claimed was a chair. They'd stopped in to hang a new IV bag. The most important thing for Olivia was rest and staying hydrated. The nurse had said as much in that hushed tone they used in hospitals that somehow seemed louder than a sideline cheer.

He glanced at his watch. It was late. Sleep was unlikely. Not because the chair was harder than a boulder in the desert. It wasn't like he hadn't slept in worse places, but every time Olivia twitched a muscle he went on alert. Finally, he nodded off for a little while.

It was the sound of the baby crying that told him it was a dream. He wanted to wake himself up but couldn't. The glow coming through the hospital room door beckoned him. His body moved without his direction. All he wanted was to stay in the room with Olivia. He didn't want to see what was beyond the door. Nothing good was ever on the other side of the door in his dreams.

As if under a spell he trudged down the empty hallway, which glowed with red and blue lights that blinked in a familiar rhythm. He got to the end of the hall and stopped. He didn't want to see what was behind that door but couldn't stop himself. His hand reached out to push the door open. The state championship ring gleamed on his finger. He hadn't seen the damn thing since high school. As far as he knew it was still at the bottom of a lake in Alabama.

The door swung open. The girl he hadn't seen in fourteen years stood on the ledge of an open window holding a crying baby. Somehow, he knew it was his and Olivia's. Tiffany looked like she did in high school, the night she died. Like she had the world by the tail. Too bad he couldn't stop her from throwing it all away.

"What are you doing?" His voice sounded slurred. If he didn't know better he'd say he was drunk, but he hadn't been drinking.

"You took something from me. Now I'm taking something from you." She laughed maniacally.

"I didn't take anything. You know I wasn't the one driving that night. Brandi was."

"We all know that. But the world thinks it was you. So you're the one that has to pay. You never paid."

"I lost everything even though I didn't do anything."

She shrugged. He recognized the look on her face. It was the innocent face she put on just before she did something mean to an undeserving student.

"Maybe not. Still. You know me. If I'm not happy, nobody else gets to be."

With that statement she jumped, carrying his screaming child with her.

"No." Nick bolted upright in the chair. A layer of sweat dampened his skin and stuck his clothes to his body.

"Nick? Are you all right?" Olivia's soft voice called to him from the bed. Soothing his jangled nerves.

"Yeah." He scrubbed his hand down his face. "Just a dream."

"Must have been some dream."

He stood then walked to the bed, trying to shrug off the after effects of the disturbing nightmare. Tiffany used to come to him all the time when he was asleep, but she hadn't in a while. Her last words made him think that her sudden reappearance was due less to any lingering feelings of guilt over his role in her death and more about the chance at happiness that was staring him in the face with concerned blue eyes.

"It's an old nightmare. Haven't had it in a while." He hoped she assumed it was some combat related dream and let it go. The last thing either of them needed right now was to get into a conversation about the events that led him to lose his football scholarship and join the Navy.

"Do you want to talk about it?"

Nick shook his head. "No. It's stress related. In case you haven't noticed my girl is in the hospital and she's not listening to me when I tell her our baby's going to be fine."

A hint of a smile drifted across her lips. It wasn't much, but it made him feel about ten feet tall.

"Now I'm definitely your girl? When did you decide that?"

He shrugged. "Don't know." It was probably somewhere between the moment at dinner when he'd questioned calling her his lady and the moment on the side of the road when she'd looked so still.

"What's that mean, being your girl?" Her whisper echoed with the beeps of the machine monitoring her vitals.

"Whatever you want it to mean. I know we still have a lot to figure out." He swallowed. "A lot to talk about. I'm following your lead."

"Really?"

Nick smiled. "Well for the next few weeks I'm following the doctor's lead, but after that it's your call."

"When am I going to get to go home?"

"Yeah, about that." They needed to talk about what was going to happen when she left the hospital.

The beep of the machine spiked. "How long are they keeping me here?"

He rushed forward. "Relax. Breathe. You should be able to go home tomorrow."

She inhaled and blew out a breath. "Good. Why did you get weird when I asked?"

"Cause I'm not sure how you're going to react to the rest of it." He'd come up with a plan after talking with the doc about what Olivia needed for the next few weeks.

"Rest of what?" She gripped his hand.

"I'm moving in with you."

"You're what?" Her voice sounded almost shrill.

"You're going to be on bedrest for a couple of days and the doc wants you to take it easy for a few weeks, at least until we get to the ultrasound. That means you'll need help. So, you've got me."

She looked panicked. "One of the girls — "

"Delilah has taken over the spare room at my place to help with my mom and Tess is still a newlywed."

"What about Charlie?"

A sharp pain spread from his chest to his gut. He was trying not to read too much into the fact that she wanted anyone but him staying with her.

"She's got a family thing going on." Technically, true. But from what he understood, she always had a family thing going on. He didn't need to tell Olivia that he'd let her girls know, in no uncertain terms, that he was taking care of his woman and their baby.

"Oh."

"Am I that bad?" He hoped the answer was no.

She shook her head but didn't say anything else.

There was something rolling around that beautiful brain of hers. He wished he could get her to open up to him. But, he didn't have the right to push when he was still holding back some major things himself. The big conversation was coming, the one where he laid his past at her feet and waited for her to judge him for it. Was it such a bad thing that he wanted her to be comfortable with the best of him before he showed her the worst?

Anyway, he wasn't going to push her for her secrets until he was ready to share his own. "I'll take care of you."

Her even breathing told him she'd gone back to sleep. He wasn't sure if she heard his whispered vow, but he meant it. She was the number one priority in his life and he would make sure she had everything she wanted and needed, even if one day she wanted him gone.

The next evening, Nick stared at the beach from the window in Olivia's guest room. After he'd shaken off the nightmare, the night before had been quiet, but if experience had taught him anything it was that the quiet could be deceiving. He was surprised Olivia hadn't put up more of a fight about him moving in, which showed how tired and scared she was.

He'd wanted to be able to spend more time with her. They needed to build a relationship before the baby got here. Dealing with food poisoning and a medical threat to the baby wasn't part of the plan.

Hell, who was he kidding? There was no plan. He'd been flying blind ever since he'd found out about the baby.

"Nick?"

Her soft voice washed over him. He turned around to find her standing in the doorway.

"I thought you were going to take a nap."

She shrugged. "I couldn't sleep."

There was nothing else he could do. He went to her then pulled her into his arms. "You need to get some rest."

She leaned back and stared at him. "I'm hungry."

That was a good sign. He glanced at his watch. It was just past eight.

"Do you want to order something?"

She nodded. "I don't feel like cooking."

He shrugged. "Me neither. What do you feel like ordering?"

"You cook?"

He nodded. "I've been on my own a long time. It was learn to cook or eat out all the time. I don't like eating out all the time."

"Oh." She chewed on her bottom lip. It was adorable. She was adorable.

Before he could respond, the doorbell rang. He pulled her into the hall, away from any windows. "Wait here."

He approached the door, the windows running down either side of it made him feel exposed. Too exposed. He glanced through the peep hole. It was a standard model. He was going to have to replace it with a newer, more secure one. The windows needed some security film on them too. It was time to start a list to improve security in Olivia's house.

His muscles relaxed when he saw who was standing on the other side of the door. Cade and Tess stood there with a couple of bags of food in their arms. Nick opened the door.

"Hey. What brings you by?" he asked them.

"We brought dinner from Mooney's." Tess raised one of the bags. "Virgin margarita chicken broth made especially for Olivia."

Nick stepped back and let their friends in. Tess shoved her bags into his hands before she rushed to Olivia, who was hovering at the foot of the stairs.

"How are you doing?" Tess asked her.

Olivia smiled at him over Tess's shoulder. "I'm all right."

"You're sure?" Cade asked from his position next to Nick.

"Positive. I just want to get through the next few weeks and have everything be okay." She put a hand on her stomach.

The gesture made Nick wish he could fast forward time. Waiting through the next few weeks was going to be hell for both of them, but he wasn't the one carrying the baby. How was Olivia going to do it? Second guess every twinge and freak out over every new sensation?

"And everything will be okay." Nick carried the food to the kitchen. His skin felt tight and nerves rolled through his gut. A long time ago, he'd promised himself he'd never be helpless in his life. He'd turned himself into a man of action. Even after the night when everything had changed he'd made his own choices, forged his own path. This feeling of helplessness was an unwelcome reminder of his childhood and his brief but too long time in jail.

But, if all he could do for the next few weeks was hover and be a cheerleader for Olivia, he would be the best damn cheerleader there was.

Cade followed him into the kitchen as Tess quizzed Olivia about how she was feeling.

"How you holding up, man?" Cade set his bags on the kitchen counter.

Nick looked over his shoulder to make sure the women hadn't followed them yet. "Hanging in."

"Anything I can do?"

He appreciated the offer. "It's a waiting game now. Either the baby's going to be okay or not."

"What's the doc say?" Cade pulled the food cartons out of the bag.

Nick grabbed the plates and silverware. "The good news is we figured she got sick from the food at the Italian place. Which means she was only exposed for a couple of hours before we got her to the hospital."

"And the bad news?"

"Since she developed symptoms so quickly it was probably a pretty nasty bacteria. If it spread to the baby —" He couldn't finish.

"What do we do?"

Nick appreciated Cade using the word "we." Having his friend and boss's support meant a lot. "Nothing to do. The baby was either exposed or not. Since it's so early in her pregnancy the ultrasound doesn't pick up a heartbeat. So, we hope she doesn't miscarry and that everything's as it should be when she gets an ultrasound in two weeks."

"What if there's not a heartbeat in two weeks?" Cade asked the question Nick wasn't letting himself think about.

"The doc said it won't necessarily mean anything. Eight weeks is usually the earliest you can hear it. But it's not unusual for it to take longer, which is why a lot of women don't have an ultrasound until the end of the first trimester. So, if there's no heartbeat in two weeks, but no sign of a miscarriage or fetal distress, then we give it another few weeks." The thought of that made sweat break out on the back of Nick's neck.

Nick ran a hand through his hair. He couldn't believe the words coming out of his mouth. Even when he'd been doing all the research on Olivia's pregnancy, he'd never pictured himself as the guy who would know the ins and outs of an ultrasound and what would show up when.

Now he knew exactly what to wait for and how much of a grace period they would have before the doctors told them to give up hope.

Fuck.

He prayed the baby was like her mom, advanced and doing everything ahead of schedule.

"What's the plan?" Cade was always the man to follow a plan.

"Keep her calm for the next two weeks." Nick hoped it was as easy as it sounded.

"How are you going to do that?"

"I'd like the answer to that myself."

He turned at the sound of Olivia's voice. She stood in the doorway to the kitchen with Kate in her arms. He'd forgotten about the damn dog. The damn dog that hated him. The damn dog who chose that moment to snarl at him from the safety of her mistress's arms.

"Shhh." Olivia kissed the tip of the Kate's nose and was rewarded with a flurry of licks to her cheek.

"I don't think I'm going to have to do much. You're a genius after all and you heard the doc's instructions. I'm just going to be around to make it easier for you." He wanted his presence in her life to be soothing, not stressful.

"With two jobs and a sick mother?" She sounded like she didn't believe him.

"One job," he corrected her.

"What do you mean one job?" She stepped forward. "Cade wouldn't fire you. Would he?" Olivia closed in on Cade.

He held up his hands in defense. "Whoa. I didn't fire anyone."

Olivia turned to Nick. When she got close enough, Kate nipped at him, but missed. "Well you can't get fired from the garage. You're a partner."

She was cute when she was filled with righteous indignation on his behalf and Kate was kind of cute trying to take a piece out of him.

"True, but now I'm a silent partner." He was grateful Simon had been in favor of the plan.

"Why?"

He reached out to take her hand and Kate tried to snap it off. Damned if he was going to flinch away from fifteen pounds of fur. He leaned over and locked eyes with his nemesis. The little bugger raised her lip and gave him an Elvis sneer. She snapped at him again, this time coming within a breath of getting teeth on his nose.

"Kate." Olivia gave the pup a little shake. "What am I

182

going to do with you?"

"You can put her on the floor." She was a small dog, but Olivia shouldn't be lifting anything.

"She's going to go after you again." Olivia sounded doubtful.

He snorted. "Slugger. She's not chewing through these boots."

Nick wasn't sure why he felt like this was a test, but he held his breath. When Olivia set Kate down, he let it out. The pup made a dash for his feet and attacked. She went after him like he was made of roast beef.

"What's the deal with that dog?" Cade couldn't hold in his laugh.

"She hates me."

"She doesn't hate you." Olivia moved to the kitchen table then sat down. "She's not used to people besides me. She'd go after Cade or Tess if she noticed them."

Cade went down to his haunches, held out his hand and whistled. Kate took a break from attacking Nick's feet to study the maker of the noise. After a second she launched herself off the ground and into Cade's arms. The fifteen-pound pup almost knocked him on his ass.

"Doesn't hate me my ass," Nick mumbled as Kate did

her level best to lick Cade's face off. Tess joined her husband and gave the puppy a pat on the head, who proceeded to transfer all her affection to Tess.

Nick looked at Olivia and raised an eyebrow.

"They're dog people. Tess is a vet and they have an army of animals at their house."

"I like dogs." It wasn't his fault that he never had one. Growing up a dog would have been one more responsibility his mother couldn't handle, and he'd been in the Navy for most of his adult life.

"I didn't say you didn't."

He wasn't going to get in an argument with her, especially not about her dog. He'd figure out a way to win the little terror over. A growl from behind him told him it probably wouldn't be tonight. That fact was confirmed when he felt fifteen pounds of puppy slam into the back of his leg and felt tiny teeth prick his skin. Fortunately, Kate didn't have the jaw strength to do much damage and she seemed more interested in getting a grip on his jeans than on him.

A giggle drew is attention away from the ball of fur behind him. Olivia slapped her hand over her mouth but couldn't hide the laughter bubbling over. He'd forgive the mutt. Her antics brought the first lightness he'd seen on Olivia's face since she woke up in the hospital.

"Let's get you fed. Then we can figure out what we need to do to get you through the next few weeks."

"Let us help." Tess sprang into action. "You should sit if you don't want to drag Kate all over the floor." Her humor at his predicament was obvious.

He slumped in the chair next to Olivia and Kate redoubled her efforts as she planted herself in front of him, put her paws on either side of his leg and acted like she planned to wrestle him to the floor. He had to give her credit, though. Whatever the little dog hoped to accomplish she was putting everything she had into it.

As Cade and Tess set their food in front of them he felt the puppy collapse on his legs. He glanced under the table. She was huffing and puffing and studying him with an intensity he couldn't interpret. With one last snarl, she went to sleep.

At least they were going to be able to eat in peace.

Chapter 8

Peace was suddenly in short supply. In the week since she'd been released from the hospital everyone had been so nice. How did you tell people that their kindness was suffocating?

Olivia had slept through most of the first two days she'd been home. Nick was attentive and adorable, making sure she ate and took her medications. She actually preferred those early days when her sleeping hours far outweighed her waking ones.

When she was asleep she didn't obsess about every physical sensation. She didn't wonder if every twinge was the precursor to a cramp, the beginning of the end. If she wasn't awake she couldn't fixate on the ticking of the clock on the wall.

The clock was now the focal point for all her hopes and dreams. Every second that passed brought her closer to the ultrasound and the answers to the questions that plagued every conscious moment.

It was the irrational need to destroy the clock, to rip it from the wall and dash it into a thousand pieces that finally drove her from the room. Kate at her heels, where she'd been since Olivia came home from the hospital, Olivia padded down the stairs.

Tiredness seeped through her. By the time she made it to the front hall she was questioning the wisdom of her actions. It would have been easier to smash the clock. But she was downstairs, she might as well see what was happening in her own house.

In for a penny, in for a pound.

Olivia followed the low sounds of masculine voices into the kitchen. She stopped in the doorway and stared. Her quiet, peaceful kitchen was a hive of activity. Multiple laptops were set up on the table. Two huge dry erase boards stood between the kitchen and the sunroom. One was covered with lists of names and abbreviations. The other seemed to be some kind of schedule involving all the campus sports.

Cade and Ed were on their phones on opposite sides of the room. Nick and Bob Moore stood in front of the schedule, talking quietly and adjusting the schedule as they did.

A vague memory niggled at the back of her mind. Her father used to host a monthly poker night. When she was little, before everything went wrong, she'd sometimes sneak into the room to watch the purely masculine ritual. To this day the smell of cigar smoke filled her with a mix of melancholy and anger over the loss of the man who'd appeared to the world to be a loving father but who had, in reality, been a monster.

She wasn't aware that she'd made a noise, but she must have. The four men turned to her in unison.

"Shit." Nick dropped the dry erase pen in his hand and rushed to her side. "How did you get down here?"

"I walked." It wasn't like she'd built a transporter while she'd been stuck in bed.

He scooped her up in his arms. "Dammit, Slugger."

"I can't go back upstairs. Please," she implored him.

He looked into her eyes. After a moment, he gave her a brief nod and carried her farther into the room. He set her down in the chair at the head of the table then disappeared. A few moments later he came back and slid a pillow behind her back.

"Thirty minutes," he stated.

"Until I'm tired." She made a counter offer.

He pinched the bridge of his nose. "Forty minutes."

"This is still my house." If she wanted to, she could kick all of them out.

He leaned down like he was going to pick her up. She couldn't make it back downstairs if he took her to her room.

"Two hours." The words rushed out as she pressed into the pillow at her back.

"Forty-five minutes," he growled.

188

All she wanted was a little time away from the ticking clock. "One hour and fifty-five minutes."

"For fuck's sake." Cade bit out. "We'll be here for the next two hours with this back and forth." He looked between Nick and Olivia. "Nick, she's here. You're lucky she stayed in bed as long as she did."

Olivia couldn't help it. She stuck her tongue out at her keeper, which earned her a glare from Cade.

"Olivia, you knocked yourself out puking and you have the baby to think of. You can't overdo it."

She crossed her arms and stuck her tongue out at Cade.

"Worse than Tess when she's sick," he mumbled.

"What are you working on?" She changed the subject.

"We're trying to figure out our roster for next year." Nick exchanged a look with Cade she couldn't interpret.

"Are you allowed to recruit yet?" She didn't know much about their plans, but she'd done a lot of research on college football programs when she'd prepared a presentation to the board for an alternative to the program at Cormac.

He shook his head. "Not in high schools and not with eligible transfers, not until after this season."

"I'm guessing you aren't going to get many transfers since the upcoming season is cancelled."

"That's a good guess." He shuffled some papers. "How do you know so much about it?"

"I talked to several coaches in different sized programs around the country after Brian suggested that I prepare a proposal for an alternative to the football program."

She felt the heat rush up her neck at the memory of her stupidity. It was bad enough she'd fallen for Brian's practiced charm, worse she'd put her professional reputation on the line to propose a plan that was entirely wrong for the university.

Cade joined them at the table. "I figured you just came up with an alternate plan for the funds."

Olivia shook her head. All four men were focused on her and she felt the heat creep up the back of her neck. "I needed to know how a football program should be run, so I contacted several division one programs to get more information. After the conversations I had with the other coaches, I genuinely thought that your plan was too risky, and Brian's would be catastrophic. That's why I made my proposal."

"Why did you think Backup's plan was catastrophic?" Nick shifted closer to her. A growl from under the table announced Kate's displeasure with the move.

"You saw his coaching roster." It hadn't taken her long

to learn about the reputations of the coaches Brian's father had selected.

"I did. I'm curious what you saw." Nick watched her.

She tried to ignore the fact that all eyes in the room were on her. "I saw a list of coaches who are one step away from being sanctioned themselves. If Brian's father had brought them in the sanctions wouldn't have been lifted, they would have gotten worse."

"How'd you know that?" Ed crossed his arms.

"I talked to the coaches I interviewed about them. I wanted to do my due diligence before preparing my proposal."

"So, you thought the answer to oppose a risky plan and a catastrophic plan for the football program was to get rid of it all together." There was a hint of amusement in Ed's voice.

She shrugged. "I didn't know as much about football as I should have when I suggested my proposal to the board."

Olivia glanced under the table and saw Kate had attached herself to Nick's leg in another attempt to wrestle him into submission.

"And you do now?" Nick ignored Kate and put an arm around Olivia's shoulders.

"I did more research after the board vote."

"Why?" Ed's focus on her was unnerving.

"Tess made me see how much football meant to the school. So, I learned more about the sport because this is my university and I want to be able to support my community." She'd also wanted to know more about the situation and figure out where she'd gone so wrong. Turns out her first and worst mistake was listening to Brian Gill, Jr.

"Yeah? We can use another genius on our side. Any bright ideas about how to get over our recruiting hump?" Cade leaned back in his chair and glanced at one of the white boards. His body language told her he didn't really expect her to come up with an answer for them.

"Ineligibility." She blurted out the idea she'd been thinking of ever since she'd seen a documentary on a junior college football team.

"Excuse me?" Ed's tone was mostly skeptical with a hint of indulgent.

"How many talented players end up off their team and out of college because of academic ineligibility?"

Ed leaned forward. "I don't know. Probably at least a handful at every division one and two team across the country. Why?"

"Well, academic eligibility determines whether a player on the team can play. Right?" She'd done a lot of research on the academic standards for college athletes. Was the air conditioning turned off in the house?

"Yeah." Nick squeezed the back of her neck as if to encourage her.

"And if a player can't play because he is academically ineligible then it can mean he's cut from the team."

"Not always, but usually." Cade shifted in his seat. All four men were looking at her intently. It was disconcerting to be the focus of all their attention.

"So, recruit the players who are going to lose their eligibility and their scholarships."

"Are you serious? They aren't eligible to play." Nick looked from her to Cade.

"Next season. But you don't have a next season. You have a season after the next season. You can recruit some talented players who need extra help getting their grades up."

She took a deep breath and waited for someone to interrupt her. When none of them did she decided to continue. "If they come here, they'll have a year to get their grades up and a guaranteed spot on the team if they regain their eligibility. You'd be competing with junior colleges where they'd get to play next season, but the advantage in coming here is they'd be guaranteed a spot on a division one team the year after this." She was out of breath by the time she'd rushed through her idea.

Cade was silent for a moment. "That's kind of a genius idea. We'd have to clear it through the new academic advisor, because that would mean more work for him and his staff."

"Did Rush accept the job?" She hadn't talked to him since the meeting in her office.

"Yeah. Professor Avery's on board." Cade gave her a look she couldn't interpret, and Nick growled.

"What?" She looked at Nick.

"Rush?" he asked.

"That's what he asked me to call him." That was his name. She didn't see a problem calling a colleague by his name.

"Before or after you told him Nick knocked you up?" The humor in Cade's tone made her want to smack him. The slight tightening of Nick's grip on the back of her neck told her that he might want to do something else to his friend.

"Do you guys take a class somewhere?" she wondered.

"Huh?" Nick looked confused.

"A class on how to be irritating in ten words or less." Nick and Cade probably had PhDs in the subject.

Cade laughed. "Something like that."

"To answer your question. Rush is well aware of my relationship with Nick and is fine with being my friend."

Cade snorted. "Right."

"Not every man has an agenda when offering friendship to a woman." She wasn't sure why Nick and Cade thought she was suddenly irresistible to men when she hadn't been before.

"Olivia, you're a gorgeous woman. Almost every man with a pulse is going to have an agenda when it comes to you," Cade observed.

She glanced at Nick.

Was that him growling or Kate?

"What about you?" She looked at Cade.

"I said almost every man. My agendas are reserved for Tess." His smile was so smug she made a mental note to tell Tess what an arrogant bastard her husband could be.

"Well, Rush doesn't have an agenda with me." She wanted to smack the smug off Cade's face.

"If you say so."

This was going nowhere. "Why don't you call him and run the idea by him if you like it. I'm assuming he's going to have to approve any plan that involves making a group of academically ineligible players eligible in a year."

195

Cade snorted and pulled out his cell phone. He hit a button.

"Hey Professor, it's Cade." He paused. "Fine. You?"

Olivia listened as Cade outlined the plan. He started to set up a time to discuss it when he paused. "You are?" He gave Olivia a look that she couldn't identify, but it made her ball up her fist.

Nick laughed. "Easy, Slugger. I'm the only one you're allowed to punch."

Cade ended the call. "The professor will be here in a minute."

"What do you mean he'll be here in a minute?" She wasn't expecting anyone.

Why was Rush coming here?

"He wanted to check on you." Cade left the kitchen when the doorbell rang.

How had her life spun so far out of control? Her life used to be perfectly boring and she didn't mind. With a career she loved, she'd floated through her predictable days like they were a calm lake on windless day. Then she'd met Tess, Delilah and Charlie, which had led to meeting Nick.

Now her life seemed more like a ride down white-water rapids. It was exhilarating and terrifying at the same time. It reminded her of when her mother was alive, and life had been about adventure and love. Could she reach out for that kind of life again? Was it possible? Was Nick the secret to her new start? Or was her baby the only happiness she'd ever have?

"Olivia?"

She jumped at Cade's voice. When she turned to face him, she realized that Rush had joined them. When was the last time she'd been so lost in thought she hadn't heard someone come into a room and greet her?

"Sorry. I was wool gathering."

"Obviously." Cade was clearly trying not to laugh.

She ignored Cade's smirk and turned to Rush. "Good to see you, Rush."

"You too, Olivia. How are you?" He stepped forward and took her hand.

Olivia ignored the slight tightening of Nick's hand on her neck. "I'm fine. The rest is helping." Even though he knew about the baby she didn't want to voice any possibilities. She shifted closer to Nick hoping to absorb some of his strength.

"I'm glad you're all right." Rush let go of her hand and stepped back.

"Thank you. It was nice of you to come visit." She didn't know why he'd come, but it was still nice of him.

"I'm still new to the area. You're one of the few friends I have. It seems my timing worked out well." Rush turned to Cade. "What was this plan you wanted to discuss?"

"Olivia had a great idea for recruitment, but we're going to need your help." Cade nodded toward an empty chair at the table.

Rush sat down. "My help? I think we've established that I know nothing about American football. I barely know anything about actual football."

Fortunately, the other men in the room let the jibe slide. Olivia wasn't sure she wanted to sit through any kind of discussion on soccer versus football.

"We're looking for academic expertise." Cade briefly laid out Olivia's idea.

Rush asked a lot of questions. Most of them Olivia had thought about when she'd been thinking about the idea. For a man who didn't understand the finer points of American football, it was obvious he'd been doing his homework on the various sports programs at Cormac.

"That would mean a lot of work for the program next year." Rush leaned back in his chair and crossed his arms. "It wouldn't be just about monitoring all the student athletes and helping a few struggling ones. You would be bringing in, I'm assuming, a fair number of students who are already behind and would need a great deal of one on one attention to make them eligible to play the following year."

"Do you think we could come up with a workable plan?" Ed joined the conversation.

"I think it's possible. I would need detailed information on the players and their academics and I would have to have a significant amount of help making sure the players get the one on one attention they need to regain their eligibility. I've been researching some tutoring programs that work well for student athletes at other universities."

"You're also going to need a source for scholarships." Bob had been silent so far.

Cade turned to Olivia. "Shit."

"What?" Rush glanced around the table.

"If the players are academically ineligible to play, they aren't eligible for athletic scholarships."

Olivia bit her lip and faced Rush. "If Cade gets the players here, do you think you can help them? Not just maintain eligibility. Really help them get the education they need to build a life after football?"

Rush nodded. "I've always believed that everyone can be educated. It's a matter of finding the key to their individual potential."

She turned to Cade. "How many academically ineligible students do you think you could recruit?"

"No idea. Could be none, could be as many as thirty."

Olivia closed her eyes and did some basic math in her head. "So, you'd need about a million dollars in scholarships."

"That would probably cover it," Ed said.

"Okay." She would have to make a few phone calls.

"Okay?" Cade's eyebrows practically hit his hairline. "The conference cut the number of football scholarships we can offer and it's not like there's a scholarship tree on campus. The administration has made it pretty clear that we're back to basics in the football program until we make some progress. Even then the funding probably won't get back to a normal level until we're done with sanctions."

"What's the definition of progress?" Rush leaned forward.

"It's a little hazy at the moment. With next season cancelled, we're flying blind and on a shoestring until January. Once we're eligible to recruit again, we're going to reassess, but we're still going to be short thirty football scholarships the first season we're back in the game."

"So, you'd probably need another scholarship fund to

draw from for a couple of years." Olivia nibbled on her bottom lip. It was doable.

Cade scrubbed his hand down his face. "Damnit. We need a scholarship forest, not a tree."

"Or someone with a foundation that supports education." She twisted her hands in her lap.

"Got someone like that in your contact list?" Nick gave her an indulgent smile.

Moment of truth. "I look at someone like that in the mirror every day."

Nick leaned closer to her. "What are you talking about?"

"I'm talking about the fact that I have a foundation that focuses on education and I can have an endowed scholarship fund in place here at the university in time to cut the checks for fall tuition."

With a whoop Cade stood and swooped Olivia up in his arms. He danced her around the room.

"What the shit, Cade?" Nick's voice boomed from his seat. He rose up so quickly he knocked his chair over and plucked Olivia from Cade's grasp and cradled her in his arms like she was made of spun glass.

"What is wrong with you?" She wrapped her arms around Nick's shoulders to steady herself.

"What's wrong with me? You're supposed to be resting,

not have him tossing you around the room like a football."

"He was doing no such thing." She was a little dizzy, but the moment Cade had swung her around had been the first moment in a week where she'd let go of everything and been able to breath.

"You're pregnant." Nick didn't need to remind her.

Cade stiffened. "Shit. I'm sorry."

"Oh, for goodness sake. He picked me up and swung me around. He didn't hurl me across the room."

"You were sick last week." Nick continued to glare at Cade and Rush too for some reason

"You're being ridiculous. I've been resting for week. I'm still a little tired, but I'm fine." In this moment, she believed it.

Nick tightened his arms around her and stayed silent.

She huffed out a breath. "Really? You just insulted your friend and made him feel bad. You should apologize."

"He should keep his hands off you." There was a tone in Nick's voice she wasn't sure she recognized. If she didn't know how close he was to Cade she would swear it was jealousy.

Was he serious? She studied him as he continued to stare at Cade and Rush. Was this some territorial male thing? If so, she should be really angry about it. Why was it kind of exciting?

"Nick. He was happy." She tried to reassure him.

Nick snorted. "I'll bet."

She smacked his shoulder. "He's happily married to one of my best friends. You know it wasn't like that."

"What about the professor over there?" Nick lifted his chin toward Rush.

"I was just sitting here?" Rush choked out.

"Are you going to put me down?"

Instead of putting her down, he moved to her chair and sat, arranging her on his lap so they were both comfortable. His eyes were lit with something she couldn't quite identify. Amusement. Definitely. But something else was there. Something she'd never seen when anyone had looked at her before.

Olivia wasn't sure what it meant, but the charge that raced through her body was a good sign she wanted to find out.

He wasn't sure what had come over him. Between the professor being on his way to see Olivia for no apparent reason and Cade tossing her around, Nick understood what the expression "seeing red" meant. Still, he could have handled it better.

"Well?" Olivia smacked him on the shoulder.

He knew Olivia was waiting for him to apologize. He probably would, but the looks on both Cade's and Rush's faces told Nick the other two men understood where he was coming from. "Well what?"

She huffed out a breath that made him want to do things that could only be done in private. Exhibitionism wasn't one of his kinks.

"You should apologize to Cade and Rush."

He tipped his chin in their direction. A universal sign of apology among men. Their answering nods told him they were cool.

"Now let's get back to discussing this plan of yours." He studied her.

"That's it?" She looked from him to Cade and Rush and back again. "Some weird chin thing and everything's fine."

"Pretty much."

Olivia smacked him on the shoulder again. "That's ludicrous. In this house, we like to use our words."

He laughed. He could totally picture Olivia with their child telling them to use their words.

"What's so funny?"

"You are, Slugger." His laughter died when reality intruded, again. They were still waiting for confirmation there still was a baby.

She crossed her arms, as if she was waiting for something more to be said.

"We're guys. They know where I was coming from. Now tell me more about this foundation."

She shrugged. "I inherited a trust from my father's family. I created a foundation in my mother's name. It's an educational foundation that focuses on helping students reach their full potential and offers scholarships to colleges, junior colleges, trade schools. Basically, it takes financial burdens off the table so recipients can follow their dreams. My mother believed everyone should have a chance."

"You run a foundation?" She was a rich girl. He wouldn't have pegged it. Wouldn't have gone near her in the first place if he'd known it.

"I don't really run it day to day. I oversee it."

"So, you have a lot of money." His throat felt tight and he tried not to grit his teeth.

She leaned back. He wasn't sure what expression she saw in his eyes, but it was obvious she didn't like it. She moved to get off his lap and he let her. The revelation that she was from a wealthy family sent him back into the past

205

when he'd thought the girl of his dreams cared more about him than her family's money.

"I don't. The foundation does." She acted like there was a difference.

"What's that mean?" As far as he knows, only rich people ran foundations.

"It means that I inherited a trust when I turned twenty-one and repurposed it to support education because I didn't want anything from my father or his family." She moved to another chair at the table. He let the comment about her father go. There was no way he was going to talk about something so personal with so many other people in the room.

Shit.

He'd put his foot in his mouth again. Nick rubbed the back of his neck. Thoughts of Brandi always messed him up. If he didn't think fast, he would mess up what he and Olivia had going too.

"Sorry. I didn't mean to snap at you." The silence in the room made him shift in his seat.

"Rush, why don't you let Bob, Ed and I take you to lunch. We can go over what we need to build this kind of program. Start making some plans." Cade stepped into the silence and the four men left the house like someone had lit their asses on fire.

Nick couldn't blame them. He'd made a mess, and no one would want to watch him while he tried to clean it up. He wished he could skip this part too.

"I'm sorry." He hoped that was enough. The emotional stuff was not his strength.

She wouldn't look at him. "There's nothing to apologize for."

"There is. I just acted like an asshole."

The room was silent except for the sound of Kate growling from underneath the table. She reinforced her displeasure with Nick by latching on to his leg. The little mutt actually managed to sink her teeth into him. It was no less than he deserved. He was ready to say something else when Olivia looked up at him. Her blue eyes were filled with hurt.

"Why?"

He wasn't ready for this conversation. The question was, did he get it out of the way and let things play out, or did he tell her just enough to explain his behavior and delay the rest of it to another day? If he had any guts he'd lay everything out for her and deal with the fallout. The only thing that held him back was the state of her health. If he said something that made her sick or lose the baby, he would never forgive himself.

"Nick?"

"It's a long story." At least that wasn't a lie.

She sat back in her chair and crossed her arms. It was clear he wasn't going to get away with saying nothing.

"I knew someone once. She was from a wealthy family. We dated in high school. I thought she loved me and I was willing to give up everything I had for her, which wasn't much. Turns out she wasn't in love with me so much as the star football player. When everything fell apart she walked away without looking back."

All of that was true. It was a ridiculously incomplete version of the story. If she asked for more he'd tell her. Lying outright wasn't how he wanted to build a relationship with her.

God, please don't let her ask for details.

"I'm sorry that happened to you."

He wasn't sure if the pit in his gut was relief or shame. "I'm sorry I let it turn me into an asshole just now. I know you're nothing like her. Hearing about your money just made me think about that time in my life and I reacted. Badly."

"I understand. We all have issues that can be triggered whether we like it or not. You should know that, while

208

most of the money I got from the family trust is tied up in the foundation, I kept enough to make sure I would always be comfortable." She bit her lower lip.

The look of sadness on her face got him moving. He plucked her from her chair. In one motion he sat and settled her on his lap, where it felt like she belonged. The way she melted into his arms made a kernel of guilt take root. He was going to have to tell her everything. Eventually.

"It's okay. I don't know what happened to you after your mom died, but I'm sure she would be proud of the woman you are. Your grandmother would be too."

"My grandmother disowned me after my father went to prison." Her expression was blank.

He stilled at the matter of fact tone in her voice. "What?"

"She hated me. I was the mongrel child my father was forced to acknowledge because Bradshaw's didn't have illegitimate children or get divorced. When my father was arrested, she decided she didn't need to keep up the pretense anymore. If she could have figured out a way to break my trust and keep the money from me, she would have."

He wanted to take away all her pain, but he didn't know how. If he'd learned anything this afternoon it was that he couldn't even take away his own. "Do you want to talk about it?"

"She hated me. There's nothing else to talk about."

"I'm sure that's not true." He couldn't imagine anyone hating this amazing woman, ever.

Olivia looked up at him. "I'm the reason my father was caught." She rushed the words out of her mouth.

"What?" He wasn't sure he heard her right.

She looked him in the eyes and didn't flinch. "I gave the police the evidence they needed to prove my father killed my mother."

He didn't know what to say. What could he say? The best idea was to stay silent and let her get the words out.

"I had to. For my mother."

The desperation in her voice unstuck his tongue. "Of course, you did. Getting justice for her was the right thing to do."

"After my father's arrest, my grandmother wanted nothing to do with me. But, appearances were everything to her."

"Why didn't she want you?"

"She never approved of my parents' marriage. My father was from old money. He was the stereotypical big man on campus. My mother was like me."

The last sentence was a whisper, filled with an emotion

he couldn't identify. He was getting pissed. "Like you how?"

"She was a genius a prodigy like me. Her focus was on science and math, not languages. They met at the university where she taught. My grandmother bought my father a position on the board to give him something to do." She burrowed closer to him. "I look exactly like her."

"She sounds amazing." If she was anything like her daughter, Olivia's mother must have been spectacular.

Olivia sniffed. He tipped her head back and his heart shattered at the sight of the tears pooling in her eyes. "I miss her so much."

A tear slid down her cheek. He brushed it away with his thumb. "I'm sorry."

She sniffed. "I'm sorry too."

He was confused. "What do you have to be sorry for?"

"I'm sorry she hurt you."

"I'm sorry I forgot who I was with for a minute. More importantly, I'm sorry I forgot who you are. I promise to try and let my past stay in the past."

"That's easier said than done." She sniffled.

He shrugged. "Still. I had a moment and you took it on the chin. That's not fair to you."

She let out a breath and rested her head on his shoulder.

Her breath puffed along his neck. The trust in that simple gesture made him feel like a heel. What was she going to do when she found out everything about the night that destroyed his life?

"It's going to be all right. You're both going to be all right." He rested his hand on her stomach where, he prayed, their child was safe and sound. While he was at it, he prayed for himself too.

Let her want me when everything is out in the open.

Chapter 9

Olivia nodded but couldn't keep the tears from escaping the corners of her eyes.

"Shit." He pulled her closer and cradled her in his arms as he stood.

"I don't want to go back upstairs alone," she wailed. The thought of going back upstairs to the ticking clock made her want to scream.

"I'm not taking you upstairs." He slid between the two dry erase boards and carried her out to the sun porch. Once there, he sat down on the couch and settled her into his lap. He'd learned this was her favorite place in the house. Hopefully, it would soothe her.

She couldn't stop her sobs. It was as if they'd been pent up for a week and were unstoppable now that they'd exploded. He held her while the emotions she'd been holding in roiled around and left her hollow.

"Olivia, honey. You're going to make yourself sick again."

His words penetrated the cloud of misery that had settled around her. He was right. They didn't know anything, yet, except she hadn't miscarried. That didn't mean they were out of the woods.

"I can't help it." She hiccupped.

213

"I know. It's scary. But you're not alone. I'm here." He rocked her.

She took a deep breath. She couldn't identify his scent, but it comforted her the same way the smell of French fries and chocolate did. It wrapped around her like a blanket filling her with a feeling of warmth and safety.

Olivia let out a breath. "Okay."

"Okay." He pulled her close and tucked her head against his neck.

They sat there, the sounds of the quiet house surrounding them, the view of the ocean waves rolling against the beach. For the first time since she woke up in the hospital, she believed in her heart that she and the baby would be all right.

She pulled back to look at him. "You should get back to work. I didn't mean to intrude." She didn't want to be a burden to him.

"You're not intruding. Besides, you're more important to me than work."

She smiled then rested her head on his shoulder. The quiet of the room was more comforting than the relentless ticking of the clock. Her eyelids started to droop.

"You want to go back upstairs?"

Her eyes popped open and she pulled back to look into

his eyes. "No."

The volume of her yelp echoed through the room.

"Shhh. It's okay. Tell me what you do want." He rubbed her back, trying to calm her down.

"I'll lie down here on the couch."

He nodded and carefully lowered her to the cushions beneath them as he stood. Once she was settled with a pillow under her head, he pulled the blanket off the back of the couch and tucked it around her.

"If you need anything, holler." He leaned over and kissed her forehead.

She nodded as she snuggled into the couch. His sweet gesture made her feel warm and safe. After pouncing briefly on Nick's foot, Kate spun in two quick circles in front of the couch before lowering herself to the floor. With one last canine sneer for Nick she rested her head in her paws and went to sleep.

He studied the ball of fur. "Why does she hate me?"

"She doesn't like men?" She didn't know why Kate acted the way she did with Nick.

"Slugger, we've been working out of your kitchen for a week. If she's not attacking me, or sleeping with you, she's curled up at Bob's or Cade's feet. She doesn't like me."

"I don't know. Maybe you remind her of someone. She's

only a few months old, but she's also a rescue. I have no idea what happened to her before she was in the shelter."

As if she knew that she was the subject of conversation, the dog opened one eye, focused it on Nick and chuffed out a growl.

Shaking his head, he left the room. She reached down to pet Kate, whose grunt of approval comforted Olivia. The low rumbling of her dog's snores, combined with the faint echo of the waves rolling onto the beach, lulled her into a deep sleep where her fondest dreams and deepest nightmares were waiting for her.

It was dark when Olivia jolted awake and the dream of her mother that she'd stopped having years ago slipped away. A feeling of disorientation rolled through her. The sensation that she was in the wrong place slid through her.

The vague memory of chasing someone and being chased left her feeling unsettled and lost. The dream slipped fully from her consciousness into the void where dreams often lie in wait, until their next opportunity to prey on the dreamer's mind arrives. The faint glow from the kitchen combined with the moonlight cast shadows throughout the room, allowing her to orient herself.

"Olivia?"

Nick's voice startled her. She turned her head toward

the kitchen. The sight of him in the doorway, backlit by the kitchen light, resurrected an image that sent a shiver of worry through her. Whether the vague picture in her mind came from a dream or a long forgotten memory she couldn't be sure.

"Olivia?" he repeated her name, his tone louder, more concerned.

"Hi." She tried to shake off the feeling that something was wrong but couldn't seem to make her mind go along with what her intuition was telling her.

"You okay?"

She nodded. "I feel a little groggy."

He reached into the room and flipped on the lights. The sudden glare temporarily blinded her as her eyes adjusted to the new light level in the room.

"Ready for something to eat?"

Her stomach chose that moment to rumble. She realized she was hungry. For the first time since she got sick, she wanted to eat something. "I am."

Nick stepped into the room and gently pulled the blanket off of her. "Dinner's ready. You think you're up to sitting at the table?"

The thought of eating like a normal person instead of an invalid made her heart flutter a little. "Definitely."

He smiled as he leaned down to pick her up.

So much for being a normal person. "I can walk."

"I know. I like carrying you." He smiled.

Olivia couldn't say why she was suddenly so unsettled by his attentiveness. Not wanting to focus on any irrational thoughts she glanced around. "Where's Kate?"

As if summoned, Kate jumped from behind a chair and landed on Nick's right foot, startling both the humans in the room. The puppy wrapped her paws around his ankle and twisted, like she could take him to the ground with that one motion. All she did was roll off his foot and onto the floor. Undeterred she sprang back, attacking her foe with a few seconds of frenzied growls and nips.

Almost as soon as the attack began, Kate flopped over, panting.

"Really?" He stared at the puppy, a bemused expression on his face.

Olivia giggled.

"You think this is funny? She's always jumping out at me. Yesterday, I was in the shower and she leapt at me through the curtain like some canine version of *Psycho*."

Her giggle turned into a laugh. He loved her laugh. It reminded him of riding roller coasters.

"You should have named her Cato," he mused.

"Does that make you Inspector Clouseau?" She loved the Pink Panther movies, both the Peter Sellers and Steve Martin versions. Although, the classic Peter Sellers' movies were her favorites.

It was his turn to laugh. "I hope not. That's the last thing anyone needs."

He sat down on the couch with her in his lap. The warmth of his hand calmed her as he moved it in rhythmic circles.

"How are you doing?" He watched her carefully.

She wasn't sure how she was feeling right now. "I don't know."

He could tell something was bother her. "Want to talk about it?"

"I feel like I'm losing control of everything." Her life was turning chaotic.

"I'm not trying to take over your life," he tried to reassure her.

She sighed. "All evidence to the contrary."

"Seriously, Olivia. What's going on?" Nick sounded concerned.

"What's going on? I'm exhausted. My life has been turned upside down and I can't walk downstairs in my own house without needing someone to carry me back up.

I'm terrified for the baby and I can't get control of my emotions." Everything she'd been worried about came out in a rush.

"I've read being emotional during pregnancy is normal. Add everything that's been going on the last week, it would be weird if you weren't all over the place."

"Don't be nice to me. I don't think I can handle nice right now." She wasn't sure what she could handle.

"Slugger, you deserve nothing but nice." He leaned in until his warm breath danced along her ear lobe, sending shivers through her body. "When you're back to one hundred percent and we get the all clear from the doctor we're going to have to explore this relationship of ours."

"You're trying to distract me from being irritated with you." It was a good ploy.

"Is it working?" He chuckled.

"Maybe. Feeding me would work better." Her stomach rumbled as if to prove her point.

He laughed. "You got it, Slugger." He tightened his arms around her then stood and carried her into the kitchen. It was starting to worry her how much she relied on him. She hadn't been able to depend on anyone but herself for a very long time.

As Nick moved around the kitchen, getting dinner

ready for her, she heard Kate start to stir in the other room. A second later, she heard the clack of claws across the tile floor followed by the sensation of a warm body brushing against her legs.

She reached down and felt the soft, warm fur. Her friend licked her hand before settling in a boneless, panting heap at her feet. Olivia sat up and let out a sigh of contentment.

Nick set a plate in front of her before going back into the kitchen. She stared down at the food. Grilled chicken and steamed broccoli. It was a small serving, which was good all things considered.

A few minutes later, Nick came back with two plates, one for him and one for Kate. He got steak and potatoes. The puppy just got steak.

She watched him slide the plate with just the meat under the table. "You're trying to bribe her."

He shrugged. "I have plans. I'd like her to be on board for them."

"What plans?" Tingles zipped along her spine at the thought of him having *plans*.

"Plans that involve us spending a lot more time together, without your dog trying to wrestle me to the ground every chance she gets."

His heated gaze sent shivers through her body.

Time to change the subject.

"Why did you make something different for me?" She wasn't opposed to steak and potatoes.

"Because that's what's on your approved list from the doctor."

She huffed out a breath before taking a bite. It wasn't as bland as it looked. Nick had done something with spices that made the plain looking meal taste amazing. He was a constant surprise.

They ate in silence for a few minutes. Olivia glanced under the table and slapped her hand over mouth to keep from bursting out with laughter.

"What?" Nick leaned forward.

She shook her head and pointed under the table. Nick glanced down and started laughing. Kate had nudged her plate around, so she wasn't facing Nick. She ate a bite at a time and tossed her nose in the air, making it clear that she would eat his steak, but she had no use for the man who'd prepared it.

He laughed. "Your dog is a piece of work."

"She's not pushover, that's for sure."

"Takes after you." There was a gleam in his blue eyes.

"Is that good or bad?" Old insecurities reared up.

222

What if he doesn't like me when he gets to know me?

"I'm not complaining." He didn't elaborate.

They lapsed back into silence. Olivia finished her meal and marveled at how full she was after eating so little food.

"Your appetite's going to take a while to come back." He seemed to read her mind.

Olivia shrugged and reached down to pet Kate who was now pressed against her leg.

Nick gave the dog a look before he stood up and carried the plates to the sink. Kate sneered in return.

"What are we going to do now?" Olivia clicked her tongue, hoping her dog would settle down and stop trying to antagonize the father of her child. Once again, Olivia couldn't help but wonder how her life had turned into such chaos.

"You're going back to bed." Nick looked over his shoulder.

"No." She held up a hand. "Before you argue with me. I've spent too much time in my room and it's making me nuts."

He turned to face her. "You're still weak. You need rest."

"Rest, but not seclusion. The doctor says I can be up and around." The thought of spending any more time listening to the ticking of the clock in the bedroom nauseated her.

He must have heard the desperation in her voice. "Want to watch a movie?"

"Yes." She shouldn't feel so giddy.

He scooped her up and carried her into the living room. Nick settled onto the couch with her on her lap. He grabbed the remote. "What do you feel like watching?"

"Something funny."

He flipped through the movies on her DVR and hit play when he came to *Best In Show*. It was one of her favorites. She snuggled closer to him, wishing things were settled between them. If they were a real couple and they knew their baby was going to be all right, this would be the perfect way to spend an evening.

If they knew for sure the baby was safe, this would be the perfect night. Olivia pressed closer to him, making that cute snuffling noise she made when she was asleep. He had no idea what he was getting into when he hit play, but the smile on her face when he highlighted the movie made him choose it.

It was funny. Olivia had fallen asleep about twenty minutes into it. He was tempted to take her upstairs, but she was comfortable, and he was entertained. She'd been all over the place emotionally since she'd come downstairs. He understood stir crazy. There'd been more than one time in his life when he'd been climbing the walls because he was stuck in one place.

He made a note to help her downstairs earlier in the day tomorrow. There was plenty of stuff for her to do while she was resting. The credits on the movie started to roll and Nick shut the television off. He carefully gathered Olivia in to his arms and carried her upstairs. After he tucked her into bed, he went back downstairs to make sure the house was locked up for the night.

He finished checking the doors and pulled out his cell phone to call his brother.

"Hey bro." Simon sounded tired.

"How's things there?"

"We're hanging in there. Mom had a bad day."

"Shit. How bad?" As much as he wanted to be there for his mother, Olivia and the baby needed him.

"Spent most of the day puking her guts out. Delilah knows what she's doing. She's got all kinds of tricks to help with the nausea and Mom thinks she's awesome."

"Good. That's good. I'll try and stop by tomorrow." It was his big idea to bring their mother here. He needed to spend more time with her.

"We know you've got a lot on your plate. Things are handled on our end."

"I'm not going to leave you holding the bag. Olivia's doing well, and I'll pick a time when her girls are here to keep an eye on things if she needs help."

"Sure. I just want you to know we got this."

He didn't doubt his brother, but Nick still needed to step up for his family. "What are the doctors saying about Mom?"

"Too soon to say anything. No surprises with how she's responding to chemo. Once she's done with this first round and a round of radiation they're going to do some scans and tell us what's what."

The medical jargon swam through Nick's brain. A couple of months ago he thought he was doing pretty well picking up the lingo of a new sport to get Tess through her Ninja Warrior training. Now he was thinking of chemo, radiation, scans, fetal heart beats and ultrasounds. Fuck his life was out of control. Worse, getting it back under control was entirely out of his hands.

The next morning Nick went over his schedule for the day. Olivia was still asleep, Kate curled up on the bed next to her. The pup had lifted her head and sneered at him when he'd checked on them before coming downstairs.

He was starting to think the little dog didn't hate him, so much as she liked messing with him. It was like they were playing a game and Kate was making up the rules as she went along. When he thought of it that way, he liked the idea that the dog was so focused on messing with him.

The kitchen looked like the office for the football program. He appreciated the other coaches being so flexible with their meeting location. It meant he could be here for Olivia when she needed him.

As his coffee brewed, he pulled out his phone and dialed Cade.

"What's up?" Cade answered after a couple of rings.

"You think Tess and Charlie can make time to have lunch with Olivia today?" He needed to spend some more time with his mom.

"I can check. Everything all right?"

Nick pulled out an extra mug to make Olivia some tea. "Yeah. I need to spend some time with my mom. I figured Olivia could use some girl time."

"Let me give Tess a call. She had an early surgery this morning. I'll call you back once I know something." Cade disconnected.

A glance at his watch told him Olivia would probably

be up soon. He poured himself a cup of coffee then set about making her breakfast in bed. The caffeine kicked in as he was finishing up the egg white, mushroom and spinach omelet. After adding a few pieces of bacon to the plate, he set the dish and her freshly brewed tea on a tray to serve her. There was no way he'd admit that some of the bacon was for Kate.

Once upstairs, he knocked on the door and waited.

"Come in." Her sleepy voice sent a charge through his body. He hoped he'd hear it some day soon under different circumstances.

He opened the door then stepped into her room. It struck him again how the room was the perfect blend of the Olivia she showed the world and the Olivia he was getting to know. The king-sized sleigh bed was a dark wood that gleamed in the sunlight streaming through the bay window. Her sheets were dark blue and deep red. Bookcases lined the wall and were loaded with books. It was a mix of intellectual and sensual that suited her down to the lacy underwear she wore under her prim professor clothes.

She sat up in the bed and blinked at him. Her beautiful blue eyes were heavy with sleep.

"Hi." Her voice was husky.

Time to recite football stats to himself. She didn't need

to deal with the effect her sleep rumpled hair and barely awake response had on his body. "Morning." He cleared his throat.

Kate let out a half-hearted growl as he approached the bed with Olivia's breakfast.

"Hush." Olivia tapped the pup on the nose.

The dog settled back down, which likely had more to do with her spotting the bacon on the plate than making peace with him.

He set the tray on her lap and tossed a piece of bacon to Kate. "How are you feeling?"

"Better. I've got more energy."

"That's good. You need any help getting ready after you eat?" It would be a struggle to keep his hands to himself, but he'd managed so far.

"No. I think I'm strong enough to take care of myself."

He nodded. "Sounds good. We're going to work downstairs today. Tess and Charlie might come over to hang out with you."

"That would be nice." She smiled.

"Do you need anything else?" His skin felt itchy. Even though he'd been with her in this room more than once in the past week, she'd been a lot weaker. He needed to go downstairs and get his head screwed back on straight.

"No. This looks delicious." She took a deep breath. "Smells good, too."

"Good. I'll be downstairs if you need me."

When she nodded he turned to leave like someone lit his ass on fire. He couldn't explain why he was so nervous around her all of a sudden. It didn't matter right now. There was too much to do and no time for him to analyze the situation. Maybe later tonight when his to do list was a few items lighter.

By the time Cade, Ed and Bob showed up to get to work, he was in a better frame of mind. Of course, the calm he'd found went straight to hell when Olivia walked into the kitchen. Her white summer dress was sweet and hot at the same time. The thin straps showed off her toned shoulders. He'd have to ask her what she did to stay in shape. The dress came to mid-thigh. Her dark brown hair was piled on top of her head in one of those styles that baffled him.

"Earth to Nick." The laughter in Cade's voice was obvious.

Nick shook his head. "Hey. Olivia. You need help getting settled?"

She shook her head as she lifted her hand to show him the book she had in her hand. "Kate and I are going to sit on the porch and read for a while."

"Let us know if you need anything." He was surprised he hadn't swallowed his tongue.

She drifted by them and out to the back porch. Kate snapped at him as she pranced behind her mistress.

He barely noticed the pup since he couldn't drag his eyes from Olivia disappearing through the door.

"Dude." Cade chuckled. "You're toast."

He's not wrong. I'm in big trouble.

Chapter 10

Olivia set the book down, wondering how it was possible that she couldn't focus on the words on the page. How could she read the same page thirty times and still have no clue what it said? She'd never had a problem reading before. It would be nice if she could blame it all on cabin fever. Being stuck at home on limited bed rest for a week was frustrating. The reason for the doctor's orders was excruciating.

Still, she couldn't blame all of her distraction on the waiting game they were playing. A lot of it had to do with the man she was waiting with. Before their night in Las Vegas, Olivia had only spent time with Nick as part of the group. This past week of close quarters had been illuminating. He was more than a ridiculously gorgeous man. He was also one of the most honest, straightforward and supportive men she'd ever known.

He did what he said he would do. Taking care of her without trying to take her independence. When she didn't agree with him, he listened, and they usually found a compromise.

Was this what a partnership feels like?

Her thoughts were interrupted by Kate's yips of greeting. Olivia looked up as Tess and Charlie walked in the room. They had bags in their hands.

"We come bearing Bogart's." Tess smiled.

"Greasy burgers and French fries. Just what the doctor ordered." Charlie added.

Olivia laughed. "I'm not sure my doctor ordered that." Her dietary restrictions weren't terrible, but they were clear.

"Which is why we had Renee fix up one of her secret specials."

"Secret specials?" She'd never heard of anything like that when she'd been to Bogart's. Which is probably why they called them secret.

"Only locals know about it. It's usually recipes Renee came up with when a friend of hers needed something that wasn't on the menu."

Tess set the food out on the coffee table in front of the couch. The usual burgers and fries for Tess and Charlie and a sandwich Olivia didn't recognize.

"What's in it?"

"It's chicken. That's all I know." Tess smiled. "She made it for my gran when she was recovering from her surgery."

Cade came in and set some drinks on the table for them. "Nick took off to spend some time with his mom. You ladies need anything, let us know." He gave Tess a quick kiss and ambled out of the room.

Tess stared after him.

Charlie snickered. "You hate to see him leave, but you love to watch him go."

"Ha. Ha." Tess didn't deny it.

Olivia picked up her sandwich. It probably wasn't a good idea to get involved in this discussion because she imagined she looked the same way when Nick walked out of a room.

"How are you doing?" Charlie asked before taking a bite of her burger.

"I'm all right if I don't think too much." She took a bite of her sandwich. It was delicious.

Charlie glanced between Tess and Olivia. "Hard to do for the giant brains in the group."

"True," Olivia agreed.

Tess smiled at her. "I know it's not the same, but I remember how stir crazy I went when I was on bed rest a few months ago."

"Thank you. I just want this week to be over."

"I know everything will be fine," Tess assured her.

"How?" Predicting the future wasn't a skill set any of her friends had displayed. Olivia snuck a French fry to Kate, who was sitting patiently at her feet.

"Because I have faith in happy endings." Tess smiled.

They turned to less weighty topics as they ate their lunch and talked about Tess's veterinary practice and Charlie's recent dating debacles. It seemed like Charlie had a lot of horror stories. Olivia admired the other woman. It had only taken a few bad dates and one disastrous relationship for Olivia to give up on dating. Until Nick.

Maybe destiny didn't just exist in stories.

By the time they were finished with lunch, Olivia was exhausted. She was trying to keep her eyes from drooping when Nick walked in. Kate leapt up from her position on the floor next to the coffee table and dashed to him, launching yet another futile attack on his boots.

"How are you doing?" He didn't acknowledge the pile of fur doing her level best to take him down with anything but a smile.

"I'm good."

"She's tired," Tess acknowledged. "We should get going."

Charlie and Tess both gave Olivia quick hugs then gathered up the remains of their lunch before they went into the kitchen. Nick sat down next to her and pulled her legs onto his lap.

On hand rested on her ankles, the other just below her

knees. Warmth spread through her body, almost like he'd draped a blanket over her.

"How's your mother?"

He closed his eyes and leaned his had on the back of the couch. "Not great."

"Unfortunately, I think that's the way chemo goes. It makes things seem worse while making them better."

"It would be nice for her to catch a break."

"Did you have a chance to talk at least?" She didn't know much about his history with his mother, except that their relationship was strained.

"We talked. She hoped you were feeling better."

"That was nice of her. Is Delilah helping?"

He snorted. "Delilah's a fucking rock star."

"You sound surprised."

"You've met Delilah."

Irritation flashed through her. "She's my friend."

"I know. I'm not trying to be an asshole, but she doesn't come off as someone who comes through in the clutch." He looked at her.

"She has since I've met her. She just does it with her unique attitude." If he wanted to fight over Delilah she would. She hadn't had many friends in her life. The ones she'd made since moving to King's Folly were worth defending.

He held his hands up in surrender and she missed the warmth of his touch immediately.

"I'm sorry. I don't mean to insult her. Truth is, she doesn't seem to like me much. I'm more surprised that she's coming through for me."

She relaxed. "She's going through a tough time. It tells you a great deal about her that she's reaching out to help."

"Yeah. I don't know what we'd do without her. I think the last thing my mom wants is for her sons to be holding her hair back while she pukes her guts out."

"Do you want to talk about it?" She didn't feel as tired as she had before he sat down with her.

He brought his hands back to her legs. "Talk about what?"

"Anything." She didn't want to push him.

"My mom's been a mess my whole life. She hooked herself to my old man and thought he'd make her dreams come true. Instead, she crashed and burned."

"But she had you and her brother."

"We weren't enough to help her keep her head above water. She drank, she smoked, cigarettes and pot, and barely kept a roof over our heads." He closed his eyes.

237

"That sounds rough." The more she learned about his life, the more she admired the straight forward man he'd become.

"It was." Nick was quiet for a moment. "I want her to make it through this, but I don't know how to help her."

"You already have. You got her here and are getting her the treatment she needs. Delilah will help, but most of it's up to your mother. She needs a reason to fight."

"I like to think we've given her one, but I don't know. We weren't enough of a reason for her to get her act together when we were kids."

"Things change. Maybe she wants a second chance."

"I hope so." He turned his head and his blue eyes met hers. "It would be nice if our kid could have one grandparent."

The reminder of their baby, and everything they were up against brought tears to her eyes.

"Hey." He leaned forward and rested his hand on the back of her neck. "Our baby is fine." He pulled her forward.

"How can you be so sure?"

"Because you are one of the strongest women I know. Our kid couldn't be anything but a fighter." He rested his forehead on hers.

"I hope you're right."

"I know I am. We're going to breeze through the next week and get the all clear from the doc."

He was so perfect.

As long as he's honest with me, I can get through all of this.

A week later, sitting in the doctor's office, Nick was hoping he wasn't sweating like a pig. Today was their first chance to put the scary shit behind them with the pregnancy. If there was a heart beat on the ultra-sound then, at least for now, the worst would be over. Olivia and Nick waited for the doctor to come in. The tech told them she usually did the initial ultrasound on her own. Because of their unique situation the doctor was going to conduct the ultrasound personally.

Dr. Wyatt came into the room with a smile on her face. "How are you today, Olivia?"

"Freaking out."

"That's understandable. Let's see if we can't give you two a little peace of mind." She sat next to the examining table and rubbed some kind of jelly on Olivia's stomach. Nick stared at the monitor of the screen like he knew what all the shades of gray and squiggly lines meant.

The doctor flipped a switch and a weird alien noise filled the room. A second later it was clear what they were hearing. A soft whomp, whomp, whomp echoed off the white walls. The rhythmic beat increased his own heart rate.

"And that's the baby's heart beat," Dr. Wyatt announced.

His eyes shot from the screen to Olivia at her sharp intake of breath. Tears streamed down her eyes.

"The baby's all right?" Her voice was filled with a mixture of hope and disbelief he felt down to his gut.

"It is." The doctor narrowed her eyes. "Wait a second."

"What? What's wrong?" He grabbed Olivia's hand. He wanted to be her strength.

"Looks like there's a second heartbeat." The doctor smiled at them.

His brain short circuited. "What? Two? What?"

"Looks like you have twins in there. Both of them with very healthy heartbeats."

Twins.

Twins? Was the room hotter all of a sudden? It felt hotter?

He wasn't going to pass out. The last thing he wanted was to be one of those guys who couldn't handle their woman's pregnancy.

"Nick?" Olivia's voice sounded like it was coming through a tunnel.

"Yeah?" He couldn't focus on anything but the rhythmic heart-beats of his children.

Shit.

His children. He was going to be a dad. To two kids.

"Are you all right?" She looked at him, her blue eyes filled with a mixture of joy and panic.

"I think I need to sit down." The rocks in his gut told him he was going down, one way or another.

Clearly no stranger to nervous dads, Dr. Wyatt pushed a rolling chair toward him with her foot. He grabbed it and sat, grateful that he managed to do it without slipping and landing on his ass.

The next morning, he wanted to put his fist through a wall.

"No."

It amazed him that an English professor's favorite word consisted of only two letters.

He crossed his arms and widened his stance. "This isn't a debate."

"You're right." She shoved a stack of papers into her bag. "I'm doing my job and you're doing yours. Since our jobs are on the opposite sides of campus we will not be spending the day glued together at the hip."

"I don't have to meet with Bob until later today. I thought I could hang out with you for a while this morning." He was long past the age of being to pull off an innocent look, if he'd ever even been able to. That didn't stop him from trying.

"You can save the 'I'm completely innocent' look for someone else."

He shrugged. Worth a shot. "It's your first day back teaching. I just want to make sure you don't overdo it."

"I'm fine." She closed her bag and set it on the chair. "I have to get back to work."

"The doctor cleared you, but she said you could take a few more days if you need to." He ran a hand through his hair. "It's not a big deal if you're not up to full speed."

"I'll admit the first week was a little rough. But I feel fine now. I can't sit around this house one more day."

"Fine. Then I'll take you to work." It's not like they weren't going to the same campus.

She shook her head. "You need to get back to your life. I appreciate you taking care of me —"

He held up a hand. "If you're about to kick me out, you should rethink that."

"You can't want to stay here anymore," she sputtered.

"Why not?" There wasn't any place he'd rather be.

Olivia blinked. "Because."

"Because why?" He enjoyed watching her get flustered. She was usually so articulate and calm. It was a kick to know he could make her lose the control she showed to the rest of the world.

"You must want to get back to your family."

"Got news for you, Slugger. You and the babies are my family."

"What about your brother and mother?"

The familiar twinge of guilt slid down his spine. The sensation that made him think he'd somehow left his brother holding the bag was never welcome. "I see my mom every day and Simon has made it clear he wants me to butt out of the business. He's got everything under control."

"Still, you're supposed to be connecting with your mother." She kept trying.

That went without saying, but he was getting the idea it was easier on his mother to take spending time with him in small doses. "And I am. It can't happen all at once. Are you trying to get rid of me?"

She nibbled her lower lip. "No, but I don't want you to feel obligated because of my pregnancy. I appreciate your help the last few weeks." She walked over to him then put her hand on his arm. As always, her touch made his heart beat like he'd been doing sprints for an hour.

"I wanted to be here. I still want to be here." He was doing his best not to beg.

Olivia turned a cute shade of pink. "Well."

He glanced at his watch. "If you're determined to teach today we need to get you to class. Why don't we table this discussion until tonight? Now that we know the baby…the babies are all right, we can start talking about us." It still threw him that she was having twins.

"Us?"

"Yeah. Us." He tucked a curl behind her ear and kissed her forehead. There was a lot he needed to tell her, and he knew he was going to have to tell her some things he didn't want her to know. It would be nice if their relationship had a solid foundation before he had to bring up something that could be a wrecking ball.

"Okay." She gave him a look he couldn't interpret before getting her bag from the chair.

He watched her move. She definitely looked better than she had in weeks. It's like hearing the babies' heart beats filled her with some new energy. There was a smile on her face that had been there pretty much since the first heart beat echoed through the room. The *clack clack clack* of claws on the hardwood floor told him two things. One, Kate was nearby, probably preparing her next attack. Two they needed to take her to the groomer to trim those claws.

Nick stilled as he glanced around the room. He wouldn't admit it to anyone else, but one of the reasons he liked living with Olivia was the game he played with her dog. He also wouldn't confess that he was an active participant in their game. It felt like Kate didn't so much hate him as she saw him as a worthy opponent. At least that's what he told himself. She was a sneaky little thing. When he didn't see her right away he held out a hand for Olivia.

"Come on, Slugger. Let's get you to class."

She put her hand in his. A simple gesture that always made him feel ten feet taller than he was. He led her out of the kitchen and toward the front door.

Kate dashed out from the underneath the front hall table, where she'd hidden behind the fancy cloth Olivia covered it with. The puppy reared on to her hind legs and pounced on his boot like it was her prey. She tried to latch on to the tip of his boot with her teeth as if she could wrestle him to the ground.

Olivia laughed. The musical sound was the other reason he put up with the dog's antics. Kate's sneak attacks always made Olivia smile.

Nick let go of Olivia's hand and reached down to pluck the puppy off his leg. He held her in the air. Big brown eyes stared at him through a fluff of brown and black fur, then they narrowed. She snapped at the air a couple of times before giving him one of her Elvis sneers. It was a signal he now recognized as a temporary surrender. He had no doubt she'd be spending the day thinking of new and inventive ways to get him. It seemed fitting that a genius woman had found herself a genius dog.

He set the pup down then she dashed off to plan her next offensive. Olivia's giggle made his entire body tighten. What happened next couldn't be helped. Kissing her suddenly felt like a matter of life and death. He grabbed her hand, pulled her into his arms and lowered his head. Her lips parted, and he covered them with his. The taste of cinnamon and cream, better than any breakfast roll he'd ever had, rolled through him.

Her soft mewl had him hard, everywhere. As she burrowed closer to him a feeling of power surged through his veins. With her by his side he could do anything, be anything, finally.

It took a moment for the blaring noise to penetrate the fog of passion. When he felt her start to withdraw, he lifted his head. Her blue eyes were dark and unfocused.

"Hmmm," she purred.

A primal satisfaction rolled through him. She was his. "What was that noise?"

It took her a moment to focus. When she did, the noise sounded again.

"That's my leave the house alarm."

"Your what?"

"My leave the house alarm." She stepped back and began to straighten her clothes.

He preferred the rumpled look but wasn't crazy about the idea of anyone but him seeing it. "What's a leave the house alarm?"

"Sometimes I get caught up in my work or reading and I lose track of time. I set the alarm, so I know when I have twenty minutes to leave the house and I'm not late for my first class." She went over to the radio in the living room and hit a button.

It was logical and quirky and so perfectly her. He laughed.

She stopped in the doorway between the living room and the front hall. "What's so funny?" She stuttered a little. Something she only did when she was upset and thinking too hard about something.

247

Before she could get too far he moved to her then pulled her back into his arms. "I'm not laughing at you. I like that you have to remind yourself to leave the house." He looked into her eyes, needing her to see the sincerity in his.

She chewed her bottom lip, a gesture guaranteed to get him thinking about something other than leaving the house. He ran his thumb along the edge of her lip. "Keep doing that and we'll never leave."

"Um."

He got a kick out of being able to make her speechless. But he didn't want to push her before she was ready. If he was going to have a chance at something real with her, he knew they would have to move at her pace.

He ran his hand down her arm then took her hand. "Come on, Slugger. We have a class to get to."

She tried to yank her hand free. "We don't have a class."

"I know the doctor said everything's fine, but I can't seem to stop worrying." He squeezed her hand. "If something happened to you, I'd never forgive myself."

Olivia put her other hand on her stomach. "I understand. You're worried about the babies."

He pulled her into his arms. "Let's get this straight. I would be worried about you if there were no babies. The fact that there are babies just makes me worry more, but you are my priority. Babies or no babies."

She didn't seem to have a response. He took advantage of her moment of speechlessness and pulled her along with him as he left the house. He had no illusions this was the end of the argument, but he was going to press his advantage. Leaving her alone wasn't an option.

An hour later he was rethinking his plan. It wasn't that Shakespeare was boring, although he was more of a John Clancy fan. It wasn't the subject matter of the class that was making him nuts. It was the students. Especially that squirrely little jackass, Clay.

He hadn't made it to college himself because of the events of that night fourteen years ago, but he never imagined it would be a bunch of wet behind the ears kids trying to one up each other with their personal word of the day. He could tell Olivia was getting sick of it too, when she tried to dial back the snooty vocabulary.

"I just felt the whole scene was rather phlegmatic for my tastes," a curly haired young woman, who reminded him of someone, said as she laid back in her chair like she couldn't be bothered to sit up and participate at the same time.

"Well, I agree the scene is rather *slow*." Olivia emphasized the last word.

The student she was addressing rolled her eyes, like

having to use a word most human beings understood was beneath her.

"We're in a college English class, Professor. You shouldn't have to elucidate my point unless you want to make sure your boyfriend can follow."

Nick watched in fascination as red crept up Olivia's neck. Her blue eyes narrowed, and he wished he had some popcorn to watch the smackdown his girl was about to deliver.

"Ms. Lydell, I am not clarifying your points for the benefit of Coach Jacobs. He's a highly decorated Naval veteran and valued member of the coaching staff for the entire athletic department. He is also literate. I have no doubt he was able to follow your comments without the need for clarification." She winked at him.

He thought that was a pretty mild smackdown, but when she took a breath to continue, he realized she wasn't done.

"I was simplifying your commentary, not to make sure the rest of the people in the room understood, but to make a point to you as gently as possible. Unfortunately, you need a blunter approach. I am absolutely in favor of an expansive vocabulary. However, using polysyllabic words to bludgeon others with your perception of your own intelligence

250

does nothing to contribute to a discussion and makes you look foolish and arrogant. This is a seminar, which is different from an introductory or large class. The whole point of a seminar is for the students to share their opinions of the Bard and his work."

Nick leaned forward, sensing Olivia was going in for the kill.

"Your constant need to prove that you're the smartest in the class is killing the conversation and the chance for the other members of the class to enjoy a spirited discussion."

"This is a college course. We should all be able to rise to the same level," Ms. Lydell snarked. She tried to put on a brave tone, but she was sinking deeper into her chair as the conversation continued.

"Your level?" Olivia didn't flinch or budge.

"Well, apparently, I'm the most advanced student here." It seemed that the young woman was almost begging to be acknowledged for her smarts.

"Far from it, Ms. Lydell. There are students who are far more advanced than you, but they can't get a word in edgewise."

"I find that hard to believe," Ms. Lydell stuttered a little.

"Really? Why is that?"

Nick could tell Olivia was reeling in the snotty student.

"I've always been the most advanced student in whatever class I take." The young woman sat up straighter.

"Interesting. How do you know that?"

Ms. Lydell blinked. "It's obvious."

"Maybe to you. Perhaps you could enlighten the rest of us."

"No one ever keeps up with me in the discussion and usually has to ask the professor to explain my comments." The young woman pasted a smug smile on her face, but there was something desperate in her voice.

"I wonder why you bother spending time with the rest of us peasants."

Her student sat up slightly at the bite in Olivia's tone. "I didn't mean —"

"It's patently obvious how you maintain your veneer of superiority, Ms. Lydell. You use your rather extensive vocabulary to try and make the rest of the class feel stupid. You are little more than a bully. If you cannot curb your tendencies to try and intimidate your peers, you will be dismissed from this class. This is your first warning."

Olivia walked back to the podium and looked at her notes. In a moment she had the rest of the class engaged in a spirited discussion of the assignment. Ms. Lydell was quiet.

Nick studied her. If he'd seen anyone else get smacked down like that he would have assumed they'd be pissed. Olivia's student looked like she wanted to burst into tears, like she'd just lost her best friend. There was something about her. He couldn't place it, but there was a look on her face that reminded him of someone. He was going to have to make some calls to get some information on the young woman. His instincts told him something was off and, if there was anything he'd learned, it was not to ignore his instincts.

Chapter 11

She couldn't shake the feeling that Nick was hiding something. He was saying all the right things. After comments this morning and his odd behavior during her class, they'd gone out to dinner and had a pleasant evening. The only problem with that was that pleasant was the one word she'd never used to describe their relationship.

After dinner they'd come back to her house and she'd gone straight to her room. She wouldn't say she was hiding. Who was she kidding? She was hiding.

Nick challenged her in ways no one else ever had. Routine meant sanity to her. It had since before her mother was murdered. With the good news from the doctor, she'd wanted to get back to her schedule. Nick wanted to set up a new one for the two of them.

On the one hand, she knew she had feelings for him and he had been straight forward with her about who he was and his intentions. Still, there was always another shoe ready to drop.

Olivia had never told anyone about the volatile house she'd grown up in. When her abilities became apparent, her mother had tried to push her toward math and science. Truthfully, even as a child, certain areas of science had fascinated her. But books had been her escape. When things got bad she could retreat to her secret place with a stack of books and snacks and avoid her parents for hours, even days at a time. It wasn't a surprise that she'd focused her studies on literature.

The fact that Nick was still living in her house was unsettling. It was one thing when he'd been staying here, and she'd been too weak and tired to spend a lot of time with him. It was entirely another when he was living her with the idea of building a real relationship.

She sighed. There was no use in avoiding him. Nick had installed himself in her life and didn't appear to be going anywhere. It was at once comforting and terrifying. Taking a few deep breaths to fortify herself, Olivia left her sanctuary to find Nick. Maybe they could find a way to get past pleasant. If she was ready for it. And he was.

Olivia found him prowling around her living room. It was one of her favorite rooms simply because the walls were floor to ceiling book shelves. He stalked along the rows of books glancing from title to title. They'd never talked about what he liked to read. She knew he read Shakespeare, but he'd never told her what he had on his e-reader.

When he stopped in front of one particular shelf her heart raced.

Please don't grab one of those books.

She surged forward hoping to stop the train in its tracks. As if in slow motion she saw him take a particular book with a red jacket off the shelf. Too late. Before she could stop him, he opened the book. The choking noise he made said it all. He whipped around, book in hand and stared at her.

Heat rushed through her entire body. She must be beet red. He'd found her secret. Well, one of them.

"What...what's this?" he croaked.

"It's a book," she whispered.

Where's a good sink hole when I need one?

"Olivia. These pictures." He looked from the book to her and back again.

Thoughts crashed through her brain. Was there a way to avoid this conversation? What must he think of her? How did she let this happen? What could she say?

"Olivia." His voice was low and husky. He ambled over to her with the book in his hand. "You're a kinky girl."

The earth wasn't listening to her pleas to swallow her whole. She looked into his eyes and her breath stopped. His eyes were filled with need and desire. For her.

"It's...I —"

"How many other books do you have like this?"

She was caught in his eyes. "That whole shelf you were looking at," she whispered.

"Really?"

Why was she hiding? It wasn't all that weird. It certainly wasn't shameful. "I collect erotica." She managed to keep herself from squeaking.

"Yeah?" The heat and humor in his voice made her feel like she would dissolve.

She nodded.

"You ever try anything in the pictures in your collection?" If it was possible, his voice got even huskier.

Olivia shook her head. She was incapable of forming words. Sweat trickled down her back as heat enveloped her.

"You want to?" His voice was impossibly low as he stood as if etched in stone waiting for her answer.

She knew if she said no he wouldn't push. They'd go back to the dance they'd been doing since she'd told him about the pregnancy. He would leave everything up to her. Courage had never been her strong suit. Her one truly courageous act had cost her, dearly. Somehow, she knew right now, with this man, she could take the leap.

Olivia nodded.

As if released from a cannon, Nick shot forward. The

book dropped from his hand a split second before his arms wrapped around her and his mouth crashed down on hers. The gentleness of his lips on hers was a surprise given the force with which he'd propelled himself towards her. That was her last rational thought as sensation took over.

His kiss became demanding as his tongue ran along the seam of her lips, seeking more of her. He tasted like salt and caramel. Shivers danced along her nerves as he pulled her into his arms. The strength of his embrace calmed the last of her nerves and she gave over to sensation.

In what seemed like a heartbeat later he lifted her into his arms and cradled her close to his chest, his lips never leaving hers. The breeze ruffling her hair and whispering across skin told her they were moving. She didn't care where they were going. He could take her anywhere. Any way he wanted.

Moments later he laid her gently down on her bed. The familiar smell of lavender calmed her scrambled senses. He pulled away. Her eyes opened, and she reached for him.

"Easy, beautiful. I'm not going anywhere." He slipped his T-shirt over his head as he kicked off his shoes. His muscles rippled with every move.

"Nick." She was pleading for something, not entirely sure what that was.

"I've got you." He returned to the bed and laid next to her. His gaze roved over her.

Nimble fingers began to undo the buttons of her blouse. Some primal part of her brain wished he would rip it off of her. Instead, as he popped each button open he brushed the fabric aside. His callused fingers slid across her skin shooting darts of pleasure through her entire body.

He leaned down and left tender kisses along the skin he revealed with each open button. Inch by agonizing inch he eased her blouse open. When he reached the last button, he slid the edges of the silky fabric from the waistband of her skirt.

"Better than any present, ever." He moaned as he leaned forward and ran his tongue along her heated skin.

She ran her hands down the muscles of his back. They moved underneath her hesitant touch. Velvet coated steel. How she wished she was braver, all she could seem to do was follow in the wake of the storm he created inside of her. She wanted to be the aggressor. Maybe next time.

Nick pulled back and eased the blouse off her shoulders as if he was opening a gift marked fragile. He propped himself up and sucked in his breath.

"Perfect."

Heat rushed through her as he ran a finger along the

259

edge of her white lace bra barely grazing her breasts. She was filled with wants and needs she couldn't name or explain.

"Relax. I've got you." He leaned in and kissed her again. It was a promise.

His hand moved along her side and to her back zeroing in on the clasp to her bra. With a practiced ease he unhooked her restraint and lifted the scrap of silk and lace from her body. Again, he simply stared at her.

With a moan he leaned forward and crushed his lips to hers claiming her as his. Passion rose in her and she met his demands with ones of her own. He pulled her close, pressing her to his warm chest. The shock of so much skin against skin sent zaps of electricity shooting through her veins. She couldn't get enough of him.

She felt the button at the back of her skirt slid open and the zipper lowered then his hand slipped beneath fabric to explore what lay underneath. After a moment he pulled back, a wicked smile on his face.

"I've got to see this."

He leaned back and pulled the skirt down her hips and pushed it down the length of her body until he could pull it free and throw it aside. His fiery gaze roamed up her legs and stared at the scraps of white lace that kept him from seeing all of her.

"A garter belt," he croaked. "You've definitely got a naughty side, don't you beautiful."

She nibbled her bottom lip, unsure how to answer that question. "I like what I like."

He stood so quickly she bounced on the bed. He clawed at the button and zipper of his jeans as if he was frantic to take them off. In seconds he was pushing the jeans and his boxers down and kicking them off with his shoes.

Nick approached the foot of the bed like a tiger stalking his prey. He made short work of unclasping her garters and sliding her silk stockings down her legs. The feel of his roughened fingers dancing along her skin with the soft material that had covered her sent pools of heat into her belly.

When her legs were bare he planted his hands on either side of her calves. A moan escaped Olivia as he started licking and nibbling his way up her legs.

"Nick." His name was a whisper, a plea, a prayer.

Her breathing sped up as he reached the top of her thighs. Fire shot through her when his hands tugged her lacy panties down and out of his way.

"I need you." The admission sent her tumbling further down the vortex of passion and sensation.

"Need you to." His guttural words rippled across her

skin.

She was on the verge of something. Before she could say more his lips claimed hers in another kiss that sent her rocketing higher still.

Then he was sliding inside her, and her world shifted on its axis and shattered into a million shards. Everything she knew was gone. Replaced by this moment, this feeling, this man.

She woke later in his arms, his hands sliding along her skin as if to reassure himself she was there. Olivia burrowed deeper into his arms, unsure what to say. She thought their night in Vegas had been spectacular. It had nothing on what she'd just experienced.

"You, Olivia Valenti, are a woman of hidden depths."

Was that a good thing? "What do you mean?"

He brought his fingers to her chin and tilted her head up so their eyes met. The sudden insecurity she felt washed away at the warmth she saw in his beautiful blue eyes. "I mean you project this image, conservative college professor, which, don't get me wrong is totally hot. But underneath you're kind of a kinky girl, aren't you?"

She shrugged. "I prefer naughty." She tried to sound prim. Kind of hard to do given what had happened so recently.

His chuckle rumbled in his chest and moved across her skin like a warm blanket. "Kind of like that myself. No one would guess by looking at you that you've got some seriously sexy underwear on underneath your teacher clothes or that you've got that collection of yours."

She ducked her head and buried her face in his shoulder. They were having twins and had shared the most passionate moments of her life, but the thought of him knowing about her collection still embarrassed her.

"Hey." He hugged her. "I'm just teasing you."

"I know." He probably couldn't understand her, what with her mumbling into his shoulder.

"Olivia." Nick rested his cheek on the top of her head.

"I've never told anyone about my collection."

"You shouldn't be embarrassed."

"And yet, I am."

He laughed. "I think it's hot. I'm just curious how you started collecting erotic art."

"You aren't going to like the story." She shifted slightly so she could tilt her head and see his eyes. Looking into them was quickly becoming one of her favorite things.

"Why wouldn't I like the story?"

"Because it involves another man." Olivia wasn't sure of many things when it came to Nick, but she was certain he wouldn't want to hear about her first, and only serious relationship and the man who'd taken her virginity and left her with an appreciation of erotic art. Not that it had done them any good. Lewis was horrible in bed. His constant referencing of erotic artists seemed to be a way for him to overcompensate for his own, not inconsiderable, short comings.

"You used to look at those pictures with another guy." His words were followed by an actual growl.

"Not really."

He reared up on his elbow. "What's that mean?"

"My first serious relationship was with one a professor when I started at Columbia."

"Liv, you were a kid when you went to college." The horrified look on his face was almost funny.

"I was young when I went to undergrad. By the time I was on my second PhD, which I got at Columbia, I was in my early twenties."

"Oh." His face and neck flushed. "Go on." He settled back down, bringing her into his arms.

"Lewis was an art history professor who used to try and charm all his students by dropping the names of erotic artists randomly into conversation. You'd be in the middle of a conversation about something like cubism and he'd make a comment about how he'd love to see Tom Poulton's cubist take on the female form. That would lead to conversations about who that was with admonitions to look him up."

"Who is he?"

"He was a well-known medical illustrator. After his death hundreds of erotic drawings were discovered. They were compiled by an editor. That book you were looking at is his."

"So, this guy tried to use this stuff to pick up girls."

"He did. It wasn't a very effective ploy until he met me. I was young and lonely. When I looked up Tom Poulton, I was intrigued. Of course, after Lewis and I started dating he never mentioned anything like that again. When we broke up I asked him if he'd ever even seen one of Poulton's illustrations."

"What did he say?"

She huffed out a breath. "He said he wouldn't waste his time looking at such filth."

"Sounds like an asshole."

"He was just a small-minded man with no idea how to talk to women. I understand he changed his pick-up lines after we broke up and found an equally small-minded woman who suits him perfectly." It had been a huge blow, being so wrong about him. But now she saw him for what he was and was glad their brief relationship had ended so easily.

"His loss. So, why do you collect it?"

"I think there are some images that are quite beautiful."
She looked down, not sure if she wanted to admit the rest.

"And?" He knew. Somehow, he knew there was more.

"I'm curious," she admitted.

"About?" He rested against the pillows, holding her
close with one arm while his other hand brushed slowly up
and down her arm.

The rhythmic sensation was hypnotic. She settled into
his arms feeling safe for the first time in a very long time,
maybe ever. "Whether some of the positions were even
possible."

His lips tilted up in a slow dangerous smile. "Wanna
find out?"

Every muscle in her body seized at the thought. Images
from her collection flitted through her mind. It might kill
her, but there was only one answer. "Yes."

She was going to kill him. Who knew beneath the prim
clothes and polite demeanor was a firecracker? After her
whispered "yes" they retrieved the book he'd been looking
at when he discovered her secret and tried to recreate a few

of the illustrations.

After their night in Las Vegas, her passion hadn't surprised him. Her playfulness was another story. Since that night, when the actions of two spoiled young women, had ended his football career, he'd viewed sex as little more than a release. A bodily function that didn't require emotion or commitment. Just two people willing to spend a little time together.

Last night with Olivia changed everything. It was more than he'd ever had and more than he thought he would ever want. Aside from the amazing sex, the best parts were the moments in between when she slept in his arms or made him laugh with an adorably serious analysis of the picture they'd used for inspiration versus the actual experience.

His body started to tighten with the memories, not good since he had a meeting with Bob, Cade and Ed in a few minutes. He willed himself to simmer down by thinking about anything but Olivia. The usual hard-on killers didn't work as well as they used to.

By the time he walked into the conference room his body and mind were back under control. He was here to work, not to get into a conversation with the others about his relationship with Olivia. Walking into the room with a hard on would for sure lead to some hazing, probably some questions.

The conference room was set up as a war room for the football department. A surprising amount of work was going into putting together a program that wasn't going to include playing any actual games this season.

He tossed his planner down on the table next to Bob then fixed himself a cup of coffee. The silence was unusual enough to make him turn as he stirred the sugar into his coffee. All three men stared at him. He looked down at his shirt.

Nope. It wasn't on inside out.

He glanced over his shoulder trying to see if there was something sticking to his back.

"What?" The stares were freaking him out a little.

"What do you mean what?" Ed barked.

"You and Olivia? The baby? Ringing any bells?" Cade asked.

Right.

He hadn't told anyone about the appointment. Neither had Olivia as far as he knew. He pulled out his phone to text her.

"What are you doing?" Bob asked.

"Texting Olivia to see what your clearance is."

"Seriously?" Cade scoffed.

"Last time I released information without her okay she punched me in the nose."

The three men chuckled as he waited for her to get back to him. She should still be in her office. Her class didn't meet until later that morning. It didn't take her long to give him the all clear for the men in the room.

"Olivia and the babies are fine."

"That's a relief." Cade glanced down at the papers in front of him before his head whipped back up. "Babies?"

Nick sank into his chair. "Both heartbeats were steady and strong."

"Twins?" Ed smiled.

"Twins." The thought still scared the shit out of Nick. It had taken a lot of concentrated breathing to get used to the idea of having one baby. Now there were two.

Ed slapped a hand on the table. "That's going to be a handful, but you've got a good woman to help you through it. My daughter and son-in-law managed triplets after having seven other children. You can deal with a couple at the start of the line-up."

That much was true. After last night, he wa feeling more confident about his relationship with Olivia. He knew it was going to be time for the talk soon. Timing was everything. The better she knew the man he was now, he hoped she would be more forgiving of the boy he'd been then.

"Congrats." Cade nodded at him.

"Thanks." Nick cleared his throat. "Olivia wanted me to let you know the scholarship fund is approved by the foundation and is in the process of being funded. We should have up to twenty scholarships ready to go in a few weeks."

Cade reached for a stack of papers. "I've been making some calls. These are potential recruits." He gave a set of handouts to each man.

"Who did you call?" Nick asked as he started looking through the information.

"Rush started with the academic coordinators then I talked to the coaches."

"Why academic coordinators first?" Bob studied the list of names.

"Because all these kids were good enough at football to get recruited by a college program. Most of them division one. We needed to know if there was a hope we could get their academics up before next year."

That was a good call. Nick would have made the calls in the reverse order. Probably why Cade was going to be the head coach.

"If you look at the lists, they're ranked according to the academic coordinator's recommendation. Before we get too deep into the details, you should know I asked Rush to join us." Cade glanced at his watch. "He should be here in any minute."

"Why?" Ed leaned back in his chair.

Nick was still trying to get a bead on the dynamic between Cade and Ed. It was different then his work with Bob. It almost seemed like Cade was already the head coach and Ed was just hanging out for appearances and for the occasional word of advice.

"He's the one who's got to get these kids' grades up, so they can play. I figured he should have some input here," Cade explained.

"He appreciates it." Rush stood in the doorway, looking more put together than any man in the room. Nick felt a momentary twinge, knowing this guy had a thing for Olivia, whether he admitted it or not.

"Thanks for coming." Cade stood and held out a hand.

Rush stepped into the room to shake Cade's hand, tucking a box of files into one arm as he did. He set the box on the table as he took a seat. "I appreciate being given a chance to participate in this process."

"What are those?" Nick nodded at the files in the box.

"These are the academic records of the young men on Cade's list."

"How did you get them without consent?" Cade raised an eyebrow.

Rush cleared his throat. "I may, or may not, have spoken to some female employees of the various registrars' offices who may or may not have been charmed enough by my accent to overlook the...impropriety of my request."

Ed snorted. "He charmed the records out of them."

"Yes, well. Most universities have a policy of releasing information with consent of the student. Many of them have disclosure notices buried in their registration forms letting students know that their records may be released to other universities without consent for a defined academic purpose. It's not done often, but I convinced these departments that this was a valid academic purpose that could be a benefit to all these young men."

Nick couldn't explain why he was annoyed. The information would help them make some decisions, and it sounded like it was legal, if not completely above board. Maybe it had to do with the fact that Rush was able to use his Britishness to get something he wanted. Could he use it on Olivia?

"Any thoughts?" Cade's question drew Nick back to the conversation. He had to stop getting distracted. Olivia was important to him, but he needed to keep his head in the game. Not to mention, he needed to remember that he trusted Olivia. It didn't matter what Rush's feelings for her were.

"I have a general plan in mind, which obviously would be strengthened with your input. It should be made clear to all the young men, before they accept the invitation to attend Cormac, that they will be required to sit for several tests before the school year begins. Based on that testing, my staff and I will put together their course schedule., which will be based on their non-athletic interests and test scores. They will also have to agree to work with tutors or specialists at my discretion."

"Specialists?" Nick thought Rush would take this seriously, turned out he was taking it more than seriously.

"I believe, based on my review of some of these records, that many of these players have undiagnosed learning disorders. The testing I have in mind will not only let us know where their actual academic levels are, but also help us determine who simply needs more tutoring or academic discipline versus those students who require more specialized help."

Bob whistled. "You're not messing around professor."

Rush shifted in his seat. "I made it clear when I took this position that I would be taking this very seriously."

"And we appreciate it," Ed said, trying to ease the sudden tension in the room. "Truth is, academics usually get the short end of the stick with athletes. As long as the athletes are making grades, or can fake it, the coaches don't like to rock the boat."

"Ed's right," Cade agreed. "If there's one thing everyone putting this program together knows it's that football isn't always going to be there for these kids. I want to make sure that Cormac's putting together a stellar program that will serve our players on the field and off."

Nick nodded. "We've all heard the stories about players getting through top colleges even though they were basically illiterate. Some people think those are isolated incidents, but they aren't."

Rush relaxed in his chair. "I've spoken to Ron about something, since I would like it to be a requirement for all student athletes, but it's going to be particularly important for athletes in the football program."

"What's that?" Cade asked.

"I think they should all be required to take some basic financial management courses."

"Why?"

"Many of these students are coming from disadvantaged economic situations where they haven't had many resources to manage. A few of them will be offered astronomical amounts of money to play professionally. The stories of professional athletes blowing through their fortunes are just as, if not more, common than the stories of athletes getting through college with subpar academic records."

Nick had to hand it to Rush. He'd covered all the bases. The five men spent the next few hours going through the records of every potential recruit on Cade's list. They debated the pros and cons of each, paying the closest attention to the students that would benefit the most from this approach. While the borderline students might be closer to playing, they'd all warmed up to the idea of turning this program into an opportunity for athletes who would never get this kind of a chance anywhere else.

As they wrapped up their plans, including designating a list of players each coach was going to contact, Rush cleared his throat. "There's something else we should discuss."

Nick noticed the other man's renewed discomfort. "What's that?"

"I had a visit from Gill the younger this morning."

Just the sound of their nemesis's name set Nick's teeth on edge. "What did he want?"

"He wanted to let me know that there would be a substantial financial benefit to making sure that your students didn't achieve or maintain academic eligibility. He did make it clear his father still had plans for the program."

Ed slammed his hand on the table. "What is wrong with them?"

"They haven't learned when you're dead stay down." Cade gritted his teeth.

"I have to say Junior seems to have a particular distaste for you two." Rush nodded at Cade and Nick.

"Me I get," Cade said. "He rode the bench all through college because of me. Not sure what his deal with Nick is."

"Olivia's his deal." He wanted to wring Gill's neck, anything to make sure he stayed away from Olivia.

"Why Olivia?" Rush seemed genuinely confused.

"He tried to use her to tank our plan a few months ago. I think he might actually have a thing for her." Wasn't that a kick in the ass. He wasn't afraid of losing Olivia to Gill. She was done with the other man, but his constant hovering reminded her of bad things.

"He make any plays for her?" Cade watched Nick.

"Not since the day he made an offer to the professor

here." Nick shook his head.

"What kind of money did he offer?"

"I'm sure he thought it was a good deal of money." Rush sounded amused.

"But you don't?" Ed raised an eyebrow.

"I don't usually bring it up, but my family is one of the wealthiest families in Great Britain. I'm not inclined to take blood money for any reason, but Gill's offer was quite insulting."

"What did you say?" Bob was the only one who seemed to be holding on to his temper.

"I told him I'd think about it." Rush smiled.

"What's the plan?" Nick knew the professor was up to something. He'd done a little digging and everything he learned told him Rush was a straight shooter and would have told Gill to fuck off, or whatever the Brits say, if he didn't want to string Gill along for some reason.

"It seems your enemies are quite determined to bring this program down. I've made a few inquiries to understand the situation. I would be less concerned about Gill the younger. He appears to simply want to cause trouble for the two of you." Rush nodded toward Cade and Nick. "Mr. Gill Senior's motives are more difficult to ascertain, but he appears to be bent on making the university pay for not giving him what he wanted."

"That's an interesting read," Cade said. "What do you think we should do about them?"

"I don't believe outsmarting them will be a difficult proposition. Especially if we can get more information on their plans."

"But?" Nick didn't know how he knew there was a "but." It was something about the look on Rush's face and the tone in his voice.

"There has to be more going on than simply the fact that the board didn't follow along with Gill's plans. It doesn't make sense otherwise."

Nick didn't disagree with him. If there was anything he'd figured out it was that most people played their cards in life close to the chest. He should know. "Can you string Backup along for a while? Gather some information for us?"

Rush nodded. "I've made a commitment to the student athletes at this school. I have no intention of letting them down."

Nick was starting to like the guy. As long as he kept his hands to himself with Olivia, they might even be friends one day. Well, maybe when Rush got a woman of his own.

The five men spent the next hour going over the latest

plans for the upcoming non-season. It was hard to think of it as a real thing since their games had all been cancelled and they couldn't do anything with the players using university facilities.

Fortunately, the weight room was for all sports. Unfortunately, because of the sanctions Nick and Bob couldn't actually schedule the football players for the room. They would have to work their strength training around the other sports.

Cade had moved in with his wife after they'd gotten married and volunteered their land for training and workouts. It was a decent alternative. They had the space to simulate a football field, plus Tess was a competitor on American Ninja Warrior and had a full obstacle course behind the house. She and her brothers were always building new obstacles, which would be great for training for the football players.

All in all, the first season they were working as coaches promised to be pretty creative. Since Bob and Nick's job involved strength training for all the teams they would be the ones responsible for keeping the pulse on the campus and bringing the rest of the coaches up to speed.

Olivia's idea to recruit athletes with academic issues

added a whole layer to the plan none of them had anticipated.

"I'm going to say it straight. I wasn't the best student. I can hold my own, but some of these kids are going to need tutoring I can't help with."

Cade rubbed the back of his neck. "That shouldn't be a problem. Frankie's got a double major in education and psychology with a masters in sports management, Ben's got his degrees in business and educational leadership. I've talked to both of them and they're on board with the plan."

That was a relief. Nick was here to support the team and the program they were all trying to build, but he had too much on his plate right now to take on anything more. Besides, some of these kids were going to need a lot of intensive help to get on the right track.

They spent a few more minutes putting together their plans and assignments for the rest of the week and agreed on the time and place for the next meeting.

After they broke up, Nick decided to stop by Olivia's to see if she wanted to grab some lunch. His mother was having a good day, so she and Simon were meeting him at Mooney's. It would be nice if Olivia could join them and get to know his family better. She might be irritated at the last-minute invitation, but he'd spend time with her no matter what her mood was.

Fifteen minutes later he stepped off the elevator on Olivia's floor, about to face the lioness in her den, when he heard raised voices coming from her office. Nick bolted down the hallway and burst through the door to the secretary's area outside of Olivia's office.

"Shut up you, pedantic little twit." What's her name, the mouthy student Lydell, was right up in the weasel Clay's grill.

The little bastard was practically foaming at the mouth. "You have no business at this university, you arrogant fraud."

"Enough." Nick's bellow was followed by silence. Any fears he had of Olivia being pissed at him for dropping by with no warning vanished when he saw the look of relief on her face.

"What the hell is going on here?"

The snooty Ms. Lydell sneered at him. "None of your business."

"That's it. One more word out of either one of you and I'm going to give you both F's in my class." Olivia looked between her students. The fire in her eyes dared them to speak.

This was definitely not the time or the place, but he was

totally going to have to let her know how hot the bossy teacher bit was.

"Now. Clay. I have told you repeatedly that my office hours are by appointment only during the summer. Yet you continue to drop by whenever you want and expect me to be available."

The little bastard's mouth opened and closed as Olivia turned her attention to her other student.

"As for you, Ms. Lydell." She zeroed in on the younger woman. "Your ego is starting to interfere with your ability to be a student. If you think you have all the answers there is absolutely no point in attending classes. You are a bright, capable young woman, but if you don't temper your attitude I am going to have a serious discussion with your academic advisor about your future here at Cormac."

Olivia stopped and took a breath and turned back to the weasel. "Clay, you have an appointment with your tutor in an hour. Direct your questions to him. If there's anything he can't answer, he will set a time for the three of us to go over it."

She turned to her other student. "Your current paper topic is not approved. I suggest you rethink it and bring me three alternate topics by the end of the week. If both of you will excuse me, I have an appointment with Coach Jacobs."

Olivia turned and marched into her office. Leaving a room fool of stunned people behind her.

Nick stood rooted to the spot. Every layer of her personality that he peeled back was hotter than next. Life with her would always be a surprise. He prayed she'd want to build a life with him when she knew everything. Otherwise he was screwed.

Chapter 12

She didn't know what had come over her. It would be wonderful if she could blame pregnancy hormones, but Olivia suspected her new found outspokenness had more to do with the dark haired, blue eyed man standing in her office looking all kinds of smug.

"What was that about?" Nick's question drew her attention from her inner thoughts to the man who was quickly becoming as vital to her as any major organ.

"Those two have never gotten along. Clay interrupted my appointment with Ms. Lydell and it escalated from there."

"Why do you call him by his first name and not her?" Nick leaned against her desk.

"She insists on it." At first, she'd thought it was merely pretention. But there was something about the young woman that sparked Olivia's protective side. She couldn't explain it, but the unexplained feelings were likely the reason she hadn't kicked the young woman out of her seminar already.

"Why?"

Olivia shrugged. It wasn't appropriate to make personal comments about her students. Especially since she felt a connection to the young woman that baffled her. Until she got to the root of her student's issues, she couldn't explain anything about them to someone else.

"What brings you by?" Maybe a change of topic would help.

"Simon and I are taking our mom to lunch. I was hoping you would be free to join us." He smiled.

"Are you sure? I don't want to interfere with your time together." She felt guilty that he was spending so much time with her instead of with his mother and brother, who both needed him.

"You're not. I figured it's past time for you all to meet. After all, they're going to be the twins' uncle and grand-mother."

A sharp pain lodged itself in the vicinity of her heart. Family. It had been so long since she'd been able to claim one herself she hadn't thought about what it would mean to her children. She tried not to wish it were different. That she had close family to share with the babies.

"If you're sure I won't be intruding." She chewed her bottom lip.

He stepped forward then pulled her into his arms. "You're going to have to get used to the fact that you and the babies have a family, whatever happens with us."

Nick leaned down and captured her lips with his. The

kiss, and his words, eased the pain in her heart and spread warmth through her entire body. Visions of last night sprang in to her mind and turned the warmth into a bonfire. He pulled her closer and ran his hands along her back. She lost track of time and everything else.

When he pulled back, she felt the loss of the connection like an ache in her entire body. He rested his forehead on her.

"As much as I would like to play professor and naughty student on that couch, we need to meet my mom and brother in thirty minutes."

She smiled. "Why can't we play naughty professor and straight A student?"

He groaned. "Slugger. We're about to go have lunch with my mother and brother. I'd prefer not show up with a hard on."

Her laugh came out more like a choking sound as she stepped away from him. She took a breath. What was it about this man that made her forget everything else? Olivia tried to compose herself as she retrieved her purse from the bottom of her credenza. If they couldn't keep their hands off each other, this was going to be an interesting lunch.

Interesting didn't quite cover it. They ended up at

Mooney's which made sense. It was a favorite for all the locals. The blend of Irish and Mexican menu items was unique, and Olivia particularly liked to try the specials, which were usually the fusion dishes blending the two cuisines. Today's unique offering was a shepherd's pie taco. Olivia wasn't sure if it was the pregnancy or the fact that, after recovering from food poisoning she'd finally gotten her appetite back, but the description of the dish made her mouth water.

Nick's brother seemed more excited to see her than his mother did. Jane Jacobs looked pale. Not surprising given everything she was going through. Olivia was happy she felt well enough to go out for lunch.

The matriarch of the Mooney family, Graciela, was working the floor today. Olivia loved watching the family business in action. Everyone took a part, even Lily, the deputy sheriff, could be found behind the bar from time to time.

As if summoned from Olivia's thoughts, Lily Mooney walked through the front door. She strode up to her mother, who was in the middle of taking their orders, and kissed her cheek.

"Anyone going for the shepherd's pie tacos?"

Graciela nodded at Olivia. "The professor is trying

them."

Lily smiled. "Good to see you up and around, Olivia." She turned to her mother. "Ma, I'll have the tacos at the bar when you get a chance."

"You're welcome to join us." Olivia wasn't sure where the invitation came from and technically, it wasn't hers to make. Nick had invited her to his family lunch after all. She glanced at him.

"Uh. Sure." He glanced at his mother who was looking down at the table.

There was an undercurrent of something that Olivia couldn't identify. Maybe she should figure out a way to get to know Lily another time.

The woman in question glanced at the others seated at the table and shook her head. "I appreciate the invite, but my dad's behind the bar and we've been working opposite schedules for a while. I was looking forward to catching up with him. Maybe another time." She smiled.

"We're having a girls' night out here tomorrow. You're welcome to join us." Her mouth ran ahead of her brain again. Tess, Delilah and Charlie might not want to add another woman to the mix.

"Yeah? Sounds like fun. Your last one here was legendary." The deputy sheriff gave her mother another kiss on the cheek before sauntering away.

After Graciela left to put their orders in, the table grew weirdly quiet.

"I'm sorry." Olivia broke the silence.

"Why?" Nick took a sip of his iced tea.

"It's your family lunch. I'm a guest. It was rude of me to invite someone else." Awkward family dynamics were not her specialty.

"It's okay. You were trying to be nice." Nick put a hand on top of hers.

Nick's mother cleared her throat. "It's my fault."

The woman had barely said a word since they'd sat down. Three in a row was surprising.

"What's your fault?" Olivia wanted to get to know the woman. If her treatment went well she would be the babies' only grandmother. The thought sent a sharp edge of sadness through Olivia. Her mother would have loved having grandchildren.

"I'm not comfortable around cops," she whispered.

That wasn't unusual in Olivia's experience. "Not many people are, except other emergency responders and people who've interacted with the police positively." Her own experience after her mother's murder was a decidedly mixed bag, although she still kept in touch with Detective Harmon. The woman had saved her life and her sanity.

"Yeah. Not many people got my rap sheet." Jane lifted her head to look at Olivia. Her blue eyes, so like her sons', held a mixture of fear and defiance.

Olivia blinked. She and Nick had talked about their fathers' issues with the law. He'd never mentioned his mother had her own problems.

Before Olivia could answer the other woman spoke again. "I'm straight now. Kept my noise clean for fourteen years."

Nick's sharp glance at his mother told Olivia there was a significance to that date. It was a little disconcerting every time she realized how little she knew about Nick. He was the father of her children. In some ways, she knew him better than she'd ever known anyone. In others, he was a virtual stranger.

"That's good then." People made mistakes. Olivia had no time for those who didn't learn from them but wasn't going to turn her back on those that did.

Jane's eyes widened. "That doesn't bother you?"

"What?" Olivia asked

"My record." Jane trembled.

She shrugged. "Why should it bother me?"

"Fancy woman like you wouldn't want the likes of me for the grandmother of your baby." The defiance in the other woman's eyes gave way to pain.

Hadn't Nick told his family? She glanced at him and he gave her a nod, clearly leaving it up to her.

"Well, since your son is the father of my twins, my children are the likes of you. Besides, my father's serving life in prison. I'm not in a position to judge anyone."

Three sets of eyes widened. It occurred to her that she'd told more people about her father in the last few weeks than she'd told since being emancipated after his conviction.

"Didn't know that about your daddy." Jane leaned back in her chair.

Olivia shrugged. "I don't shout it from the roof tops. But it's one of the reasons I don't judge people. I prefer to form my own opinions." No need to say anything about how few people she'd even tried to get to know since her mother's death.

The arrival of their food prevented a response to Olivia's comments. Once their meals were in front of them, by silent agreement, they focused on eating lunch and lighter topics of conversation for the rest of their time together.

It was a fun lunch. Once everyone stopped worrying about the impression they were making, they relaxed, and conversation flowed. Simon was excited about being an uncle to twins. Jane was more reticent, whether that was her character, or her own health issues, Olivia couldn't tell.

The shepherd's pie tacos were fantastic. The combination of Irish staples with Mexican spices was delicious. She told Graciela as much when she stopped by to check on them.

"Thank you. My son loves mixing and matching. It doesn't always work." She had an expression on her face that Olivia imagined only a mother could. It was a mixture of indulgence and annoyance, that seemed to say Graciela Mooney was proud of her son, even if she didn't always understand his experimental ideas.

"This worked perfectly. I loved the fried potato as the shell for the taco."

"I'll be sure to tell him. My Lily tells me she's going to be here tomorrow night for girls' night with you and your friends." Graciela smiled.

Olivia nodded. "I'm looking forward to getting to know her. She was so helpful when I got sick a few weeks ago."

A shadow crossed Graciela's face. Olivia wasn't sure what it meant, but it wasn't any of her business. "Well then, we'll see you and your friends tomorrow night."

After the older woman left, Olivia glanced at her watch. "Lunch has been wonderful, but I have to get back the office."

"What does a professor have to do during the summer?" Jane asked.

It was a question Olivia was used to. "I'm teaching a seminar, but I'm also head of the English department. There's scheduling for the spring semester —"

"Spring?" Nick leaned forward. "We're still working on the fall in athletics."

She nodded. "You can update athletes as they arrive. We have to have schedules set in time for course catalogues to be printed. Fall catalogues were done some time ago. I also have to coordinate the staffing for the department. There are core English requirements for all students, so I have to make sure we have enough professors and graduate students to teach all the courses we need to offer for the entire university, as well as our majors."

"I had no idea your job was so involved." Nick's eyebrows drew together.

"I don't do it alone. My assistant, as much as she appears to have her head in the clouds, is very good and there are several committees within the department that handle the nuts and bolts of the organizing. I'm an excellent del-egator." She smiled.

"We shouldn't keep you then." Jane's sharp tone in-stantly deflated the mood at the table.

Olivia wasn't sure what she'd said to upset Nick's mother, but obviously something made the woman angry. She let Nick lead her from the restaurant. He was practi-cally vibrating.

Once they were in his truck she found her voice. "I didn't mean to insult your mother."

"You didn't." He gritted his teeth.

"I must have said something to upset her." One moment they were all getting along, the next Jane seemed intent on ending the lunch as quickly as possible.

"She can get snappy when she's tired. That's all it is."

"Are you sure?" She chewed her bottom lip. That last thing she wanted to do was upset Nick's mother when she was already dealing with so much.

"Of course." His clipped tone made it clear he didn't want to talk about it anymore.

She couldn't get back to her office fast enough. The sud-den and disquieting end to a lovely lunch made her wonder if she was capable of being part of a family.

What did I do?

He had no idea why his mother had snapped at Olivia, but he was damn well going to find out. Once he dropped her at her office, he would double back to his house to have a conversation with his mother. He didn't really have time for it, but he was damned if he was going to let his mom upset Olivia.

The mood in the truck was thick and filled with tension.

"Are you okay?" He shifted in his seat.

She nodded but didn't say anything.

"Really? If something's wrong, I hope you can tell me."

The silence stretched out between them. He felt like this was a test for them, for him.

Finally, she spoke. "I'm sorry."

"Why?"

"I obviously upset your mother —"

"You can stop there. If it came down to a choice between you and my mom, I'd choose you. Every time."

"Because of the babies." She sounded resigned.

"Because of you." He'd thought the job at Cormac was his fresh start. In this moment, he realized it was Olivia. She was the reason he was here, and she was his last best chance at a new life.

"Oh." Her mouth formed a perfect circle.

If he wasn't driving he would pull her into his arms and kiss her perfectly shaped mouth.

"Do you know why your mother…got mad…at me?" Her slight stutter told him exactly how upset she was.

"Doubt it was you. She's not a big fan of law enforcement." He hoped that was it but had to admit to himself he didn't know his mother well enough to say for sure.

"That's understandable. I'm sorry I invited Lily to join us."

"Don't be. We owe Lily. She was great the night you got sick." He still got chills thinking of Olivia unconscious by the side of the road.

"Regardless." She took a deep breath and let it out. A trick he'd seen her use to control her stutter. "I was at lunch to get to know your mother and brother, not include new guests in the meal."

"My brother likes you and so does my mom. She's just tough to get to know." He knew there was probably more to the story, but he was going to give his mother a chance to explain.

"If you're sure."

He wasn't sure about anything when it came to his mother. But he would get to the bottom of her reaction to

Olivia.

After he dropped Olivia off at her office, with a promise to pick her up in a couple of hours after her meetings, he went back to his place, looking for his mother. He found her sitting on the back porch.

"What the hell?" He hadn't meant to jump right into it like that, but he was pissed watching Olivia deal with being upset and embarrassed after lunch.

She sat there, silently watching the waves roll onto the beach.

"You going to tell me why you were so rude to Olivia?" He wanted answers.

She shrugged.

That wasn't going to cut it. "Seriously? You got nothing?"

She stood and moved to the sliding glass door.

"Where are you going?" Images of his childhood flashed through his mind. Images of her always walking away.

"To pack." His mother sounded resigned.

Pack? What the hell?

He needed to know what was going on. "Where the fuck are you going?"

"Back to Alabama." She wouldn't look at him.

"Why?" This didn't make any sense.

"I've worn out my welcome."

"What are you talking about? I just want to find out why you were so rude to Olivia. I'm not kicking you out." He wanted them to get along.

"This isn't working," she whispered.

"What isn't working?"

"None of it."

She opened the door and walked into the house. He followed her, closing the door behind him. She wasn't going to run away. Not this time.

"Stop." The command in his voice was clear.

It didn't work on her. She just kept walking toward her room.

"Damn it, Mom. Tell me what the fuck is going on," he bellowed.

She stopped at the door to her room, her hand on the door knob. "I didn't want this."

"What? A family? A chance?" This was the most fucked up conversation he remembered having in a long time.

"Hope." She whipped around to face him, tears running down her cheek.

He blinked. "I don't understand."

"I was ready. In that shitty trailer in Alabama. I was

298

ready for it to end." Her voice was scratchy from emotion.

"Why?"

"I didn't deserve anything else." She started to crumble.

He stepped forward and scooped her into his arms. She was impossibly light for a grown woman, whether it was the cancer or her life that had made her so frail, he couldn't tell.

He strode to the living room couch and set her down, then took a seat next to her. "I think you know how I feel about getting a break, a fresh start."

"You're a good man. You didn't throw away your first shot, it was stolen from you. By that stupid girl. And me." Shame filled her voice. "I'm nothing."

"You're my mom. You're going to be the grandmother to my children." He leaned back at the look of pain that shot across her face.

"I'm dying." She looked up at him, letting him see the truth in her ravaged face.

"Not necessarily."

The doctors hadn't spun fairy tales, but they'd given her a shot at beating the cancer.

"Do you understand what you're doing to me?" She covered her face with her hands.

"Tell me." All he wanted was for her to give him some

freaking answers.

His mother took several deep breaths, then lowered her hands and looked at him. "You're showing me everything that could happen if I beat the cancer."

"And that's a problem because?" He thought giving her something to fight for was a good thing.

"Because the odds of me beating this thing are small."

"And?" You didn't give up because the odds were against you. If he'd done that he'd probably be sharing a prison cell with his old man.

"And I was fine with dying because I had nothing left to live for. You're giving me things to lose. All my life, I never thought a woman like your Olivia would give me the time of day, much less talk to me. She sat down and had lunch with me. She treated me with respect, like the grandmother to her babies." There was a catch in her voice.

"You are." He tried to gentle his tone, but he didn't understand why it upset her to get along with Olivia.

She threw up her hands. "That's the problem."

He ran a hand through his hair. This conversation was making him nuts. "What's the problem?"

"You've shown me what I could have if things go my way. Things never go my way." She sounded a little like she was talking to a child.

"Let me see if I have this right. You're pissed because we're showing you what life could be?" That made no sense.

"Ever since your father landed me in prison, I've learned not to expect much. The less you expect the less it hurts when life kicks you in the face."

"And we've given you more than you expected." He was starting to understand.

"You've given me something to lose." The accusation was clear in her voice.

He took her hand. "No. We've given you something to fight for."

Chapter 13

"So, how big is Nick's cock?" Delilah's voice boomed through the pub.

Heat shot through Olivia's cheeks and she let her face fall forward onto the table. "Must you?" she mumbled.

Tess laughed. "She did it to me. Now it's your turn."

"It looks like I'm in time for the good stuff."

Lily's voice drew Olivia's attention away from her mortal embarrassment. "Hi."

The other woman's brown eyes glowed with laughter. "Hi yourself."

"What are you doing here?" Delilah eyed the new comer with suspicion.

"Hey to you too Delilah." Lily smiled, clearly not bothered by the other woman's attitude.

"Pull up a chair." Olivia scooted closer to Delilah.

"Tess, Charlie." Lily nodded at the other women at the table as she pulled up a chair.

"Long time no see, Lily." Charlie raised a glass.

"What am I missing?" Olivia could tell there were undercurrents between the four women, but she had no clue what was going on.

"We've known each other since we were children." Tess took a sip of her drink.

"We ran in different crowds." Delilah sneered at Lily.

"Still?" Lily's eyes widened.

Delilah glared at her. "Still."

"Still what?" Olivia looked between the two women.

"Why did you have to invite Deputy Do-Right tonight?"

Lily rolled her eyes. "Maybe I should go." She started to rise, but Tess stopped her.

"No."

"No?" Delilah turned her glare to Tess. "No? We're friends now. You have to back my play, not hers."

"I'm backing both of you. It's in the past." Tess directed the last words at Delilah.

"You weren't there. You'd moved on to college by the time everything went down."

Olivia watched the interaction between the women with fascination.

"Charlie told me everything. It wasn't Lily's fault. It happened. You need to get over it."

"I don't see why," Delilah mumbled before she sipped her drink.

"Oh for God's sake." Charlie jumped into the conversation. "Lily didn't do anything. That bitch Miranda set the whole thing up. She wanted you to think Lily did it."

"Why? Miranda was my friend." Tears pooled in Delilah's eyes.

Tess reached out and took Delilah's hand. "You know that's not true."

Delilah dashed at the tears on her cheeks with the back of her hand.

"What am I missing?" Olivia didn't grow up here in Cormac and didn't understand all the undercurrents going on between the women. On a good day she couldn't always pick up social cues. When those cues were under layers of subtext she was doomed.

"It's a long story." Delilah raised her hand and signaled the need for another round of shots from the waitress who wandered by then turned her gaze back to Lily. "It wasn't you."

Lily shook her head. "I tried to tell you, but you weren't really in the mood to listen." Lily rubbed a small scar on the back of her left hand.

Delilah stared at the pale mark in Lily's tan skin. "Shit." She looked up at Lily. "Let's get drunk."

"Really?" Lily's eyes widened.

Tess leaned in. "It's Delilah's way of making amends."

The waitress came with shots for everyone. Olivia stared at the glass Delilah pushed in front of her. "I can't drink."

"Yours is pineapple juice. No booze for you, but you have to take a shot with us. It's a thing."

Olivia shrugged and lifted the glass to her nose. She leaned over and sniffed Lily's shot to compare them. It was clear that Olivia's drink was non-alcoholic. A lit match might set the entire table on fire with the fumes coming from the other women's shot glasses.

Delilah raised her glass and the others followed suit.

"To us. Chicks before dicks."

The women raised their glasses and then tossed back their shots. Olivia had little experience with girls' nights, having only been out on one before this. Still, the refreshing jolt of juice was decidedly different than the burn of tequila she remembered. Of course, it was the burn of tequila that led to the night of passion that led to her doing pineapple juice shots tonight.

"Earth to Olivia." Delilah snapped her fingers in front of Olivia's face.

"Sorry. I was just thinking about our last girls' night here."

Lily snorted. "The staff is still talking about it."

"Why?" Olivia thought a pub like this must see more interesting nights out than theirs.

"Mostly because no one here likes Brian Gill." There was something in Lily's voice when she mentioned Brian's name that Olivia couldn't identify. "Delilah's public acknowledgement of his lack of endowments went over big."

"How has he gotten away with so much over the years?" It seemed like every time Olivia turned around someone else who didn't like Brian popped out of the woodwork.

Lily shrugged. "Senior's the big problem. He's got money to burn and uses it to reward his minions and squash his enemies. It's his weapon of choice. Junior gets caught in a lot of his bullshit."

"You starting a fan club for Junior?" Delilah asked.

"No. Just pointing out that if I had to get stuck in a room with one or the other, I'd pick Junior over Senior." Lily sipped her beer as she engaged in some kind of staring contest with Delilah.

"You screwing my ex?" It was like Delilah wanted to pick a fight.

No one could fake the look of disgust that crossed Lily's face. "No. He's...I...Just no." She shivered.

"You sure?"

"Jeez, Delilah. Just because I think his father's a bigger

asshole doesn't mean I'm bonking Junior. Get a grip." Lily huffed out a breath before taking another swig of her beer.

"Good. Because while I agree that Senior is evil incarnate, Junior is a ginormous douche canoe and I don't want any more of my girls getting messed up with him." Delilah signaled for more shots.

"Why are we wasting our time talking about him at all?" Charlie joined in the conversation. "The Gills are a sinking ship. Let 'em go under without giving them any more time."

Lily accepted another beer from the waitress and lifted in a silent toast to the bartender, her father, before turning back to the table. "Don't take your eyes off them, especially Senior. They can still do a lot of damage on the way down."

Olivia heard the warning tone in Lily's voice. "What do you know?"

Lily shrugged but didn't elaborate. As if their discussion had summoned the object of their disdain, Brian stepped up between Olivia and Lily. Every woman at the table stiffened.

"We need to talk, Olivia." He focused on her.

"We don't need to do anything." Olivia turned away from him.

"Baby." He grabbed her arm.

"Dude." Lily's tone was low and held a warning. "Not a good idea. I'd have to arrest you if she asks me to."

"You're not on duty, Deputy." Brian glanced at Lily and let go of Olivia, but he didn't back away from the table. "I need to talk to Olivia, and you all need to back off."

Lily looked at the ceiling and counted to ten under her breath. "Dude. Let…it…go."

Delilah pushed Brian away from Olivia. "You need to leave."

"Delilah, this has nothing to do with you. There are things Olivia needs to know."

"Don't forget what we all know." Tess stood and moved to stand by Olivia. "You're not going to bully any of us any-more."

"Fuck me," he mumbled. "I'm not trying to bully any-one. I just need to talk to Olivia for a minute."

That was it. Olivia stood, kicking her bar stool over as she did. "Enough. You artless ill-nurtured lout" She poked a finger in Brian's chest. His eyes widened as he stepped back. Olivia was pissed. She'd been pushed around enough for ten lifetimes and her mother had died at the hands of a man who'd believed his way was the only way that mat-tered.

Olivia advanced on Brian as he backed away, poking

her finger into his chest with every word. "For the last time. I don't care what you have to say. What you have to say is immaterial to me. You used me. You lied to me. You insulted my intelligence."

Olivia barely saw the crowd parting as she backed Brian towards the exit. She knew without having to look that her friends were following in her wake, backing her up.

"We, and by we, I mean this entire town, is fed up with the machinations of the Gills. You and your villainous swag-bellied barnacle of a father have run rough shod over this town and its citizens for far too long. You have two choices. You can keep pushing yourselves where you don't belong, or you can go back to your house, sit on your piles of money and think about what you can do to become better human beings."

With the last word he stumbled out of the pub and the bouncer yanked the door shut. Olivia was almost out of breath. She hadn't even seen the bouncer open the door in the first place. The pub was silent for a second before a roar filled her ears. She turned around and found the entire room cheering.

Warmth shot through her entire body. They were cheering for her. Charlie and Delilah hooked their arms through hers as the women returned to the table.

"That was spectacular." Tess smiled as they all took their seats.

Olivia felt a slap on her back that almost sent her face first through the table. "Drinks are on the house tonight," Lily's father announced before giving his daughter an affectionate hug and returning to his place behind the bar.

Olivia didn't know what had come over her. The next few minutes were filled with the other patrons of the bar stopping by to thank her for telling Brian off. It seemed the Gills had taken advantage of the town for long enough and with each setback the beleaguered citizens were stepping forward and finding the strength to push back.

Once things had settled down, and Lily' father had sent over another round of drinks, Olivia took a breath.

"First, that was awesome." Delilah lifted a beer to toast Olivia.

"Thank you." Olivia sipped her soda water.

Charlie put her elbows on the table. "What's second?"

Olivia turned to her. "What do you mean?"

"She said 'first.'" Charlie nodded at Delilah. "That means there's a second. So, what's second?"

The other women at the table exchanged glances.

Lily sighed. "Watch your back. Junior will likely lay low and let that go, but it's going to get back to Senior. He doesn't take kindly to the Gill name being tarnished. The empire of terror he took over from his father is crumbling, and he's getting desperate."

Olivia's hand went to her stomach. She hadn't thought about the danger.

"Don't scare her," Delilah snapped.

"I'm not trying to scare her," Lily returned. "I want her to be careful." She looked at Olivia and seemed to be choosing her words carefully. "I'm probably overreacting. But, I see a lot in my line of work I wish I could unsee. So, just, be careful. That's all."

Delilah, Tess and Charlie continued to scoff at Lily's dire warning, but Olivia was all too familiar with how far a cornered bully would go to protect what he thought was his.

"I understand." Olivia reached out and squeezed Lily's hand. "Nick barely leaves me alone as it is. This is going to have him going into overprotective overtime."

"What's the story with you two?" Lily asked.

Olivia thought for a moment about how to answer the question. The other women at the table and Nick's friends and family knew about her pregnancy. She was still a few weeks from her second trimester and didn't want to make a public announcement until she was well past that stage. But

Lily had probably heard Olivia was pregnant the night she'd gotten sick and knocked herself out on the side of the road.

"We're having twins," Olivia blurted trying to keep her voice down.

Lily blinked and then blinked again. "Wow. Twins." She took a breath and smiled. "I'm a twin. Good luck with that."

I'm going to need it.

"I'm going to kill that son of a bitch." Nick paced the small office he shared with Bob. It was in the main portion of the athletic department, a few doors down from the football staff's offices.

"Calm down." The older man sat in his chair, watching Nick.

"Calm down? Calm down? That bastard came up to her in a public bar. He's always lurking around campus. He's fucking stalking her."

The town was buzzing with the story of the confrontation between Brian and Olivia. Everyone was praising the feisty English professor who'd given the one of the town bullies a piece of her mind.

"I wouldn't go that far. Seems he's got something say to her, but she's not willing to listen."

Nick stared at Bob. "And it's all right for him to try and get her alone when she wants nothing to do with him?"

"Didn't say that."

"What did you say then?" He wanted to put his fist through something. Preferably Backup's face.

"I'm trying to keep you from going off half-cocked." Bob crossed his arms.

"Believe me. When I find that son of a bitch I'm going in fully loaded." It would be a cold day in hell before that bastard went near Olivia again.

Bob blew out a breath. "That's what I'm trying to avoid."

"You're protecting him?" Nick couldn't believe Bob was sticking up for Backup.

"No." Bob's firm, quiet voice echoed in the office. "I'm protecting you."

"From what?" He could handle Backup with one arm tied behind his back.

"From blowing your shot here."

"Gill's a threat to this program. I'm going to get fired for dealing with it?" That was ass backwards.

"I'm not talking about the program."

"What are you talking about?" He wished Bob would just spit it out.

"I'm talking about Olivia. She's a good woman. The kind of woman that can give a man a solid base. You got a raw deal fourteen years ago. I admire you for taking the bullet for the women in your life then, but it cost you your first shot. This job. It's not your second shot. She is."

Bob was right. Nick took a deep breath. "So what am I supposed to do? Let Gill slink around and harass her?"

"No. You're supposed to keep your head. You've been in combat. When shit hit the fan did you lose it and go berserk?"

Nick took another deep breath. Bob was right. He needed to keep it together. Letting emotion or frustration take over would only lead to mistakes, which could get Olivia hurt.

"What do you think I should do?"

"You make sure she's protected, and we need to figure out what else the Gills are up to."

"The protection I can handle. The question is how we figure out what's going on with the Gills." It's not like they were sitting around staring at walls, they were trying to get a bead on what the Gills were planning.

"I mean there's more to this than a university football

314

program. There has to be," Bob observed.

"Like what?" It hadn't occurred to Nick to look beyond the program, but then he'd been focused on his responsibilities and not the big picture.

"Don't know. The Gills have been around King's Folly almost as long as the Kings. They've spent that much time trying to prove they're better than the founding family and just about everyone else who set foot in this town."

Nick had heard some stories about the Gills. It was hard to avoid them the way Senior and Junior were making moves on the program. He hadn't realized their bullshit went back that far.

He ran a hand through his hair and down to the back of his neck "So right now we what? Play defense until we figure out what's going on?"

Bob nodded. "All we can do. We go on offense without enough information we're asking for trouble. We've got feelers out, trying figure out their game plan. When we know more, we can do more."

Nick nodded. He didn't have to like the fact that Bob was right. Protecting Olivia and the football program was all that mattered. Nick glanced at his watch. It was almost time for him and Bob to interview assistants for the strength program. Then they were meeting with Cade and

Ed to go over the status of recruiting.

He pulled out his planner. There wasn't enough time to run across campus and check on Olivia.

"You want to go see her," Bob observed.

Nick should be upset that he was that obvious, but he couldn't be. "Yeah. But I don't have time. Besides. She's got a class in a few minutes."

Bob laughed. "Pick up the phone. Check on your professor. Get your head on straight. We've got a lot of work to do."

Nick nodded. He tried calling Olivia, but her cell phone went to voice mail and her assistant said she'd already left for class. He'd have to see her later at home. Home. Had he ever had one of those?

That evening, Nick walked into Olivia's house. She was right behind him. It had been a crazy, but uneventful day, at least as far as the Gills were concerned.

Things were getting busy with the football program. Cade and Ed had lined up ten players willing to take a shot on Cormac in exchange for a guaranteed spot on the team, if they brought their grades up. They still had another couple of dozen young men to contact. There were ten more scholarships to fill.

The house was quiet when they walked in the front

door. Too quiet. Kate had taken to lurking around corners and pouncing on him. She didn't get between him and Olivia and she never attacked to draw blood. It might be nuts, but he got a kick out of her games. The pup was cute as hell trying to take him down.

She didn't disappoint tonight. He walked by the living room and, as he passed by a chair near the doorway, Kate bounded over the top of the chair and onto his back. She bounced off him and landed on the floor, then proceeded to latch on to his jeans with her teeth.

Olivia giggled behind him, reminding him why he put up with this game. Because Olivia's laugh was the best sound he'd ever heard and anything that made her laugh was alright with him.

"Is your mother mad at me?" She nibbled her lip.

Her question seemed to come out of the blue, but the look in her eyes told him she'd been stewing on it since lunch the other day.

"No. She's not." He tried to reassure her.

"Why did she start acting so short with me?"

"She was freaking out. It's been a long time since she had anything to live for. And with the cancer, she's afraid she's getting a glimpse at something she's never going to get." It made sense when she'd explained it to him. He'd clued Delilah in who'd patted him on the head and told him to let the grown-ups handle it.

"Is there anything I can do?" Olivia asked.

If there was, he didn't know what it was. "Delilah says she's got it covered, but I think she's going to have to figure out her stuff on her own. She knows she's not alone."

"That sounds like part of the problem. I understand it."

"Why?" He didn't think Olivia and his mother had anything in common.

"I've been on my own for a long time. I was let down by all the people I was supposed to be able to trust." She set her bag down on the chair in the front hall and moved into the kitchen.

"Which is nothing like my mom, who let down everyone who was supposed to be able to trust her." He followed Olivia.

"That's not what I'm saying." She pulled a couple of glasses out of the cabinet. "Sweet tea?"

He nodded. "Thanks. What are you saying?"

"When you find yourself alone, you either learn to live your life that way or fade away. She learned to live that way. Now, she's surrounded by people telling her she's not alone. It can be daunting. Add her illness and it must be terrifying to have so much in front of you that you're not sure you'll be able to have."

"Are you feeling intimidated or something?" He couldn't imagine she was.

She smiled. "Or something." Olivia opened the fridge and pulled out a pitcher.

He stepped forward and took the pitcher out of her hand. "Do you need to work it out on your own, or can I help?"

"You've already helped."

"How?" He poured their drinks then put the pitcher back in fridge.

"By being someone I can trust."

Her words felt like a gun shot to his gut. They still hadn't talked about the night that changed his life. He'd been putting it off because he was terrified that she wouldn't look at him the same way after she knew the truth.

"Listen —"

The doorbell interrupted his attempt to bring up the subject.

"Hold that thought." She smiled. Olivia went to answer the door with him right behind her.

Lily was on the other side with her egotistical student, what was her name? Lydell?

"Sorry to bother you had home, Olivia. We have a situation."

Olivia stepped aside so Lily could escort the young woman inside.

"What's going on?" Nick came to stand behind Olivia and put an arm around her waist.

"We caught this young woman trying to break into your office."

"What? Why?" Olivia stared at the young woman whose face was red and splotchy from crying.

The young woman tried to speak, but stared sobbing again. Olivia led her into the living room and ushered her to the couch.

"Did she say anything before you got her here?" Nick looked at Lily.

The woman nodded. "She has something to tell Olivia."

"What? That she' a freaking stalker?" Nick's raised voice made the young woman cry louder.

Olivia glared at him. "Shhh." She turned back to her student. "Ms. Lydell. Claire. You have to calm down and tell me what' wrong."

After a few minutes, the young woman finally got herself under control.

"You're my sister," she blurted.

Olivia sat back and stared at the woman on her couch like she was an alien.

"She's your what?" Nick looked at Olivia. She'd never mentioned having a sister.

Olivia took a deep breath. "You'll need to explain that."

"We have the same father," Claire whispered.

Olivia hadn't talked about her father much, but the little she did tell Nick made him believe that it was certainly possible there was a secret family out there somewhere. Hell, there could be more than one.

"Why didn't you tell me before?" Olivia took her hand.

"My mother said…well she said a lot of things about you and your mother that made me think you wouldn't welcome a younger sister."

"I see. Why did you come here?"

It looked to him like Olivia was taking her time processing the information Claire was sharing. He stood, muscles rigid, waiting for any sign Olivia needed him for anything.

"I always wanted an older sister. I just…wanted to get to know you. I thought if I could show you I was smart too, you'd see we have something in common and you might like me a little bit."

That explained why she was always trying to dominate

Olivia's class. Claire wanted to be the star student and impress her big sister.

"And why were you breaking into my office?"

The young woman blushed. "I found out about you and Coach Jacobs, about the baby. I wanted to leave you another present," she whispered.

"The teddy bear was from you?" Nick stepped forward. This was getting weird.

She nodded. He wasn't crazy about the situation, but the young woman looked miserable and if it was all as innocent as she made it sound that was one less potential threat he needed to worry about.

"I...so all this time, your attitude in my class. It was to show me how smart you were? So I would like you?" Olivia sounded confused.

The young woman nodded and burst into tears again. After a moment, Olivia scooted forward and took the crying girl into her arms. Lily nudged Nick and they both stepped out of the room.

"What are you going to do?" He led Lily into the kitchen to give Olivia and Claire some time.

"I have to file a report, but it's going to say she freaked out about a late assignment and broke into the building to try and turn something in. I'll say I took her to her professor to address the situation. That should be the end of it." Lily stopped just inside the kitchen and kept her eyes on the living room doorway.

"Thanks." He was grateful Claire wouldn't get into any trouble.

"No problem. Kid's got a lot on her plate, Olivia too." Lily voiced Nick's thoughts.

"Let me know if there's any blowback." He wasn't sure what he could do about it, but Lily had had his and Olivia's back since the night they'd met. He'd have hers if she needed him.

She smiled a smile he could only call predatory. "Always have blowback in my job, but I doubt I will over this."

There was a story there, but not one Nick would worry about tonight. Tonight, he needed to deal with the soap opera in the next room. A long-lost sister. Who'd believe it?

Chapter 14

A sister. She had a sister. Ever since Claire had showed up in the first class of the summer there had been something about her that had niggled at the back of Olivia's mind. When Claire confessed her secret, Olivia finally realized what had been bothering her. Clair had their father's eyes.

"I don't know what to say." Olivia reached for a tissue and handed it to Claire.

Claire dabbed at her eye and blew her nose. "I know I've messed everything up and you won't want to get to know me."

"Why now?"

"I didn't know who you were. My mom told me all these stories about why our father couldn't marry her and that he loved us very much. Last year I found a scrapbook she kept hidden about him, his trial, everything. I confronted her, and she lost it."

"Why?" Olivia knew she was repeating herself, but she couldn't process this information fast enough to come up with more in-depth questions to ask.

"She's not a person who deals well with reality. She built up this whole fantasy over the years that took the place of what really happened. When I confronted her with it, she didn't handle it well."

Olivia grabbed Claire's hand. "What did she do?"

"A lot of yelling and throwing things."

"Did she hurt you?" Olivia wanted to hug her sister. Sister. That was easier to get used to than she would have thought.

"Not physically."

"I'm sorry." Olivia squeezed Claire's hand.

"It's not your fault."

"I wish I'd known about you. I always wanted a sister."

Claire smiled for the first time since Olivia had met her. It was another feature she shared with their father, and Olivia.

"I should have just come to you and told you who I was." Claire sounded frustrated with herself.

"Yes, well, that certainly would have been easier on all of us. Why didn't you?"

"My mom said you wouldn't want anything to do with me because I was the reason your mom died." Claire's voice dropped to a whisper so quiet Olivia almost didn't hear her.

"Why are you the reason my mother died?"

Claire took a deep breath. "My mom gave our dad an ultimatum. He had to marry my mom or stop seeing her. I

325

guess he killed your mom so he could be with mine."

Claire's stared at her hand, fisted in her lap. The woman's agony called to Olivia and her words answered a question that had plagued Olivia for thirteen years. Why, after sixteen years of tolerating his life with his wife had her father decided she had to die. Olivia knew divorce wasn't an option in her father's family, even if he had another family that he wanted to be with.

"I'm so sorry I got your mother killed."

This was too much. "You didn't." Olivia scooted forward and pulled Clair into her arms.

"If my mother hadn't given him an ultimatum because of me your mother would still be alive."

"I hate to tell you this, but our father was a bastard." Olivia's vehement statement cut through Claire's sobs. "I doubt he would have married your mother if he'd gotten away with killing mine."

Claire pulled back and stared at her wide-eyed. "I don't understand."

"Our father was a spoiled, entitled bully who didn't listen to anyone but his mother. And he only listened to her because she held the purse strings."

Claire looked down. "I only saw him every few weeks. He didn't pay much attention to me."

"He didn't pay much attention to me either. He was a selfish man. If he got away with murdering my mother, he planned on buying a beach house in Malibu and setting himself up as a film producer, so he could have access to lots of young women desperate enough to trade sex for a shot at stardom." The memory of his plans still made Olivia nauseous.

"What?" Claire's shock was audible.

"I overheard a conversation between him and our grandmother a few days after my mother's funeral." Olivia put her hands on either side of Claire's face. "Your mother's ultimatum wasn't the reason he killed mine. I think he was feeling trapped by both his families, and he needed to get rid of my mother to escape."

"He wasn't going to stay with us?"

Olivia heard the desperate little girl in Claire's voice and recognized it. She'd been that little girl once, too. Desperate for a father's attention, a father's love.

"No. He wasn't."

Claire was silent for a moment. "Do you want me to go?"

The broken little girl in Olivia cried out at the thought of losing a sister she just found. "No. I want you to stay so we can get to know each other. Nick has a brother, so my babies will have an uncle. I think they'll need an aunt too."

The hope that bloomed in Claire's eyes told Olivia she'd made the right decision. For a woman who'd been resigned to spending her life alone, especially after she fell for Brian's lies, she was acquiring a lot of family and friends.

"Really?" Claire's whispered question was full of hope.

"Absolutely." Olivia grabbed another tissue and dabbed at the corner of Claire's eyes before handing the tissue to her to blow her nose.

"Okay."

Olivia glanced at the clock on the mantel. "It's late. Why don't you stay in the guest room tonight. We can talk in the morning."

Claire nodded. "I'd like that."

Breakfast the next morning was less awkward than Olivia anticipated. Kate adored her new playmate and, when she wasn't sneering at Nick, danced around Claire's feet with a look of adoration in her eyes.

Claire confided she'd always wanted a dog growing up, but her high strung mother didn't want anything that would mar the perfect home she tried to build to entice their father to stay.

Nick cleared his throat. "What's the plan for the day?"

Olivia smiled at him. He'd had a lot to say about welcoming Claire into her home, but he'd told Olivia he would back her up. Having someone in her corner as reliable and trustworthy as Nick was a new and heady experience.

"We're going to drop Claire off at her apartment on our way to campus, then I have a couple of meetings."

"Any more surprises?" Nick watched Claire.

She shook her head.

"You sure?"

Kate took that moment to abandon her new friend and pounce on Nick's feet.

"Really?" He looked under the table.

Olivia didn't know what got into Kate whenever Nick was in the house. If it looked like she was really trying to attack him, Olivia would be worried. But so far it seemed like the puppy loved to rough house with Nick.

"Claire and I are going to work on getting to know each other. No pressure on either of us."

He nodded. The rest of breakfast passed quickly and before she knew it, Olivia was sitting at her desk between meetings.

The door opened. She looked up expecting to see her assistant. Instead, Brian stood in the doorway.

"I'm calling security." It was getting creepy how he kept

showing up. She reached for the phone.

"Wait."

The desperate sound in his voice made her pause, but she left her hand over the phone. "Why won't you leave me alone?"

"You have to listen to me," he begged.

She ignored the thought at the back of her mind that said Brian wasn't the type to beg. "I don't have to do any-thing."

"I won't come any closer. Just listen to me. Let me say what I have to say then I'll go. I won't come near you again unless you call me."

She couldn't imagine any reason why she would volun-tarily call him. She left her hand resting on the phone. "Say what you have to say, then go."

He took a step forward.

"From there. No closer."

He sighed, like he was the one being imposed on and closed his eyes. "You need to watch out for Jacobs."

"Oh, this is too much." If he was going to start insulting Nick this was going to be a very short conversation.

"Do you know why he ended up in the military?"

They hadn't discussed it. She knew Cade had chosen the military over football for some reason and assumed Nick had done the same. Although there had been a mention about some problems in high school.

"He enlisted, like most people do."

"He had a choice. Prison or the military."

"That's ridiculous. I won't sit here and listen to your lies." Nick was one of the most straight forward men she knew. He would never be close to going to prison.

"He killed a girl."

"Get out." Olivia stood so quickly her chair toppled back in to her credenza.

"Everyone knows about it." He pulled an envelope from his back pocket. "The stories are all here."

"Get out." She reached for the phone.

He put the envelope down on the chair closest to the doorway. "Call me if you need anything."

She stared at the empty doorway, shaking. Had he just accused Nick of being a killer? Olivia stomped over to the envelope and picked it up to throw it away. She didn't care what lies Brian had concocted.

An article fell out of the envelope and drifted to the floor. She looked down and saw Nick's face staring back at her in what was clearly a high school football picture. It was the ubiquitous pose of a player in full pads and on one knee. Next to his picture was the picture of a young girl, smiling and full of life. Olivia picked up article and read it.

The paper drifted from her fingers and floated back to the ground. She sank to the floor, oblivious. After a moment she realized that she still had a full envelope in her hand. She looked inside and pulled out the stack of articles. Each one more gruesome than they last.

There were tributes to the girl, Tiffany, who died instantly in a drunk driving accident with Nick behind the wheel. There were stories from her friends about how Nick had always been jealous of her friendship with his girlfriend. There had been two bags of marijuana in his truck, found after the accident. Through it all he remained silent.

The prosecutor was going for the maximum sentence. He should still be serving time. Then there was a small article noting that the charges had been reduced and Nick had agreed to join the military. In exchange, his record would be expunged after his first tour of duty.

Nick was a killer. Oh, God. She really was her mother. Memories of the time right after her mother's death assaulted her. The pain of her loss. The confusion. Her father's lies and his refusal to take responsibility, even at the end.

"Olivia?"

She barely heard his voice. It felt like there was a mound

of cotton between her and the rest of the world.

"What's all this?" He squatted down next to her. His hand stilled over one of the articles.

"Where —" He yanked his hand back like it was burned.

"Is this all true? Did you kill this girl and get away with it?"

He sighed. "It wasn't me. I wasn't driving."

The world rushed back in and through her. The words "it wasn't me" echoed in her brain. The memory of her father saying the same thing to Detective Harmon right before he'd pointed the finger at Olivia.

"Get out." She couldn't control the pain and the rage that roiled inside her.

"Olivia, we need to talk about this," he begged.

"You need to get out. I never want to see you again." She couldn't even look at him right now.

He sucked in a breath. "You don't mean that. The babies —"

She stood in a fluid motion she didn't know she was capable of. "You won't go anywhere near my babies. Do you hear me? Get out." Her yell was probably audible through the rest of the building, but she didn't care. She couldn't let anyone hurt her children the way her father had hurt her.

The memories from her childhood were all she could see. All she could feel.

"Please, let's talk about it." He held out his hands, palms up, pleading with her.

"There's nothing to talk about. I won't have my children raised by a killer." She spat the words, wishing her mother had the courage to walk away from her father before she was born.

His face turned cold as he closed himself off. She'd never seen him look like that before. "I won't bother you. But if you need me, you only have to call."

She wasn't going to call. She couldn't. The similarities between her and her mother ended today.

◀🏈▶ ◀🏈▶ ◀🏈▶

Looks like he was going to turn into his old man after all. Nick took a swig of scotch. It burned his throat and gut. Until tonight he'd always limited himself to a couple of beers when he wasn't driving. Seemed like a good night to stop being so controlled. What did he have to stay sober for anyway?

Somewhere along the way he'd fallen in love with Olivia and she'd cut him out of her life with more precision

than a laser. He could push the issue about seeing the babies, but why bother? He didn't want to set his kids up for
some drawn out custody battle that would only hurt them.

Besides, Olivia was right. He was no good. Why should
he get a happy ending?

"What the actual fuck?"

His brother's voice sounded farther away than the
waves crashing against the beach. He didn't bother to respond. There was no point. No point to anything really. After all the years of fighting for a chance to prove he was a
good man, the only person whose opinion he cared about
believed it wasn't true.

He took another swig from the bottle. No reason to answer his brother. No reason to do anything anymore.

"What the hell are you doing?" Simon yelled.

"What's it look like?" Nick bit out.

"Looks like you're getting shitfaced. Not hard to do considering it looks like you've downed half a bottle of scotch
and you're a complete fucking light-weight."

"Olivia and I are done." The words hollowed him out.
Even when he'd been staring at serious time in prison he'd
never felt this empty.

"What does that mean?"

"Means she found about what I did, and she wants

nothing to do with me."

"That's nuts. You didn't do anything." His brother's anger whipped at him, stronger than the wind coming off the ocean.

"I didn't stop anything either." He'd been glad when Brandi and Tiffany left the party that night. Hated it when they got that way. It was only when he realized Brandi had grabbed his keys that he'd gone after them. More worried about the truck he'd gotten from a Bama alum than the girls.

"Dude. Get off the fucking cross, somebody else needs the wood." His brother ripped the bottle out of his hand.

Nick blinked. "What the fuck does that mean?"

"It means you got a raw deal. You tried to stop your spoiled girlfriend from doing something stupid. She did it anyway and killed her best friend. You ended up taking the fall for her."

Nick didn't really need a recitation of the night. But the way his brother was winding up, it didn't look like he was going to let himself get interrupted.

"Instead of being a human being, she proved she was a selfish brat and not only let you take he fall but put herself front and center of the whole cluster fuck as the tragic heroine. Add to that getting busted with Mom's pot in your truck and you got royally screwed by the women in your life."

"You're not really telling me anything I don't know." The ocean breeze and Simon's anger were cutting through the fog of booze and self-pity.

"Well quit acting like an idiot then." Simon hurled the half empty bottle into the ocean.

"What the fuck is your deal?" He was the one who'd been dumped by the woman he loved. Simon had no reason to be this pissed.

"My deal is that the you're the best fucking man I know. You've taken the scraps life has thrown at you for fourteen years and acted like you don't deserve more."

"I don't." It was the truth. If he hadn't been such a dick to Brandi and Tiffany that night, everything might have been different.

"Why? What great sin have you actually committed that you don't deserve to be happy?"

"I didn't stop them from driving away in my truck." Did he have to keep saying it to make people understand?

Simon pinched the bridge of his nose. "Did you leave your keys in it?"

"No. Brandi fished them out of my pocket." It had been one of her better moves, seducing him to snag his keys or sometimes his cash from his pocket. He'd been a horny seventeen-year-old who fell for it every time.

"What did you do when you realized she had them?" Simon hunkered down in front of Nick.

"I followed them, but they were pulling away from the house?"

"What happened next?" Simon pushed.

Why was he making him relive this? "I jumped in the back of the truck. I wanted to stop them."

The night came rushing back. He could still feel the bed of his truck, hear his voice screaming at Brandi to stop and her answering laughter. Then the screeching tires, the screams and the slam of the truck that propelled him forward and left him with bruises over the right side of his body.

"But you couldn't."

His brother's quiet words ricocheted through his head. He couldn't stop them. He'd been so sure of his own superiority. Drunk on the power of being a teenage athlete, sure of his own invincibility, he'd been sure he could stop the train wreck unfolding in front of him. It had been a huge blow to his ego that he hadn't.

"No."

"Then, the cops found Mom's stash in your truck and

338

you were screwed." His brother finished the story.

Nick flopped onto his back. "Story of my life."

"Only because you let it be."

"When did you turn into Yoda?"

His brother snorted. "Listen, you will."

"Fine." Nick let out a breath.

"You've been punishing yourself for fourteen years because you couldn't control events the way you wanted to. Maybe it's time to let go of the shit you couldn't control and focus on the shit you can."

"Which is exactly nothing." Everything in his life was up to other people.

"Bullshit." Simon stood and kicked Nick's boot with his own.

"She wants nothing to do with me." Saying the words made Nick's stomach turn.

Fuck me, I'm going to puke.

"How did she find out?"

Nick rolled over and took a few deep breaths. "No idea. I found her in her office surrounded by clippings from all the local newspapers that covered the accident and aftermath."

"Who the fuck gave her that garbage?"

That was a good question. Olivia wouldn't have gone

looking for it. Someone had to give it to her. Someone who'd gone digging themselves, because those clippings were from fourteen-year-old Alabama papers. No fucking way would someone find those without doing some serious investigation, or without a connection in Alabama.

Nick sat up. He regretted it when the scotch he'd been drinking curdled his stomach.

Simon jumped back. "If you're going to puke aim that way."

Easier said than done. As the contents of his stomach came roaring up from his stomach he was reminded of one of the many reasons he rarely drank. He couldn't handle his fucking booze. That was his last coherent thought before everything went black.

If the tiny dwarves in his head didn't top their pounding, he was going to lose what was left of his mind. Nick thought dying was preferable to the noise. A flapping noise followed by a blinding light made the sadistic dwarves look like fuzzy bunnies.

Nick blinked. The hazy figure standing in front of the, now uncovered, window shimmered before it turned into his brother.

Nick covered his eyes with his forearm. "Go away, fucker."

"Rise and shine, buttercup."

Nick reached blindly for something to shut his brother up. He found one of his boots, grabbed the heel and hurled it at the smirking man. His brother was sober and wide awake, so he easily sidestepped the boot.

"You've got shit to do. Get up." Simon showed no mercy.

Memories of the night before came rushing back. "Fuck off."

"Nope. You're going to get up, shower and get your life together."

"How the fuck am I supposed to do that?" Olivia wanted nothing to do with him.

"Dealing with the smell first would be a good idea."

Nick tried to ignore his brother, but a deep breath told him Simon was right. He stank. He rolled over and put his feet on the floor. He felt like he'd been run over by an entire defensive line. Multiple times.

"Get moving," Simon barked.

Since when had his little brother turned into a drill instructor? "What the hell?"

"Like I said, sunshine. You've got shit to do. Your little tantrum last night was it for your wallowing."

"I can do what I want." He sounded stupid, even to

himself.

"Sure. You can piss your life away, turn into a drunk like the old man. Or you can get your shit together and get your woman back."

"Those my only two choices?" One wasn't appealing. The other was impossible.

"You really want another one?"

No. He didn't want the first choice his brother had offered. He wanted Olivia and their life together with the babies they'd already created and any others that came along. He wished he knew how he was going to get it.

"Shower first. Strategy next." Simon seemed to read his mind.

Nick felt almost human again after his shower and found his mother and brother still in the kitchen, eating.

"No Delilah?"

"I'm taking Mom to her appointment. Delilah's..." Simon looked like he was finding the words.

"Pissed and staying away?" Nick wouldn't be surprised if Delilah was creating replicas of him to burn in effigy.

His mother snorted. "Something like that. Should have told Olivia the truth."

"Thanks. It's not like I don't know that now." He had no one to blame but himself, because he'd had lots of chances to give her the whole story.

"Knew it before, too." His mother studied him over her coffee.

"Yes. I should have told her from the start. I am a dumbass. Is there anything else?"

His mother shrugged. "That about covers it."

For weeks he'd been telling himself that he should sit down with Olivia and tell her everything. Having his family's "I told you so's" shoved in his face on top of his own wasn't helping.

It was taking his booze crippled brain a little longer to catch on than usual.

"Anyone have any bright ideas on what I should do next?" He'd take all the help he could get.

"Talk to Olivia," his mother said at the same time his brother said, "Find out who's gunning for you."

Nick sat back in his chair. He had a feeling he would need more to convince Olivia that he deserved another shot, and he wanted to know who had fed her the story before he had a chance to tell her himself.

He looked at Simon. "Any clues on how I can figure out who tipped her off?"

Simon shrugged. "Who's got an axe to grind and something to gain?"

Nick stared at his brother. They were good questions. Who wanted him and Olivia apart? Who could get their hand on copies of those articles?

There was only one person who came to mind.

"I've got to have a conversation with Gill."

Thirty minutes later, Nick parked his truck in front of the McMansion Gill called home. He reached for the door handle for his truck.

"Careful." Simon grabbed his shoulder. "You don't want to make things worse."

Nick didn't think things could get any worse, but he knew he wouldn't have a shot of getting Olivia back if the situation escalated. "I'm just going to talk to him."

"Right." His brother hopped out of the passenger side of his truck. "Then I'm just along for the ride."

He would never say it, but Nick was grateful for his brother's presence. It was good to have someone watching his back.

The front door of the house opened before they made it up the front steps.

"What do you want, Jacobs?" Brian stood in the door-way, eyes bloodshot. It looked like he hadn't shaved in a couple of days and he was moving like he'd been run over by a truck, or a freight train.

"I want to know what the fuck your problem is." What had he done to this man, besides accept a job?

"Fuck off. She's better off without you."

How the hell would this douche know? "You don't know me."

"I know your kind." Brian sounded tired. And done.

"My kind? My kind? What the fuck is my kind?"

"You and Maguire and that team of losers you're putting together. You're all the same. You think you're hot shit and the world owes you. You don't care about anyone but yourselves."

The level of shit this asshole was spewing was in danger of choking them all.

"Are you fucking kidding me? Everything you've ever gotten you've gotten because of your rich daddy."

Brian blinked. Something like pain flashed in his eyes but was gone so quickly it might never have been there. "You don't know shit about me."

"Right back at ya' pretty boy. The only difference is I didn't feel the need to step up and fuck up your life for you."

"Are you fucking kidding me? You and the whole crew you're running with have been fucking up my life for years. Starting the day Cade "the all mighty" Maguire signed with

345

Cormac and stole my shot at getting the fuck out of here."

This was going nowhere. "Where did you get the clippings?"

"What clippings?" The other man studied his fingernails.

"How about we not do this anymore. Okay, Gill? Instead of never ending rounds of screwing with each other, how about you just play it straight for once in your fucking life."

Gill looked up and stared at him as if he was thinking. It would be a shock to know this guy had one unselfish thought a day. He looked over Nick's shoulder and narrowed his eyes. Nick and Simon turned around to see Gill Senior step out of the backseat of a Cadillac.

"Fine. You want to know?" Brian nodded at his father. "He gave me the clippings. Got 'em from your ex-girlfriend." Brian turned around and walked back into his house, slamming the door behind him. The sound of three locks clicking into place echoed in Nick's head.

"You're trespassing, Jacobs." Brian Gill, Sr. looked nothing like his son. The older man's dark hair was greying and receding. His paunch was pronounced.

"We're leaving." Nick stared at the older man. There was something in his eyes that gave Nick the chills. Junior had always struck Nick as a waste of potential. Senior just gave off an air of menace that made Nick think he'd never had any real potential to begin with.

Nick and Simon ambled to the truck. They needed to get out of here, but he'd be damned if he showed Gill Senior any weakness to exploit. As they pulled away, Nick could see Senior standing at the front door banging on it. Junior didn't seem inclined to let him in. As he pulled out on the street, he saw a sheriff's cruiser pull up, Lily behind the will. She gave him a wave of her hand before she pulled into Brian's driveway.

Did Brian actually call the cops on his father?

Maybe there was more going on than they all thought. Whatever. The Gills weren't his concern at the moment. He needed to talk to Brandi and find out why she'd torpedoed his life.

Again.

Chapter 15

Olivia was numb as she sat in Dr. Wyatt's office. It was her first appointment since Nick had left her office and the first one he'd missed since she'd told him she was pregnant.

It hadn't taken long for word to spread among her friends. Tess, Charlie and Delilah had shown up on her doorstep within hours of Nick leaving her office. Claire hadn't been far behind them.

She was too numb to do more than be led around the house and eat and drink whatever was put in front of her. They asked her what happened, but she couldn't respond. The memories of her past were muddled up with the memories of the life she'd been building with Nick. Rational thought wasn't something she was capable of. Fortunately, they didn't push. They just stayed with her. Claire had assumed the role of protective sister and spent the night.

It was nice. Not being alone. But they weren't Nick.

At least the need to pee was distracting her at the moment. She'd had to drink multiple glasses of water this morning to ensure the best visibility for the scan. Olivia sighed and shifted in her chair.

"Deep thoughts." Lily's voice pulled Olivia back to the present.

"What are you doing here?"

Lily shrugged. "Little birdie told me about your appointment. Thought maybe you'd want some company."

"A little birdie? You mean Nick."

"Simon." Lily sat next to Olivia.

"Why would Nick's brother send you?"

"Because you're still family to them."

"I'm not anything to them." If she said it enough times, maybe she would believe it.

"Not my business. You are my friend. That means I'm here if you need me." Lily leaned back and stretched her legs out in front of her, like she wasn't planning on going anywhere.

Olivia thought about asking her to leave but decided against it. The last time she'd felt this betrayed, she'd retreated behind a wall, determined to spend her life alone. She rubbed her belly. Alone wasn't an option, and she refused to raise her children isolated from the world.

Since coming to King's Folly, she'd built a life and a community here. There was no reason to cut herself off from all of it because of Nick's lies.

"Thank you."

Lily smiled.

"What's with you and Brian?" The other woman's attitude toward Gill Junior had niggled at Olivia since their girls' night out.

"Why do you think there's something between us?" Lily looked at her.

"I don't know. You just seem…protective of him."

"Olivia Valenti." The nurse's call prevented Lily from responding. Not that it looked like she was going to. Olivia made a note of Lily's reaction and promised herself she'd get back to this discussion another time.

Twenty minutes later, the ultrasound tech was rubbing jelly on Olivia's belly, preparing to administer the second ultrasound of her pregnancy. As excited as she was to see the babies, she was almost more excited that she'd get to go the bathroom in a little while.

I don't remember having to pee this badly the last time?

"There we go." The tech's voice drew Olivia's thoughts from her full bladder to the screen where a picture of her babies was fuzzy and gray.

"Wow," Lily whispered. "Look at those little jelly beans."

It felt wrong. Nick should be here. Olivia pushed the thought away and focused on the image of her babies. "Are they all right?"

The tech nodded. "They look good." She hit a few keys on the keyboard, taking measurements. "Good size. Development looks normal."

"Can you tell their sex, yet?" She and Nick hadn't discussed finding out during the pregnancy. Would he want to know? Why did she care?

"Sometimes." The tech narrowed her eyes and focused on the screen. "Usually you get a clearer view of the sex at thirteen to fourteen weeks."

"Are they giving you and signs?" Lily asked. She glanced at Olivia. "Sorry. You're deal, not mine."

"That's all right." Olivia laughed. The twinge from her bladder made her wish she hadn't.

"Looks like yours are going to take a little time before announcing themselves." The tech looked from the screen to Olivia. "Do you want a copy to take with you?"

"Yes, please." Olivia couldn't believe it. The first picture of her children.

"Better make it a dozen." Lily added.

"What?" Olivia looked at her.

"Whatever is going on with you and Nick, these babies have a big family. Better get used to it now."

Lily's words still ran through Olivia's mind a few hours later as she studied the picture of her babies. They were

Nick's too. Could she really keep him from them? Did she want to? She set the picture down and stared at the envelope full of articles sitting at the corner of her desk. If lay there, like a snake, coiled up and ready to strike.

Ready to? It struck yesterday and ruined everything.

A knock on her door interrupted her thoughts.

"Come in." She wasn't sure she was up for company, but she could use the distraction.

Rush walked in. His perfectly tailored sport coat clung to his shoulders, giving a hint of the muscles that must be hidden by the fabric. He moved with a dancer's grace, which made sense. She'd learned he was a competitive ballroom dancer before coming to Cormac. A fact that one of his students had discovered and shared with her friends. Which meant the entire campus knew.

She stood. "Hi, Rush. What brings you by?"

"I wanted to check on you. I heard you and Nick..." His voice trailed off.

"Word really spreads quickly." She'd never been on the inside of a story that spread through the Cormac grapevine.

He smiled. "Small town and a university. Two time-tested and guaranteed conductors of gossip. Combine them and stories spread exponentially faster."

"Is that a scientific finding?" She wished she could

laugh.

He shrugged. "We'll call it Avery's Law."

She nodded toward the sofa. "Would you like to have a seat?"

"Thank you." He moved to the couch, then sat. "I wanted to see how you were doing, and, if it's not too impertinent, give you some advice."

She sat in the chair opposite him. "I'll be happy to listen."

"But you won't guarantee you'll take it." He studied her.

It was her turn to shrug.

He blew out a breath. "Some time ago, I met an amazing woman." He rubbed his chin. "I met the woman."

Olivia leaned forward but didn't interrupt him.

"There was something I didn't tell her. Unfortunately, when she found out, because of the way she found out, she believed things that weren't true, about me. About us."

"I don't know what —"

He held up a hand. "I'm not equating my secret to Nick's. What I can tell you is she stormed out of my life and refused to hear me out or give me the benefit of the doubt. And said some unforgivable things on the way out the door. We hadn't been together for very long. Logically, I can understand her anger. Her sense of betrayal. But if I saw her again today, I don't think I could forgive her."

"Forgive her? You kept something from her. It sounds like it was something important."

"It was. I'm not excusing it." His eyes met hers.

"Why didn't you just tell her everything."

He ran a hand through his perfectly trimmed hair. "Probably the same reason Nick didn't talk to you. Insecurity."

"Insecurity?" She choked out. "What do either of you have to be insecure about?"

"I can't speak for Nick. What I can say is that men are human. We make mistakes. Some of them are terrible mistakes, some of them are simply so stupid we can't believe we ever made them. For me, I wanted the woman I loved to see me for who I was when we met. Not who I was when I made such a ludicrous mistake. I thought if she could see me for the man I was, not the boy I'd been, everything would be all right."

Olivia didn't know what to say. There was something in Rush's words that made sense. Nick had been seventeen that night. Old enough to think he knew everything, too young to realize he didn't.

Rush stood. "I'm not telling you what to do. And I'm

certainly not equating your situation to mine. When Francesca left me, she didn't take my children with her. Easier to put that relationship in the past."

With that final thought, Rush moved by her, squeezing her shoulder briefly as he passed, then left the room.

She was alone. Again.

But do I have to be?

Fourteen years ago, Nick had sworn he'd never speak to Brandi again. Now he was back in his hometown, trying to do just that. He stopped by the judge's house, figuring he'd know where Nick could find Brandi.

He rubbed his hand down the side of his jeans as he waited for someone to answer the door. A moment later the door opened, and the man who'd saved Nick's ass fourteen years ago stood there. He didn't look like he was in his eighties. As far as Nick knew the old man was still on the bench, one of the good guys.

"Judge."

The man held out a hand to Nick, who shook it. "Call me Paul."

Nick didn't think he'd be able to do that, but he followed the man who had saved him from prison into his home.

"Sorry to bother you, but I was looking for Brandi. Not sure where to start." Nick hadn't kept up with anyone outside of his family and had made a point of staying away from any place that he could run into Brandi.

"She's not far from where you grew up."

Nick blinked. "What do you mean?"

"Her family had a run of bad luck right after you left. She made some bad decisions after that. Lives in a trailer not far from the one you grew up in."

Nick wasn't sure what he expected, but this wasn't it. After spending some time catching up with the judge, and promising to get him tickets to Cormac's first regular season game, he found himself back in the trailer park where he grew up.

He stood in front of the run-down trailer that looked worse than his mom's ever had.

What the hell happened to Brandi?

The front door creaked open. "You going to stand there all day?"

The voice was the same one that had followed him into his feverish adolescent dreams, yet it was also shockingly different. He stared at the woman in the doorway trying to see the girl she'd been. Her once bright blond hair was lank and almost greasy. Her complexion, that used to remind him of peaches was mottled and red.

"Brandi?" he croaked out her name, still not believing this woman was the girl he'd known.

"Figured you'd show up."

"Why?" He hadn't tried to see her for fourteen years.

"You never could leave things alone." She sounded resigned.

"No, I couldn't." If he had he wouldn't have been anywhere near the truck that night when the cops showed up. "Why did you do it?"

She didn't even ask him what he meant. "You deserved it."

"I deserved it?" He'd saved her from drunk driving charges. "I took the blame for you."

She sighed. "Might as well come in. No point in standing outside and doing this." Brandi shuffled back into the trailer.

He guessed that was a signal to follow or leave. He followed. The trailer looked worse on the inside. It was filthy. What the hell had happened to her?

Brandi slumped in a chair by the dirty window that let just enough light in to show off the trailer's grungy interior. She poured a shot of cheap whiskey into a glass and held the bottle out to him. He shook his head.

"What the hell happened to you?" He couldn't reconcile the girl he'd known with the woman sitting in front of him.

"Karma. That bitch."

"I don't understand." None of this made any sense.

"Course not. You got out. Always knew you would. I was stupid enough to think you'd take me with you."

"You stopped speaking to me after the accident. How the hell was I going to take you anywhere?" He'd tried calling before he shipped out. Her father told him not to call again. As far as he knew, Brandi was done with him.

"I had to. If I hadn't turned my back on you then they would have known. I couldn't go to prison," she whispered.

"You wouldn't have. They let me choose the military. You probably wouldn't have gotten more than probation." There was no way the perfect daughter of the richest man in town would have done any jail time.

"Because somehow Judge Strong figured out you weren't driving, and the pot wasn't yours. He found you a loophole. He would have thrown the book at me."

"You don't know —"

"I do. He told me." She poured herself another drink.

"What? When?" Had he entered an alternate reality?

358

"Right after you left. He came by the house. Told my dad he found out he'd tried to pay off the prosecutor to throw the book at you and that he knew why. He looked me right in the eye and said I should be grateful for you. If you hadn't been willing to take a stand for me he would have sent me to prison."

Nick ran a hand through his hair. "Fine. But it's not like that happened. You didn't have to — "

"To what? Pay a price? I paid. Believe me." She took a swig of her drink.

"What the hell happened to you?" He still couldn't believe this woman was the girl he knew. How had he never heard about what happened to her?

"You really kicked the dust of this town off, didn't you? Even when you came back, you didn't."

He pinched the bridge of his nose. "What does that mean?"

"You were big news for about thirty seconds. When you were gone the town latched on to an even bigger story."

"What's that?"

"Turns out my daddy was a crook. Left town before the prosecutors could get him and took all the money with him. He left us with nothing, but a black mark on our reputations and a mountain of debt we couldn't pay."

A lot of things clicked into place. "How much did you get for the clippings?"

She blushed. "Doesn't matter."

"I'd like to know what it was worth to sell me out this time."

"This time? This time?"

"You were driving the car that killed your best friend. Not me. You did that." He wasn't going to let her hide anymore.

"Don't you think I know that? I see her every night. I haven't had a good night's sleep in fourteen years." Tears pooled at the corners of her eyes.

"My heart bleeds for you." He did feel sorry for all she'd been through, but her inability to see beyond her own bullshit was pissing him off.

"You never saw it," she croaked.

"Never saw what?" He threw up his hands.

"You were the golden boy. I was the one hitching my life to your star. Then you crashed and burned."

He couldn't take much more of this. "Because of you."

"I know." She threw her glass. It hit the wall over his right shoulder and shattered, filling the air with the smell of cheap whiskey.

"What is wrong with you?"

"You blame me for costing you your ticket out. Did it ever occur to you that you were my ticket out?"

It hadn't. He didn't know what to say to that. Especially since she'd refused to see him before he left for the Navy.

"I killed my best friend and destroyed my life in one night. From what I can tell, you're doing just fine." The bitterness in her voice was thick.

"Am I supposed to apologize for that? You cut me loose." He'd tried to talk to her, even thought about asking her to go with him, but she'd acted like he no longer existed.

She was silent, so caught up in her own self-pity she didn't see what she was doing to herself or to him.

"This was a mistake." He turned to leave.

"Sure. Run away. Again."

"I didn't run the first fucking time. I chose to stay out of prison for a crime I didn't commit. You chose to turn your back on me. You chose to let me take the blame."

"I didn't know what would happen," she whispered.

"Meaning you didn't know you would still need me." It was all so clear. She'd kicked him to the curb thinking some other sucker would come along and get her where she wanted to go.

"That's not fair."

361

"How much did you get?" He wanted to know how much his happiness was worth to her.

"Five grand, for all the good it did me."

"What's that mean?"

"My boyfriend took it. Cleared out last night leaving me right back where I started."

He wanted to feel sorry for her. He really did. The girl he remembered was bright and energetic. She'd take on the world and make it hers. This husk of a woman bore almost no resemblance to the girl she'd been. This woman had long since given up on life. He never thought in a million years that Brandi would turn into the woman his mother had been. He was getting a headache.

He reached for the door handle. "I'm sorry."

"That's it? You're sorry. You owe me."

"Exactly what do I owe you?" He stared at her.

"You're where you are because of me," she spat.

Here she was. The girl he remembered. The selfish, vain piece of work that saw herself as the center of the world and the rest of its population as her servants.

"No. I'm here because of me. I chose to protect you. I chose the Navy over prison. I chose to build a good life instead of letting life run me over."

"I was drunk. I didn't mean for any of it to happen."

"I'm responsible for my decisions. You're responsible for yours." He could finally see what his brother had been trying to tell him all these years.

"You were supposed to save me," she whined.

"Shit. Tell me you haven't spent the past fourteen years waiting for someone to rescue you."

"What else was I supposed to do?" She looked confused, like she really had no idea she had any other choices.

"Save yourself. The Brandi I knew would be able to do it." He ran a hand through his hair. Olivia wouldn't pull this shit. She'd been through her share of garbage and had pulled herself up and out of it. Was the girl he knew all those years ago a figment of his imagination?

"I don't know how. You have to help me."

"I've helped you more than anyone else in your life. I gave you a shot to build a life free of a criminal past. You've done your level best to make sure that bullshit follows me everywhere. Even now, you've fucked up my life with it."

She snorted. "How have I fucked up your life? The people that hired you knew about everything. It wasn't going to change anything."

"My woman didn't know and now she's threatening to keep my kids from me, you selfish bitch," he bellowed. He was done. Getting in some circular argument with her

wasn't doing any good. She was still the same girl that ignored his wants and needs and did exactly what she
wanted to do.

Nick left the trailer.

"Where are you going?"

"I'm going home. This, whatever it is, is over. You stay
away from me and my family."

"You can't just leave." She turned on the water works.

"I can do whatever the fuck I want." He turned around
and faced her. "Word of advice. Get your shit together.
You're still young. Sober up and figure out how to make
your life better by yourself. The Brandi I remember could
do it. Be that girl again."

He got in the car and pulled out of the trailer park.
There was no need to ever come back here again.

Chapter 16

Olivia sat on the sun porch watching the waves break along the shore. The sounds of the beach weren't soothing. She missed Nick. Kate did too. The little stinker. Olivia found one of Nick's T-shirts tucked away in one of Kate's beds. The puppy had snapped at her for the first time when she tried to take it. Olivia couldn't blame her. She slept with another one of his T-shirts under her pillow.

She'd been so sure kicking him out was the right thing to do. It wasn't that he'd made a tragic mistake when he was younger. It was the fact that he blamed it on someone else. When her father had murdered her mother, he'd made it look like an accident. Plan "B" was to make it look like Olivia had killed her mother. When Nick shirked responsibility for what he'd done, she lost it.

After thinking about it for a few days, and missing him the entire time, she wondered if she had over reacted. Whatever the mistakes of his youth, she knew he was a good man now. Kate growled at her before burrowing into Nick's T-shirt. Olivia was going to have to get out of the doghouse somehow.

She sighed. What was she supposed to do? A knock on the front door saved her from staying on the hamster wheel in her brain.

Olivia went to answer the door. She was shocked to see Delilah and Nick's mother standing there.

"You going to gawk all day or let me say my peace?" Jane asked.

"Um." Did she have a choice?

"Better let the old bat have her say." Delilah winked.

"I'll old bat you, missy. When these drugs stop kicking my ass I'll show you a thing or two."

"I live for the day." Delilah ushered Jane inside and into the living room. Once they were settled on the couch, Olivia sat down in the chair opposite Jane.

"How are you?" Olivia was surprised Jane was here. She thought she had a chemo appointment today.

"Just got pumped full of poison. But I've got some things to say before I start puking my guts out."

Olivia nodded. She had a feeling she wasn't meant to contribute much to the conversation at this point.

"He wasn't driving the car that killed that girl."

"What?" Olivia and Delilah spoke at the same time.

"His girlfriend and her best friend took his truck. The two of 'em were drunker than skunks. Nick jumped in the back trying to stop them. Brandi drove it right into a tree. She got thrown from the car. Tiffany got her neck broke and my boy got bruises up and down his right side from getting slammed around in the bed of the truck." Jane looked down at her hands, which were twisted in her lap.

"What else?" Olivia could tell there was more. The magnitude of her mistake made her want to throw up herself. But she needed to hear all of it.

"I used to stash my pot in his truck." Jane's admission was so quiet, it was barely audible.

"No." Olivia covered her mouth with her hand.

"I was a two-time felon. Didn't want to get popped again. They found my drugs when they searched the truck and Nick got charged with that too."

"I don't understand how he didn't go to prison." Vehicular manslaughter and drug possession? He should have done some time.

"The judge the case was assigned to figured out the lay of the land. Tiffany's daddy tried to buy the prosecutor and he started rumbling about maximum sentences. Judge Strong got the goods on the DA and told him he could stay of jail by accepting the deal he proposed and resigning. Only bought him a little time. Ended up in prison for fraud a few years later."

"And Nick?" He'd protected his mother instead of turning her in. He was exactly who she'd thought he was.

"One tour in the Navy and Judge Strong wiped his record. He served longer because he found a place there."

Olivia felt sick. He'd been telling the truth. He really hadn't done it. She'd spent so much time trying to avoid her mother's mistakes she'd made a monumental mistake of her own.

She put her hands in her face. "What have I done?"

"You're not the only one." Delilah's voice was laced with regret. "I gave him a hard time, too."

"Nobody owes that boy more apologies than I do." Jane leaned back on the couch as if all her energy had been sapped from her body.

"I should get her home." Delilah leaned over.

"Why don't we take her upstairs. She can rest here until she feels better."

Delilah studied Jane. "That could be a while."

"Would it be easier to get her upstairs or back to the Jacobs' house?"

"Upstairs." Delilah's tone told Olivia it was a stupid question.

"Then I'll help you take her upstairs." She'd find Nick once she made sure his mother was all right.

"Better get me to a bathroom first."

Olivia and Delilah shared a glance before jumping into

action. They spent the next several hours taking care of Jane and getting her through the worst of the reaction to her chemo. Once she was settled in the guest room and asleep, Olivia and Delilah sat in the kitchen.

"You're good with her." Olivia observed.

Delilah shrugged.

"What's wrong?"

"I got it wrong with Nick," Delilah admitted.

"So did I."

"Yeah, but you've had the hots for him since you met. You were bound to screw up at some point. It's the dance everyone does in a relationship. I always look before I judge."

Olivia thought that might have something to do with the fact that everyone constantly judged Delilah by her appearance. "You're cautious with people. It's natural."

Delilah didn't seem comforted.

"What's really wrong? It can't just be that you misjudged Nick."

"Brian's fighting the divorce." She sighed.

That made no sense. "Why? I thought he wanted to split up. He told me he wanted it final as soon as possible."

"Probably his father."

"What's his father got to do with it?"

"Everything."

"Delilah —"

"I'm going to go upstairs and crash. I try and nap while Jane does. Makes it easier."

With that, Delilah was gone. Leaving Olivia with more questions she couldn't answer.

A few hours later, Jane and Delilah had woken from their naps, thanked Olivia for her hospitality and left. It happened so fast, Olivia felt like she had whiplash. She was in the kitchen making dinner when the doorbell rang.

The skitter of Kate's claws across the floor told Olivia who was at the door. She went to the front hall and opened it to find Nick standing there. He looked tired. Amazing, but tired. His beard was a little scruffier and his hair was longer. It stood up in places liked he'd been running his hands through it since the last time she'd seen him.

His eyes were wary. "Can we talk?"

She nodded and stepped back so he could come inside.

"Do you want to sit on the sun porch?" She thought it would be a good place for their conversation.

"Sure." He followed her into the room.

As soon as he crossed the threshold Kate sprang out from under the couch and landed on his boots.

"Really?" He looked down at the puppy who had attached herself to his jeans and was twisting like she thought she could take him down. He leaned over and scooped her up. He held her in front of him. Kate gave a little snarl before she licked his nose.

Nick smiled. "I missed you too." He tucked Kate in his arms and settled on the couch.

Olivia sat next to him. "I'm sorry."

His eyes widened. "Why are you sorry?"

"I should have let you tell me your story. I was so blinded by my own that I couldn't hear you."

He looked confused. "What do you mean?"

"You know my father killed my mother." She swallowed.

He nodded.

"What you don't know is that when his plan to make it look like an accident failed he framed me for her murder." The words rushed out of her mouth. She prayed she'd never have to say them again.

"What?" His raised voice got a yip out of Kate.

She sighed. "I was arrested, and he had a whole plan where I would plead not guilty by reason of insanity. I'd spend a few years in a mental institution and get out and live my life."

371

"Shit."

"The detective who arrested me believed me. She knew he was the one behind it all. With her help, I got the proof and they arrested my father. His family cut me off after that."

He put his arm around her. "I'm sorry, Slugger."

"So, when you said your girlfriend was driving that night —"

"You flashed back on your old man trying to stick you with the murder of your mother."

She nodded. "I've been letting him get in the way of our relationship from the beginning, and I'm sorry."

He took her hand in his. "No. I'm sorry. I should have trusted you with everything from the beginning. If I had, we wouldn't be here." He pressed his forehead to hers.

"Maybe." She sighed. "Maybe we're where we're supposed to be."

"Slugger. I've missed you like crazy. Tell me how to fix this. Tell me what to do and I'll do it. Please, just give me another chance to prove I'm the man you and the babies need."

"You've already done that." She squeezed his hand. "From the moment we met, even before we were together you've been there for me. You've shown me in a thousand different ways that you're the kind of man I can rely on. The kind of man who will be an amazing father to our children."

He slid off the couch and onto his knees, facing her. Kate nipped at him until he set her down and she scampered away. He took both Olivia's hands in his.

"I love you. I never knew what that word meant until I met you. I'm going to love you until the day I die."

She squeezed his hands. "I love you to. I thought I understood what that meant, until I met you. I'm going to stand by you for as long as you'll have me."

"Forever, Slugger. I'll have you forever." He leaned in and kissed her. His warm lips brushed across hers, softly at first then more demanding.

She dug her fingers into his hair, loving the silky feel against her skin. He slid his arms along her sides and then up her back, pulling her close.

He trailed kisses along her check and down her neck. "Missed you so fuckin much."

She leaned back on the couch, pulling him with her. She ran her hands up his back, under his T-shirt. His muscles rippled at her touch.

He kissed her again. Warmth spread through her entire body. He was home. She barely heard the growl. She pulled back from the kiss and looked over Nick's shoulder in time to see Kate flying through the air. She landed on Nick's back and bounced to the floor.

"What the —?"

Olivia laughed. "I think she's glad to have her playmate home."

Nick looked at the puppy who sneered at him before dashing off, his T-shirt in her mouth. "Is that mine?"

"She missed you too."

He looked back at Olivia a smile on his face. "I can't believe I'm saying it, but I missed her crazy sneak attacks."

"I'm sure she's got plenty planned for you now that you're home." Kate was nothing if not resourceful.

"Am I?" His blue eyes met hers.

She tilted her head. "Are you what?"

"Am I home?" The question was filled with hope.

She brushed her knuckles across his cheek before cupping it in the palm of her hand. "As long as we're together. We're both home."

He smiled. "I've never had a real home."

"Neither have I. I didn't realize what makes a home until I lost you." She kissed him.

He rested his forehead on hers. "What makes a home?"

"Love."

He smiled. "We got that, Slugger." Nick kissed her. It was filled with all the promises he'd just made to her.

She returned his kiss, giving him all the promises she'd just made to him. Olivia wrapped her arms around him, letting his strength surround her.

Olivia smiled. Turns out tequila and Las Vegas had been the means of uniting them.

Thank God for tequila.

Want to get the latest news on King's Folly and Cormac University? Interested in who's up next?

Sign up for my newsletter:

http://elizabethspaur.com/landing-page-newsletter/

Thank you for reading *Shotgun Romance*. I hope you enjoyed Cade and Tess's story. If you did, please leave a review.

If you haven't read Cade and Tess's story, *Second Chance Option*, turn the page peak to read Chapter 1:

Chapter 1

It was a view Cade Maguire hadn't seen in almost fourteen years. The trees on the edge of the South Carolina National Forest showed signs of spring as the branches sprouted buds. If memory served, the forest would be a riot of color in a few weeks.

"What the hell are we doing here?"

Not surprisingly, neither of his Bernese Mountain Dogs responded. Sonny and Sam were great companions but hadn't mastered the art of speech. Yet.

Mostly black with patches of light brown and white, they were almost identical. The only way to tell them apart was the white strip of fur between their eyes. Sonny's was a little narrower than Sam's. Their light brown eyebrows sometimes made their expressions almost human.

He dropped the last of his boxes in the front room of his new cabin. All his worldly possessions fit neatly into the small corner between the bay window and the back wall. The boxes he was expecting from his grandfather would probably fit in the hall closet. Moving around his entire life had taught him not to hang on to things, but this was pitiful.

The year lease he signed made him jumpy. Especially because that agreement had him living in King's Folly, a town he'd never in a million years thought he'd see again, much less plant roots in. But stubborn didn't pay the bills and the chance to get back in the game was too good to turn his back on because things had ended badly here.

The room was bare except for the boxes. Someone had come through and cleaned recently. Hardwood floors shone in the early morning light. There wasn't a dust mote to be seen in any of the rays of sun shining through windows so clean birds might smack in to them. A fresh coat of white paint covered the walls and left behind a smell that reminded him of being transferred to a new base.

Thanks to the Navy, he'd had access to three squares and a place to sleep for the last fourteen years. Starting from scratch wasn't new. Usually, his assignments came with furnished apartments, not bare rooms with no amenities.

Shit. I don't even have a coffee maker.

He rifled through his duffle bag, which had the necessities and found his planner. It was an old school, leather bound, refillable notebook, a gift from his grandfather after his graduation from Officers Candidate School. A little something from one type A personality to another. The book was the one thing that had survived all his moves and deployments. The list of things he needed to make this cabin more habitable was a mile long. It wasn't like he knew where to buy some of this shit, either. When did he ever think he'd have to buy kitchen appliances?

"I guess Maguires never say never, right boys?"

Sonny barked as if in agreement and Sam pressed against Cade's right leg burrowing close, but careful not to put too much weight in to his comforting move. It always amazed him how attuned they were to the residuals of his injuries.

He reached down and scratched them both behind the ears. They were still puppies at almost a year old, but they were big. The three of them had been through a lot together since he'd gotten them six months ago.

"On to the next adventure."

They chuffed their agreement and followed him as he limped toward the door. Sonny and Sam danced around him, clearly looking forward to another chance to go outside and play. He didn't blame them. The three of them had been cooped up in his truck for the last three days driving from San Diego to South Carolina, only stopping long enough to get a few hours of sleep when he needed it or a bite to eat when they all got hungry.

As he opened the door, the dogs bounced outside like they were spring loaded. He inhaled taking in the smell of pine and yellow jessamine, trying to ignore the faint hint of sea salt in the air. The sound of woodpeckers in the distance was oddly soothing.

A pair of barks signaled that the boys had found something to occupy them. The muscles in his back and side pulled tight sending an ache along the edge of his nerves. It was one of those days that he felt closer to a hundred years old instead of thirty-six. Rotating at the waist helped and he studied his new quarters as he worked out the kinks left behind by the long road trip.

He'd deliberately avoided the beach properties. Too many memories. Instead, he'd found a two-bedroom cabin at the edge of the woods. Plenty of room for Sonny and Sam to run and fewer ghosts for him to trip over. Maybe he could figure out what it meant to make a place a home.

The first notes of Queen's "We Are the Champions" interrupted his thoughts. He pulled out his phone, then hit 'accept.'

"Ed." He greeted his former coach, first true mentor, and new boss.

"You in town yet?" The old man got right to the point.

"Yeah." Cade stretched, trying to work more of the pain and stiffness out of his right side. After so much time driving, his scars were tight. He was going to need to use that lotion his physical therapist had hooked him up with. "The boys and I got here a little while ago. Just finished unloading the truck."

"The boys?"

"My dogs." An itch at the back of his neck made him go taut. He took a quick look around.

Where did Sonny and Sam go?

"Right. I hate to bug you since you just got to town."

The itching sensation intensified. "What's up?"

"We've got a situation brewing. We need to meet this afternoon in Ron's office."

"I'll be there." He needed to get off the phone. Something was up.

"Knew I could count on you." Ed disconnected the call.

Always a man of few words. It was one of the things that made the man a great football coach. When he had something to say, you listened because Ed King used his words so sparingly.

4

The dogs weren't barking anymore, which meant they were sniffing after something. Probably on the trail of some local wildlife. Still, he needed to find them. They weren't familiar with the area and there were wild animals in the forest around them and swamp land not too far from here. The problem was figuring out which direction they went.

A sudden screech of tires followed by a yelp and the sound of a vehicle peeling away came from the direction of the road and catapulted Cade into action. He ran down the driveway toward the sound. His heart beat like a pair of hummingbird wings and his chest felt like it might explode. When he got to the spot where his land met the road, he found them. Sonny lay motionless, but whimpering. Sam hovered over him barking at the retreating SUV as it screeched around the corner.

Cade dropped to his knees. Sonny's breathing was shallow, and there was blood. A lot of blood. Too much blood.

"Hey. That truck just took off." A lanky kid came out of nowhere and took a knee on the opposite side of Sonny and reached out as if to pet him.

"Don't touch him," Cade barked, fear coiling in his stomach like a viper waiting to strike.

"I know where the nearest vet is. It looks bad, but the Gallagher clinic is the best. If anyone can patch up your dog, they can." The kid sounded out of breath, but confident.

Cade nodded. He knew something had to be done, but he was,

for the first time in his life, incapable of action. Things were moving too quickly for him to think.

The next few moments were surreal. It was like he was watching the scene unfold through a Vaseline covered lens. The kid hustled Sam into the cabin and locked the front door after he'd closed it. Then he rushed back to Cade and helped him bundle Sonny into the backseat of Cade's truck. His dog's whimpers tore through his body like the IED that had ended his Navy career.

Looking at his buddy fighting for life made his stomach turn. He'd seen more than his share of blood, but this? This much blood? Because some stupid asshole couldn't slow his fucking car down?

Cade buried his fingers in the long black fur at Sonny's neck, careful to avoid his obvious injuries. He curled over until his mouth was next to the pup's ear.

"Easy, boy. I've got you. It's going to be okay."

Please, God. Please, let it be okay.

Sonny's whimpers echoed through the cab of the Avalanche. The truck must have been moving. He heard the engine and felt the movement as the kid rocketed around corners like a race car driver.

Cade didn't care about the truck. All he cared about was getting Sonny to help.

"We're almost there, boy," he whispered. His voice sounded like he'd been gargling shards of glass.

Please God, let us be almost there.

6

Sonny and Sam had gotten him through the worst days of his life. Recovering from career ending injuries had taken him to the edge. The puppies had pulled him back from it and helped navigate his new normal. There was no way he wanted to map out another one. He was too old for that shit.

The viper coiled in his gut balled up tighter and settled as if waiting for the perfect moment to lash out and destroy everything. He didn't know what he would do if Sonny didn't make it.

Please God, don't let me find out.

Ninety-nine point nine-nine percent of the time Tess Gallagher loved her work. Being a veterinarian was her calling. She loved animals and taking care of them was a joy and a privilege. Serving her community at the same time was the gravy on top of the French fries.

However, since hiring her part-time assistant, there was that other point zero one percent of the time.

"Is it just me or does this new cage make Mr. Wigglesworth look fat?" And there it was. Her former nemesis, unlikely new friend and recently hired employee, Delilah Derringer, and her total lack of a filter struck again.

Tess glanced over her shoulder to make sure she'd closed the door to the examination room. The last thing she needed was for Mrs. Milton to hear any insults to her beloved parakeet.

"Really?" These were the moments she wanted to smack the

sass right out of Delilah. "You know how Mrs. Milton is about this bird."

Delilah shrugged. "She hates me anyway. I ran into her in the grocery story last week, and she spent fifteen minutes telling me what an embarrassment I am, and it was my lucky day when 'that nice Tess hired my lazy behind.'" She held up her fingers to make air quotes and mimicked the woman in question perfectly.

Tess closed her eyes, inhaled deeply and counted to ten, letting the slightly antiseptic smell of the room soothe her.

"It's hard enough to get some of our older clients to take me seriously. All we need is for Mrs. Milton to start telling the entire town we were making fun of her baby." She'd worked hard to build her reputation and didn't want Delilah's lack of tact to tear it down.

Delilah laughed. "You really need to lighten up. You don't want to main line Pepto-Bismol again."

It was probably wrong to want to strangle her. No, it was definitely wrong. Still there were moments, like this one, where Tess gave it serious thought. Instead, she focused on Mr. Wigglesworth's annual physical, counting to ten again, and once more for good measure.

"How old is chubby anyway?"

Tess studied the soft pink plumage of the gentle bird and did her best to focus on her patient and not the woman who seemed to delight in tormenting her, even though lately it was good natured instead of nasty.

"He's fifteen. His initial appointment was one of the first ones I assisted Dad with before I started vet school." Tess smiled at the memory. She'd been thirteen and a mixture of excited and terrified that had made her want to shout and puke at the same time.

"Fifteen? I thought parakeets only lived like five years."

"Technically, this is a Bourke Parrot, but their called parakeets. The average life span is fifteen to twenty years, depending on whether they receive the proper diet and care."

"Well, the whole town knows Mrs. M is a fanatic about the care and feeding of anything but husbands."

Tess couldn't stop the giggle that escaped. She tried not to encourage Delilah's more outrageous commentary, but sometimes she couldn't help herself. The woman was funny. Unfortunately, halting one of her rants against some of the more disapproving citizens of King's Folly, South Carolina was like trying to stop the bulls at Pamplona. Since they had gone from enemies to friends, she had learned that it was essential to distract Delilah before she got on a roll and from the look of her, she was winding up for one hell of a tantrum.

"Speaking of husbands, any word on your divorce?" She felt a little bad using her friend's personal drama to change the subject, but these days it was the easiest way to put the brakes on the freight train that could be Delilah's mouth.

"Did I tell you what that cock knocker is doing now?"

Tess tuned out the rest of the speech, because yes, in fact, Delilah had told her what her soon be ex-husband was up to now. In

9

excruciating detail. Three times. This Morning. By the time she finished her examination of Mr. Wigglesworth, the room had gone strangely quiet. She turned around. Delilah was standing in front of the door, arms crossed, a spark of irritation in her blue eyes.

"What?"

"You did that on purpose."

"I have no idea what you're talking about." Tess kept a gentle grip on the parakeet as she turned to put him back in his cage before returning her attention to her irritated friend.

"You brought up the lying, double-crossing bastard so I would stop making fun of the bird."

"That doesn't sound like me." She maintained eye contact with Delilah. There wasn't time for a staring contest, but there was less time for the drama. After a moment, her friend smiled and stepped away from the doorway to let Tess pass.

"I have no idea how I always got the better of you when we were growing up. Can't get anything by you these days."

"When we were growing up, I thought you were scary." Tess stepped outside of the exam room, knowing her words would, oddly enough, soothe her friend. Given that she was the one who had gotten Delilah worked up over her ex, it made her feel better to be the one to calm her down.

Tess had to admit that since she started spending more time with her three younger brothers and Delilah she was getting better at picking up on people's more subtle social cues and expressions.

10

It was still a lot like trying to decipher an ancient, unknown language, but more and more she was building a translation key.

She took her patient back to reception where Mrs. Milton and Sheila were still trading the latest and greatest in local gossip.

"And do you know what the uppity English teacher said to me?" Mrs. Milton broke off from her tirade when she spotted Tess coming down the hall. Her pink tinted lips, the exact same color as her bird tilted up and, with a high-pitched coo, she moved away from the receptionist's desk and waddled towards Tess, who held the cage out for her client.

"And how's mummy's wittle baby waby?" She smashed her nose up against the cage and made kissy noises.

"Mr. Wigglesworth is doing very well, as usual. You're taking excellent care of him."

Mrs. Milton beamed at Tess and pinched her cheek.

"You're a good girl."

Tess smiled and ignored the fact that Mrs. Milton spoke to her in the same tone she used with her bird. It was better than the people who spoke to her like she was still a child. "Thank you. You keep doing what you're doing, and we'll see you and Mr. Wigglesworth next year."

As Mrs. Milton and her parakeet left the building a black Avalanche screeched to a halt in front of the clinic, smoke blowing from the tires. Tess had a split second to appreciate the large, muscular man who jumped from the back seat of the truck before all her attention shifted to the large, bloody animal cradled in his

11

arms.

She threw open the door. The bitter smell of burnt rubber filled the air.

"I need a doctor." His voice sounded raspy and thick.

"I'm Dr. Gallagher. Follow me." She led him to the nearest empty examination room and watched closely as he laid what she could now see was a Bernese Mountain Dog down on the table as if it was the most precious thing in the world to him.

With years of experience she ran her hands along the dog's body and found the source of the bleeding and looked up to see her veterinary technician, Charlie, and Delilah, standing in the doorway, waiting for instructions.

"Charlie, prep the OR and have the portable x-ray standing by. We've got internal bleeding and possible broken bones. Delilah, bring in the gurney, we need to get…"

She focused on the man, whose oddly familiar, piercing green gaze never left his dog.

"Sonny." He seemed to know what information she needed.

Tess nodded. "We need to get Sonny in to surgery."

The next few moments passed in a flurry of activity. Sonny was quickly transferred to a gurney, then wheeled back to the OR. There was no question that her staff would settle the distraught, and sexy man out front. This wasn't their first ball game.

Once in the operating room Tess and Charlie worked in concert to save the big dog's life. Delilah stood by the door, eyes looking anywhere but at the injured dog, hand over her mouth,

12

doing nothing to disguise the gagging noises she was making. She waited for an update on Sonny's injuries that she could share with his concerned owner.

It took Tess a few minutes to study the x-rays they had taken while Charlie finished making sure Sonny was prepped for surgery. Tess hoped she could send Delilah out to the waiting room with an update before she tossed her cookies.

"Let him know Sonny has a broken right hind leg and some internal bleeding. The break is in two places, but it's clean so we are going to set the leg after we stop the bleeding and repair the internal damage. He's welcome to wait, but this is going to take a while, three to four hours at least."

Delilah left the room like someone lit her ass on fire.

"I still don't know why you hired her."

Tess smiled beneath her surgical mask. She and Charlie had been friends since infancy and she wasn't ready to give Delilah the same pass Tess had. "She needs the job and she's a hard worker."

"She can't stand blood, she's disrespectful to the clients, she's…"

It was a familiar refrain. Tess tuned it out momentarily when she spotted a bleeder. "Retract this."

Charlie didn't stop her litany of complaints against Delilah as they continued the surgery. She paused occasionally to take Tess's direction and the occasional breath, but lately Charlie reserved her diatribes for the OR because she knew no one would overhear

13

her. Tess sighed.

"You do know the definition of insanity, right? Cauterize that."

Her assistant expertly followed her instructions. "Doing the same thing over and over again and expecting a different result."

"Right? How are his vitals?" They'd been growing steadier as the bleeding was controlled.

"Stable. So, I'm insane now?"

She set the last clamp in place, confident she'd identified all the bleeds. "Let's stitch up these bleeds. You do keep repeating yourself."

"What type of sutures are we using? I'm worried about you."

"Internal, absorbable." Tess held out her hand for the sutures. "I know you're worried. I even understand why you keep bringing it up. I have, historically, been very slow with social cues and Delilah has, historically, been nasty to me."

"But you think she's changed." It was a statement, not a question. Charlie checked Sonny's vitals.

"I believe in second chances and I think she deserves one. If I'm wrong – "

"I'll kick her ass."

Tess laughed. Charlie had always been her biggest defender and was far from convinced that Delilah had turned a corner. "And if I'm right?" She scanned the now closed incision, pleased with her work. Sonny's vitals were stable, and he'd responded well to the anesthesia.

14

Charlie sighed. "I guess I'll have to be friends with her."

"You already are friends. I know social situations aren't my forte, but I believe the two of you enjoy baiting each other. Let's cast this leg."

The two women worked in concert to finish Sonny's treatment. Now that he was clearly out of danger and Charlie's latest issue with Delilah had been dealt with, Tess took a moment to focus on the man who had brought Sonny in. Those familiar green eyes had finally sparked a memory.

Cade Maguire.

He was back, and he had great taste in dogs.

Gridiron Knights

Second Chance Option – Cade and Tess's Story

COMING SOON IN 2018

Romancing the Receiver – Ben and Lily's story – September 28, 2018

Love in the Zone – Frankie and Rush's story – October 26, 2018

Bootleg Love Affair – Boomer and Delilah's story – November 30, 2018

Loving the Lineman – Deke and Emma's story – December 28, 2018

COMING IN 2019

Meet the Knights rivals in *Gridiron Dragons*